rum sips and salty lips

WENDELL BEACH

BOOK ONE

REBECCA V. ARCHER

GOLDEN ALE PRESS LLC

 Created with Vellum

For Wesley
Always my best friend

content note

Absentee parents in childhood (not abusive, but not nurturing), gaslighting in the workplace and by previous partner, secondary characters experience infidelity, tropical storm, discussions of body image, discussion of kayaking accident.

This book is also high heat with multiple explicit scenes.

This list may not be exhaustive. Please contact the author if you have any questions or concerns. Any updates will be posted to:

https://rebeccavarcher.com/rum-sips-content-notes

one

ORION

I don't want her on my boat. Fuck. I don't want anyone on my boat. But especially not Carina Webb, the woman I'm not allowed to disappoint.

It doesn't matter if my personal vessel was accidentally added to the inventory of my newly purchased boat charter company. I'm in charge on the boat and pay everyone's salary, but even with that authority, I'm still told it would be a mistake to cancel on Carina. A major faux pas. A black spot on my name before I've even been in town twenty-four hours.

I stand at the end of the dock, next to the stern of my beloved sailboat, the *Twisted Rigging*. The Florida sun is already beating down even though it's only midmorning. I watch a blond figure walk down its length, past the few dozen other sailboats in this small marina, assuming it to be her.

I tried negotiating my way out of this earlier. Nathan, the deckhand who had shown up ready for duty, made the situation as clear as the water surrounding this island. "Captain, she's basically Wendell Beach royalty."

"Orion is fine." I've never been formal with my crews. "And what does that mean?" I scrambled, cleaning up the galley.

"She owns the yoga studio. And everyone loves her clothes." Nathan gestured like it was self-evident. I blinked at him, wondering how a yoga studio was the center of a beach town, especially one with more tourists than residents. "She's friends with the Barneses and Foleys. She did a whole sea turtle thing last year."

With the additional context, I sent Alex a text.

ME

The booking office messed up so I'm chartering Carina Webb today. You know I hate people on my boat. Give me one good reason to not cancel on her.

ALEX BARNES

She'll be the easiest charter you've had. She's likely bringing her friend Haley. Haley's food will change your life.

And I'll ban you from Paradise if you upset Carina.

My skin itches with the threat. It's more than exclusion from the bar he and his family have owned for generations. The message is clear: fuck up this charter and my future in Wendell Beach is in jeopardy. Alex is close with the Foley family who own Coastline Beach House, a luxury resort at the south end of the island. And part of my strategic plan is to get an exclusive contract with them.

I've been independent my entire life. Sailing around the world. Never staying more than six months in one spot. Sure, I end up with my family in Boston for a few months at a time. But I'm tired of the cold and the shuffling. I want a new anchor point. A place to be year-round.

I've always craved the heat, so Florida was an easy choice. I could have gone anywhere in the state. But I know Alex and the influence his family has on the tourist industry. I'm not quite starting from scratch here. I have connections. I bought the sailing company and a house to remodel. If ocean kayaking was going to get me killed, I might as well be warm.

After docking late last night, I haven't even had time to go to my house yet. The one so close to the beach I can throw a rock over my neighbor's yard and hit the sand. I had planned to go today, but when I woke up this morning I had an email confirming the Nebula Athletics charter.

Four women. They will provide the booze and food. They want to spend the day paddleboarding and sailing on the *Twisted Rigging*. The boat was technically available for charter since I told the Lost Craft Charters office manager I would be arriving today after sailing her south myself, unwilling to let someone else touch her.

I tried to tell everyone she is my personal vessel and not available for charter. They apologized for the mix-up and talked in circles about why Carina was such a VIP we couldn't put her on a different sailboat. They said they might have been able to make other arrangements if I had spoken up sooner. But during my weeks at sea, I'd only been skimming my email.

"She's the nicest boat on the island," Nathan said. His flattery worked, to my annoyance.

So, I'd ground my teeth, hidden the lotion and tissues and all evidence a thirty-five-year-old single guy had been alone on this boat for weeks. Then loaded up the sail locker with inflatable paddleboards.

I had a second to peek at her Instagram profile. Just long enough to get the sense none of it is candid. As she walks closer, I check her out in the most professional way I can. My eyes go to her feet first. No shoes on the boat. I can tell how my day will go based on a client's reaction to the rule. She has on what looks like a pair of lightweight sneakers.

Practical.

It doesn't mean anything. I've had guests tell me their sneakers cost the same as my new car payment.

Her legs are long and tan. I really shouldn't be noticing them, but I suddenly can't help myself. It must be the weeks at sea, because I've never ogled a guest before. I reset my mind. I will be professional all day and then get out my kayak to blow off some steam when she leaves.

She's carrying an oversized tote bag, which can't be heavy because she's holding it with ease. Someone else must have the alcohol and food. I prefer to get those things on board quickly, so everything is stowed long before we sail.

She's finally close enough I can get a good look at her face. I should have looked more carefully at her Instagram. I should have prepared myself better. She's absolutely stunning. Her sunglasses cover her eyes, and I'm hit with the need to know what their color is. She smiles and I wonder what her lips taste like. She's tall, so she doesn't have to tilt her head up much to look at me. She has a stray lock of hair framing her face from her otherwise neat ponytail. I fight the urge to push it behind her ear.

She extends her hand for me to shake. "Hi, I'm Carina Webb." Her soothing voice reminds me to stay in the moment. "I know I'm early. I'm here for the Nebula Athletics charter." I shake her hand, holding on to it longer than I should, appreciating her soft skin.

Her face is already flushed pink. It's barely ten a.m., but the sun bakes everything early. I make a mental note to find sunscreen. And why doesn't she have a hat? Shouldn't that be the first thing to grab before heading outdoors in Florida? "I'm Orion Edwards, captain of the *Twisted Rigging*. Let me take your bag. Your shoes can go in this basket, and I'll show you around."

I catch the way she looks at her feet and the gap between the dock and the stern. I swear she tries to calculate how to balance so she can keep the bag, take off her shoes, and step aboard. She reluctantly hands the bag over. It's heavier than I expected. It can't be towels or a change of clothing. Maybe it is the liquor.

I move to the stern and turn to offer her my hand as she's bending over to pick up her shoes. I catch the faintest hint of a baby blue bikini under her white tank top before I have the good sense to look away. When she extends her leg to step aboard in bare feet, I try not to stare at the way her pale blue shorts travel up her thigh. There is an exploding star near the hem—the logo for the clothing company everyone is apparently obsessed with. I thought I gave her enough space, but she steps right up to me, so close she almost bumps me, her breath hitching. The cutest flush crosses her cheeks as she smiles.

Right. This will be a long day. I lead her below deck. "Is there anything we need to do with this?" I ask, setting the bag on the table next to the galley. I gesture for her to sit.

"Oh, it's wine and glasses. I didn't know what you'd have on board. And I have reusable wine tumblers. Plus, I didn't want to bring glass on a boat, so I put the wine into other bottles. It's already chilled, and since everything is double-walled it'll stay that way. Your office said it would be fine. I didn't want to use refrigerator space the food needs."

I've never heard so much overthinking in one breath. And she's clearly looking for my approval, her eyes wide and expectant.

"That sounds great." She's already proving to be a thoughtful guest. Unfortunately, I've seen so much shit in my seventeen years of giving tours that my approval bar is low.

I scan the space one last time, making sure I didn't miss anything while cleaning. My existence has been erased. The boat looks great. If I am forced to sail with strangers, I want to make sure she looks her absolute best. The interior of the boat is done in cream and beige, making it appear more open than the space should. The table has sofa seating against the hull side, allowing us to be comfortable as we have this conversation. It also has a small galley where I've been cooking my meals. I can get pretty creative after I've been at sea awhile. "I apologize," I tell her, "I only found out about your charter this morning. What are you envisioning for your day?"

She looks me straight in the eyes. I'm shaken by their gray color and with the potency of her attention. They should be cold, and I can see how someone else might think that. But they feel like warmth to me and simultaneously like my sea legs have been removed. Like I'm heeling without warning. I suck in a breath and hope she doesn't notice she's making the hairs on my arms stand on end. I'm not sure anyone else has ever looked at me with such intent before. I feel unnerved and safe at the same time. She's not splitting her attention between me and her phone or thinking about her grocery list. She's not watching the radar and the wind and scanning for other boats. It makes me excited and feel like I should do everything I can to keep her attention on me. I'm not worried I don't deserve it, or I won't hold up to her scrutiny. Only about keeping her attention.

I would have preferred my first trip to be with a tourist. Someone enjoying the Cultural Coast for a few days and then moving on. An uncomplicated way to start.

But this woman is a pillar of the community. This is "fuck up and face consequences" territory. And I haven't had time to prepare so I don't know what she's expecting. And she's making me flustered. I can't count the number of charters I've done in my life. I'm a professional who doesn't cross lines. It's been years since I've been tempted. I don't know why it's her, but I need to shut down my attraction.

I won't let it ruin the plans I have for this business and this move.

"I'm bringing out my top two executives. They've been with me since the founding. I want to treat them to celebrate the last ten years."

Ten years? She looks to be in her early thirties so she must have gotten started right out of college. I wish I'd had more time to google her. I'm curious. But I can wait.

I show her a map on my phone. "I can take you down to this island here. The water should be good for water sports." Nathan filled me in on the popular spots. I've done research but this is an art—knowing where to go based on the conditions of the day and what's least likely to be crowded. I'll figure it out in time. Until then, I hate relying on someone else.

"Sounds great," she says brightly, her excitement contagious. "I've never chartered a boat, so I'll leave it up to the experts." I expected her to be high-maintenance, but she's not.

"Great. I need to do a few more things before we're ready to sail. Feel free to hang out down here, or on the deck." I stand, ready to get back to work. Less because I have work to do, and more because I need extra air when I'm around her.

She looks around the galley. While I've picked up everything personal, she has an exacting eye and will find the dirty sock I missed. Her gaze stops at the small bookshelf next to the radio. "*Sailing in the Mediterranean*," she reads. "Have you been?"

"I have. A few years ago some friends and I took the *Twisted Rigging* across the Atlantic." I don't want to leave now. Not when I have the chance to share my passion with her.

She nods, not quite impressed with my sailing record. "*Circumnavigating the Globe?*" She names the next title.

"I haven't done that. Maybe one day," I muse. But I won't. I don't think so, at least. The urge I've felt to move from place to place as quickly as the tide is gone. I should mourn the sense of adventure I've lost, but I don't. I'm ready for calm seas and the same bed every night.

If I find the right life partner to share everything with, I'd try it again. But I've made my choice. I'm tied here, to Wendell Beach. To the house and the company I bought.

I'll always come back here.

Carina looks at me with her whole attention. It's fierce and I don't think she means it to be. She's so still, her eyes steady and a little guileless, like she's found something captivating drawing her in, stealing her attention. I'm suddenly comparing it to my interactions with other people. We're always fidgeting or distracted in some way. Carina isn't.

I'm intrigued. I want more. I want to know everything about this woman. I want to give her all my time and attention.

She opens her mouth, but Nathan's voice on deck greeting someone cuts her off.

"That must be Haley," Carina says. "She's the chef." She stands quickly and heads up to the deck.

I follow, the muscles in my jaw tensing. I didn't want her on my boat. I can't be lusting after a client. And I really can't when it's this woman.

<h1 style="text-align:center">two</h1>

CARINA

I FEEL THE CAPTAIN ON MY HEELS AS I RUSH TO GET MY HEAD ON straight. I'm supposed to be calm and collected. I am. Or at least I try to be. But Orion washed over me like a wave I wasn't expecting. There's no way it affected him like he affected me.

He's tall, with broad shoulders and biceps that go on for days. A storm could hit him, and he wouldn't notice. He has a short beard that's more likely him not shaving for a few days.

I don't generally think I have a type. I haven't dated seriously in years, preferring flings. Most of the time, I go for men as different from my MBA-having, suit-loving ex as possible. Which is easy to find on a yoga retreat and at athleisure wear conferences.

This man's chocolate eyes hint at a wild side I'll never be able to match. His brown hair under his ball cap is on the longer side, brushing his chin, and I can tell he runs his hands through it all the time. I'm not thinking about running my hands through it. It would be so soft if I did.

He's so fucking handsome.

I don't understand how I'm suddenly so horny.

"Haley!" My voice sounds too high even to my ears. I've put

9

my sunglasses back on since the sun reflects off the water and the white of all the boats. "Thank you so much for doing this." Nathan has already stepped up to help her with the coolers of food she's brought.

"Of course! Any chance to be on the water, especially when I don't have to reel in or gut fish." She's dating a fisherman and loves catching something and cooking it the same day. She introduces herself to both Orion and Nathan. Which is helpful because I'm sure I would have stumbled over my words under Orion's watchful eye.

I truly don't understand what's going on with me. I'm around attractive people all the time. Maybe my previously unknown pirate fetish has decided to rear its ugly head? It's been six months since I've had a fling. Maybe this is my body telling me Orion is a prime candidate.

My mind isn't opposed.

The thought doesn't go away as Stacy and Jeannette arrive, and Orion prepares the boat for us to leave. I'm aware of his presence even when I can't see him. Of course, I watch as he guides the boat from the dock with minimal help from the deckhand. Anyone would. And I notice the way his biceps fill the sleeves of his polo shirt as he raises the sails.

I make clothing. I pay attention to how it fits people.

Now he's at the wheel—the helm, he calls it, which is right next to where I'm sitting. We're moving along faster than I expected. We tilt as the sails catch the wind. The boat is beautiful, and seeing his face light up with joy while he's sailing makes me happy.

The sails power our movement, but it's also him. He's the one adjusting the angle of the sails and constantly watching the wind and the water. It's baffling to me that he's able to keep track of so many things at once. I can see his attention moving around. And it's doing something to me I didn't expect when I decided to take my team out for a day of sailing.

It must be the competence I'm attracted to.

But I have competent male friends who don't do anything for me. Alex is an expert bartender. I've seen women forget what they're doing while he shakes a cocktail. Christian, my closest male friend, turns heads wherever he goes.

Neither of them affect me the way Orion does.

We sail down the island, just far enough out that we won't encounter any swimmers. I watch my beautiful beach pass by and the miles of sand that I love so much. The wind blows my hair, and I'm constantly pulling the loose strands back behind my ears. It's still incredibly hot out—there's no way to avoid that in August—but I feel better here, out on the water, than I have anywhere else in a while.

Haley passes the rosé around. I brought plenty, so we won't run out, but I keep my sips superficial. This is a celebratory trip but I'm still the boss. I don't get to cut loose.

"You're not having any?" I ask Haley when I notice she's not taking any either. "I know it's not champagne."

"I'm working," she protests.

"Please. You're barely letting me pay your hourly rate." It's an old argument. She thinks since she cooked for me when we were college roommates, she could never ask me to pay her even though she does charge other people for this exact service.

"I'll have a little now. I want to be sober for paddleboarding," she says. I raise one eyebrow. We're both experienced enough that one glass of wine won't affect either of our abilities on a board. "What's your excuse?" She points to my nearly full cup.

Jeannette and Stacy sit on the bow flirting with Nathan. Orion can probably hear us, so I'm careful. "I'm just watching today. You all have fun."

"You okay? Is it your hamstring again?"

My hamstring feels fine. I overstretch it from time to time. Haley probably has a mental log of every injury her friends have ever had. But that's not what's on my mind.

It's the anxiety no meditation has ever been able to fully quell. *What if I fail?*

If we're stand-up paddleboarding, that means falling. I have years of experience with the sport so I should be fine. According to Nathan, the conditions should be calm where we're headed. But falling in the Gulf of Mexico, even if unlikely, isn't something I can risk.

I could handle falling in front of any of the women, and probably Nathan too. But Orion has clearly seen a lot. I will do anything to make sure he has a high opinion of me. I need him to keep thinking of me as the in-control business owner I am.

"It's fine. I'm tired from my class this morning," I answer.

I know what my reputation is around town. I give back to my community as much as possible. I organize beach cleanups every month and helped plan last year's Sea Turtle Rescue 5K. I've worked hard for the image I have.

It's real too. I care deeply about the environment and built my business around sustainability. But one misstep, no matter how small, can destroy everything I've built. One bad review can go viral. One out-of-context quote can blow up. People who don't know me always judge. My friends are amazing, but I constantly wonder how long they'll stick around.

When we get to the planned spot, both Orion and Nathan jump into action to lower the sails and drop the anchor. I tuck my feet under me to make myself as small as possible.

"You're fine," Orion says as he brushes past me.

"I don't want to get in your way."

"Trust me, you could never be in my way." He winks. My insides shouldn't quiver at his casual flirting. He does this with every guest, I'm sure. It earns him better tips. I don't mean anything to him.

I wish I did. Even for a night.

They inflate the paddleboards and I pass on Nathan's tour of the mangrove forest. "I did a lot of sun salutations this morning,"

I tell him and Orion. It's not a lie but it's not the reason I'm staying behind.

The waves rock Haley, and she kneels to maintain her balance. I also notice the way Orion watches her like a hawk, worried he'll need to jump in for a rescue. But Haley finds enough stability to paddle after Nathan. I wave goodbye, but they're already focused on what's ahead of them.

It feels sudden, the way they're gone. I'm left with Orion, the boat, and not another soul in sight. I sit on the stern, dangling my feet in the water.

"Mind if I join you?" he asks, as a formality.

I'm next to a bowl of shrimp ceviche. I'd told him he could help himself to anything we brought. I always order extra rather than risk running out. So far, he hasn't taken me up on the offer.

"This is a nice perk you've given them," he comments, eating a cracker from the plate set between us.

I shrug. "They've worked really hard to get us where we are."

"You founded the company, right? You must have worked hard too," he says.

My skin prickles. I know what he's getting at because I've seen him watching. Not just me, everyone. He notices I've barely had a sip of alcohol and held back from the gourmet snacks, letting everyone else have their first pick. I take a bite from the tray, savoring the way Haley creates the perfect blend of seafood, citrus, and avocado.

I've worked hard. The company is my brainchild. My ex would tell me since the risk was mine, the reward should be mine as well. But I got the startup cash from my father, or rather his investment firm, the Webb Group. I built on what I was given. It doesn't feel earned. I'm not a rags-to-riches or a bootstraps story.

"It's just nice to be away for the day," I muse.

"What all does your company do?" he asks.

I'm not insulted he hasn't heard of Nebula Athletics. We're

incredibly successful, but only in certain circles. I'm not sure there's much overlap between yoga and sailing.

"We primarily make yoga clothes and athleisure with a heavy focus on sustainability and fair labor practices." He nods along, like he agrees with my message. I'm a businessperson first, even though I also have years of yoga practice and as a yoga teacher. I've given this elevator pitch to enough people to know if they're waiting to ask about my profit margins.

But Orion looks genuinely interested.

"I also own a yoga studio under the brand in town. We stream classes online so that more people have access to movement."

"That all sounds great," he says. "Do you teach too?"

"I do. Started in college." He nods but doesn't respond. Anyway, I don't want to talk about me. "How long have you been sailing?" I ask. I'm curious about him. I saw the way he lit up when I asked about the Mediterranean. He has to be new to Wendell Beach, otherwise we would have crossed paths. It's a small town, and I've been a year-round resident for seven years. We don't have a large permanent population, relying on tourists and seasonal residents. I doubt this man, who is constantly looking at the horizon, would stay in one place long.

"I've been sailing since I was a kid. I grew up in Boston. Bought my first boat at eighteen." He gestures with his hand. "Now I have a fleet there and a fleet here."

A few pieces fall into place. I hadn't heard of Lost Craft Charters until Alex suggested I use them. The office informed me they'd been bought recently, and the name changed. I was assured they are locally owned. That's important to me.

"You own the charter company?"

"I do. And its sister company in Boston."

"How long have you lived here?" I should have seen him around.

"Technically, since last night." He leans against the side of the boat. "I sailed down from Boston. When the *Twisted Rigging* pulled into the slip, this town officially became my home."

He lives on this boat?

"You sailed from Boston yesterday? Why are you even out today?" I ask, not yet ready to process that I've invaded his home.

He takes his hat off and runs a hand through his hair, exactly like I imagined. "It took more than a day. But yes, the *Twisted Rigging* is my personal boat. No one else captains her."

"I could have gone out on another boat."

"Nothing but the best for Carina Webb." He says it evenly. It's the way it is.

I've heard it before. But it's not how I feel. I would never ask to put Orion out. "You really didn't have to do this."

He shrugs. I wonder if anything fazes him. "So far it's been worth it." His gaze turns from the vast sea until he's focused on me.

My breath hitches, which it never does. Years of yoga and pranayama breathwork have me always in control. I want it to mean more than simple flirtation as part of his job.

I hold back my smile, suddenly afraid it doesn't mean anything to him, when it means something to me.

three

ORION

I DON'T KNOW WHY CARINA IS HESITANT TO GO PADDLEBOARDING. I can tell from Haley's comments they both go often. But Carina looked at me like I would prevent her.

I personally prefer kayaking, but paddleboarding has always looked fun. The water is warm so falling isn't a big deal. It's possible to swim in the Charles River back in Boston, but you couldn't convince me to risk it, so I'd never tried it there. And I love a good risk.

After about an hour, Nathan brings them back from the tour, and one of the women, Jeannette, attempts a few yoga poses on her board and quickly falls in the water. I laugh along with them as soon as I realize she's able to climb up easily and doesn't need a rescue. It makes me more curious about Carina. I want to see her attempt one of the poses Jeannette tried.

I shouldn't be thinking about how flexible she probably is.

I'm a professional and she's a professional. I've done thousands of day and overnight charters. I've never reacted to a guest the way I'm reacting to Carina.

"You joining at all?" I ask her.

She sits up straighter. "Maybe in a bit. Like I said, this is for them, not me."

She told me she was tired from her workout earlier. She avoids eye contact, suggesting something else.

Jeannette paddles up to the boat. "You can do better than I did," she playfully taunts.

Carina shrugs.

"Oh, come on," Haley calls from her board. "That would make a great video, and you need content from today."

Carina looks at me.

That's when I see it. The smallest hint of fear in her eyes. I don't know what it means, but I hate it. I'd love to see her try something brave even if it doesn't work.

"A few nautical poses. Like boat. Or mermaid!" Stacy suggests.

"Fine." Carina grabs the paddle and helps Jeannette onto the swim platform, handing over her phone and sunglasses. She eases herself onto the board, and while kneeling paddles a few yards away. Jeannette holds up Carina's phone as she moves into position.

I've done a few yoga classes, but I don't know anything beyond the basics. It's enough to be impressed with the way Carina bends her body into position. She looks off into the distance in exactly the way a mermaid would if a sailor spotted her sunning herself on a rock.

I would absolutely run my ship aground if it meant getting close to her.

She looks to Jeannette and smiles while the other women cheer her on. Carina's gaze turns to me. Suddenly, all the fear I saw before is gone. I'm sure my jaw drops. I school my features back to neutral, but she saw me. She knows what she's doing to me.

"You don't want to go out more?" Haley asks when Carina paddles back a minute later.

"No, you go. I'm fine on the boat." Once again, she makes eye contact. This time she smiles. I'm not as opposed to her staying back since I get to be with her.

At the same time, I wish she would do more. I want to know her through the way she moves. She's so strong and capable. But she's hiding something, and it's obvious to me. Everyone else appears to miss it. She's not what I expected. It isn't because I assumed wrong. It's that no one sees what I'm seeing.

I can't do anything about these feelings while we're on a charter. But It's a small town. I'll run into her.

We could grab a drink at Paradise.

It's clear Alex knows her. I don't need him as a wingman. At least not yet. But if I'm at the bar enough…

"Can we jump off the front?" Jeannette asks, dragging my attention from Carina.

"The bow." I run through the safety protocol in my head. The water is ten feet deep. No visible rocks. The current isn't strong. Everyone swears they are fantastic swimmers. "Sure."

"You should jump with us." Jeannette lightly brushes my arm with her hand, giving me a flirtatious grin. Behind her, storms appear in Carina's eyes.

"I would, but as captain I'm required to stay on the boat. Regulations." It's a lie. But it's the best answer I've found for letting down a guest who wants more from me. Jeannette is pretty, but she's not doing anything for me the way Carina is. "Nathan is more than welcome to."

"Sure thing, Captain!" He practically leaps to the bow, where he holds Jeannette's hand. They count to three and jump together. Haley records on a phone.

Everyone else takes their turn, except Carina. "It's fun," I tell her. "I'll even jump with you."

"What happened to regulations?" she asks. Her skin is warm as we stand side by side. As close as we can be without touching. I could shift and then know what she feels like against me.

"Sometimes the risk is worth it." Her discerning gaze watches my expression. "But you got me there. Next time."

I need to focus on settling in town before considering a relationship. There is something about Carina that makes me want to try. I want more than one night with her. I want to learn everything that makes her tick. Really see how far we can take this. But she's a part of this town and now so am I. I can't sail away if it goes wrong. I have to be sure. I've been sure so many times before. This time the risks are higher than they've ever been.

It's late afternoon when I help her off at the dock. The sun still bright in the sky, but the radar tells me we're about to be hit with a thunderstorm, and I see clouds forming in the distance. I hold her hand a second longer than is strictly necessary. I tell myself this is only the beginning. I won't miss anything letting her go now. And I won't mess this up by jumping into something at full speed like I have before.

"Thank you," she says with a half smile I want to spread across her entire face. "It really was a beautiful day. And I owe you so much for imposing on your space."

I didn't mind her as much as I thought I would. "Next trip," I answer with a wink.

She shakes her head, but her smile grows when she turns to walk down the dock.

* * *

LATER THAT NIGHT, as I'm cleaning up the galley after dinner, I find a phone tucked between the cushions of the couch. The beach on the lock screen doesn't help me identify the owner. I grab my phone to send Carina an email.

"Orion?" The sound of her voice from the boat steps startles me so much I almost drop both devices.

"Fuck," I mutter, hopefully not too loudly. I turn to face her, so happy she was summoned by my thoughts.

"I'm so sorry. I didn't mean to... I shouldn't have... I'm so sorry." She starts to step back like she'll leave before accomplishing whatever she came here for. She's wearing leggings and a different tank top. The faintest sheen of sweat covers her skin.

"It's fine. I just didn't expect you." I hold out the phone. "This yours?"

"Yes. I can't believe I left it behind. It got passed around so much, I didn't even notice." She takes it with her brows scrunched like she expects judgment out of me for the simple mistake and taps away at the notifications.

"No problem," I say in the silence that follows. "I was about to email you."

She holds it to her chest and looks at me, giving me her full attention the way I've begun to crave. The lights are dim in the boat. She was beautiful in the sun, but she is radiant in the low light of this space that means so much to me.

"Thank you. I really appreciate it. And again, you were great today." She moves to leave. I wish she'd move to touch me. "I'll see you around."

"Do you want to stay for a drink?" I felt a connection with her earlier. We were flirty. I'll be around her again. But I'm desperate to not waste this opportunity. "Or did you drive?"

She bites her lip, looking around. She doesn't appear hesitant. Only calculating. She smiles. "I walked. A drink would be amazing."

I gesture for her to take a seat at the table. My personal belongings are out. The door to my cabin is open. I keep it neat and don't have a lot of stuff, but my life is exposed to her. I've lived on this boat for the past six months, and on and off for years before. It is the only home I've known as an adult. Now everything that matters to me is available for her viewing. I wonder how I measure up. She sits on the sofa bench at the table like she did this morning. Instead of looking around, or back at her phone, her gaze follows me as I remove a bottle of rum from the cupboard. I pour a glass and hand it to her.

"Is this straight rum?" she asks, picking it up, her expression neutral.

"Yes, it's a blend, and aged. Try a sip. If it's too much, I unfortunately don't have much else to offer." I bet she drinks a lot of wine, since she holds it to the light, examining the color. "I swear it's not a test if you can handle it or not. I'm just a bad host."

She smiles and takes a sip. Her eyebrows raise. "Wow, that's a lot better than I thought. I only ever drink rum in cocktails."

I pass her the bottle so she can inspect the label. I wait for the pirate joke that always comes, but she doesn't make it.

"Have you been to Paradise yet?"

"I haven't, no." I should tell her I know Alex, the owner, but I don't. I want this interaction to be about the two of us. She's concerned how people see her. She'll find out eventually, but I don't want to pop this bubble we've created.

"It's super cheesy, so you might wave it off. But there is always space in the locals' section and the food is amazing. Haley helps with the menus."

"It's on my list," I say. "I loved what she made today. I'll check out her recipes."

"You have to try her fish tacos. It's her most popular, and they're amazing."

As much as I find talking about bars and her friends fascinating, it's not what I'm interested in. "Did you have fun today?" The interior of my boat is spacious enough but it's still tight. I sit down on the short side of the L-shaped bench to not crowd her. She's settled into the long side. Her posture is a little slouchy and she tucks one foot underneath her.

"We did, yes. I feel so bad we took over your boat."

"Don't be. It worked out, and no one puked in my cabin so it's fine."

"I don't want to know why the bar is so low," she says with a laugh.

"You have no idea. Did you get the content you needed?" Social media is important to brands. I've been told I could monetize my travel by posting more than sunrises. But it was always for me and so my family back home could check in on how I was doing. I have someone else manage the social media for both charter companies. I never deal with it. Now content creation will always be the way Carina moved her body with strength and ease.

It was so fucking sexy. I could have watched her for hours. I still don't know why she hesitated to get out on the boards. I'm so glad she took the risk, even if it was only for a moment. I understand not jumping off the bow. She might be afraid of heights.

I must have failed in how I asked the question because she gets defensive. "Content is how I sell my products and make a living," she argues.

"I know, I wasn't judging. It seemed like the only time you let yourself have fun was when there was another reason behind it," I answer.

I see her tense as she considers me.

I want her at ease. "Never mind. It's none of my business."

I'm surprised she doesn't back down, but she softens a little. "You're not wrong. Which is a little annoying. I'm trying to be a good boss. And this trip was for them. Not me."

"Well, at least you're not working now."

"And here I thought you asked me to have a professional drink," she says, her tone light. She doesn't think I've misled her. She knows exactly why I asked her to stay.

For all her hesitancy about things, I have a feeling I know what she wants from me tonight. I just have to give her the opportunity. She's making sure we're on the same page before she takes a risk. She wants me to say it.

"It could be a professional drink. We can talk about business issues and plan future collaborations." I use a mock serious voice. "Exactly whose ass do I kiss for prime advertising at the local coffee shops?"

"It's the ice cream shops you want to get in with," she responds with a smile and a whisper, like she's revealing state secrets.

While I'm sure we could share business tips for hours, that's not what either of us want.

I don't want to have a professional drink. Neither does she. "Great, tip taken. Now business is over. Let's have a personal drink," I suggest.

"What's the difference between a personal and a professional drink?" she asks.

"Personal drinks are fun for the sake of fun. Not fun for the sake of marketing or product testing."

"I have done that before." She's defensive. "I can take time off."

"Really?" I'm skeptical. "Prove it. Let's play a game."

She looks at me over her glass, taking another sip. "What kind of game?"

"Two truths and a lie."

"This seems like a bit."

She sees right through me. I can't think of a better way to let her know exactly what I'm thinking and give her a chance to be vulnerable and safe. So I shrug and sip my rum. "It's up to you. But you should know, Carina, I expect honesty. You're mistaken if you think I don't notice all the little ways you hide."

She looks at me like she's hungry but doesn't react. I wonder what she expected when she walked over tonight. If this is what she was looking for.

I could be ruining absolutely everything right now. She could be imagining tossing her rum in my face and storming off. Telling Alex Barnes and the Foleys I'm a fuckwit they shouldn't do business with.

I'll be driven out of town by morning, if my conversations

with Alex and Nathan are any indication. The beautiful house I've remodeled, where I hear waves crashing on the beach, I'd have to convert to a vacation rental.

I won't have the anchor point I've sought since my accident all those months ago. I'll be cut loose and left to float with the current.

But if she wants this. If she's here the same way I am…

It'll be worth it.

"Fine." She pulls a metal water bottle from her bag and takes a drink. "You go first."

"My favorite place to sail is Santorini. I'm left-handed. I think you're beautiful." My glass is down so she can't tell which hand I prefer from that. But she watched me raise the sails earlier.

"You're definitely right-handed," she says.

I take a sip of my drink in response. "Your turn."

She flushes and looks at me, her mind calculating. This woman thinks everything through. She doesn't jump. Have I given her enough for her to trust me?

"My favorite yoga retreat was in Thailand. I'm not wearing panties. My eyes are green."

I almost don't catch the lie. My brain cut out when she said "panties." I can't help it. I look down at her lap as if I could see through the fabric.

"These leggings are Nebula Athletics," she says. "They're squat proof. No way you can see through."

"Do you always wear your own clothes?" I ask.

"Of course." She blinks a few times at the silliness of my question. "You haven't answered yet."

"I've sailed through storms the color of your *gray* eyes."

She takes a sip.

This is it. It feels right. It's not a risk anymore. The wind has blown me toward her. It's my turn again, and I'll place my lie in the middle. "I got tested after my last girlfriend and don't have any health concerns. I don't have any condoms. The sheets on my bed are clean." My wallet is on the shelf next to me, and from it, I take out the one condom I have.

"You can do laundry on this boat?" she asks quickly.

"I don't. I have a spare set."

"The obvious lie is the condom." Her eyes move from the condom to my face. "We should establish expectations."

I laugh, my whole body falling into it. I didn't expect her to swoon for me, but how quickly she switches from flirtation to business is unexpected.

Maybe it shouldn't be. I should have realized even a hookup is something she thinks through.

"What are your expectations, princess?"

She reacts to the name, sitting upright and inching closer to me. "Did Nathan say something about the 'princess of Wendell Beach' title? It's not really a thing. I organize a beach cleanup a few times a year. A few local business owners started calling me that in their posts. This town is too easy to impress."

"Expectations, princess." She's not easy to distract, until she is. I shouldn't admit how much I want to hear more about her volunteering.

"This is a one-time thing. Just a fling. No feelings. No commitments. We tell no one. We don't even need to bring it up with each other."

"I'm a big secret for you to keep." I'm hard thinking about what comes next—I can barely pay attention to what she's saying.

"We'll see," she says, not batting an eye for a second at my innuendo. "It's easier this way. You're new in town. We don't know how much we'll be interacting in the future. I'm not looking for anything serious. I bet you're leaving at the end of winter anyway. Heading back to Boston and your other company or wherever you decide. There's plenty of fish in the sea for you to occupy yourself until then."

"I agree to your terms." I do. I have no reason to expect this will go any further than tonight. I'm open to the idea. I'd like to get to know her more. I have a history of burning hot and then burning out. I don't want to anymore. If I date—and I wasn't planning on dating so soon after my move—I want it to be something meaningful. Maybe even permanent.

Maybe this doesn't go anywhere after tonight. Right now, I'd be open to exploring her again in a few months.

I don't correct her where she's wrong. I won't be leaving at the end of the winter and have no plans to occupy my time with anyone else.

I fully intend to take the night I get with Carina and make the most of it.

She inched closer to me as we had our little game. But she's not close enough to touch. We watch each other. It's another game to see who'll move first.

I won't. I can't.

She's been playing it safe with me all day. I won't let her do that now.

I look her in the eyes, and she looks at me for what feels like a solid minute in silence. Then she crosses the space between us and kisses me.

She's tentative at first, exploring the way my lips feel against hers. She's soft and sweet from the rum. Her tongue traces the seam of my lips and I'm done being gentle. I plunge into her mouth. This is supposed to be about her, but I'm selfish. So I take.

I cup her cheek, holding her exactly where I want her as her arms go around my neck and she climbs onto my lap. I need her closer. I need our clothes gone.

Nothing has ever felt this good.

four

CARINA

THIS BASTARD MADE ME MAKE THE FIRST MOVE.

His body rolls in waves beneath me.

I should have known he could get under my skin and sense what I need. As I straddle his lap and grind into his hard dick, I don't care how he did it. Not when everything about him feels good.

I didn't plan on this when I walked over here. I wanted my phone back. But Orion is so fucking hot, and I was open to the idea if it happened.

Nothing about this is permanent. That's why I only do flings. I know the expectations. He doesn't think he's leaving me on his pile of broken hearts. Both of us walk away as equals.

He pulls back and brushes a strand of hair that escaped my ponytail behind my ear and cradles my head so I'm looking at him. "Let's move to my cabin."

"Yes, please. And so you know, I was tested recently too." He gave me the courtesy of telling me his health status and I want to do the same. I also have an IUD, but I won't mention it. I believe him, but going without the condom requires far more trust than I have. "This is a one-time thing."

"You already said so. No need to continue trying to convince me."

"And don't get any ideas in your head about leaving me brokenhearted behind you." I can do this and be flirty with him. It's also the stubborn streak in my back. I refuse to be someone's conquest, the fool who fell in love and got left behind.

"Wouldn't dream of it." His smile is devastating.

I scramble off his lap with far less grace than I would like, and as soon as I'm standing again, he is right there with me. Kissing me like he's on a schedule and has only a little bit of time to possess me. My hands drift over his body, cataloging every muscle sailing has given him. We move to the cabin where he shuts and locks the door.

"For privacy," he says. "Anyone can wander onto a boat."

I nod. I trust him enough for that.

The cabin is small. The bed takes up most of it and there isn't any space on either side of it, just more storage benches. I climb up and he follows, pulling off his T-shirt as he hovers over me. He has a tattoo of an anchor over his heart, a compass by his hip and a few others scattered that I don't have time to examine because he's kissing me again.

"If we're only doing this once, then we're doing it my way," he says.

"Does that mean you want to tie me up?" Sailors must have a knot fetish.

"Absolutely not." He licks my neck and I close my eyes at the sensation. "There is a time and place for that, but I want you wild and free."

God, he feels so good against me. "What does that mean?" I ask.

"You seem really buttoned up," he says, pulling back from me and tugging at the hem of my tank. "I'm guessing everyone you've been with has treated you like a princess. I saw you today. I know how strong you are, how flexible you are. You won't break."

I remove my sports bra as he goes for my leggings. I hate that he knows this about me already. This man who has been in my life for a few hours already sees so many things people I've been friends with for years have missed. Things the man I was with for years didn't see.

"I don't know if I'll like it rough."

"It doesn't have to be rough. Just not restrained." He has my leggings around my knees and pauses, blinking rapidly as he takes in my body. "Is the panty thing for me or a normal occurrence?"

I laugh as I help him pull the leggings off. "No, they leave lines. My leggings are designed—"

He waves me off, tossing the leggings to the floor with the rest of my clothes. "Shhhh…explain clothing manufacturing to me after orgasms."

He stretches across the bed and moves me to my side, placing himself behind me. I shiver in his arms as he does nothing except hold me for a moment, his erection hard against my back.

He kisses my neck, seemingly fascinated by the skin there. "This only works if you're honest with me, okay?"

"Okay," I say. He's constantly asking for my honesty. I didn't realize how much I had been denying it to everyone or understand why I'm willing to expose myself to him when I was so afraid of him seeing weakness before.

"I have a feeling I know what will make you feel good, but I can be an ass, so I might be wrong," he continues.

"I'll tell you." My legs shake as he moves his callused hand down my side, momentarily stopping to trace my constellation tattoo, the only one I have, then to my waist and between my legs. My breath catches. Instead of going where I want him, he hooks my leg over his, so I'm spread open.

His touch is light as he resumes his journey, happy that I'm now completely where he wants me. "You're so fucking sexy," he says. His fingers brush my clit and where I'm wet. After the heat that brought us here, I expected rough and fast. But he's slow and gentle and it feels so good.

His other arm goes around me so I'm plastered against his chest. I can't move. I'm trapped with him. And I feel so completely safe.

Not necessarily because of him. No, he's dangerous. He could make me fall in an instant. I could drown in him without realizing it. But I've made my rules. They will keep me afloat.

"How's your endurance?" he asks.

"Hmmm?" I don't understand. He dips a finger at my entrance but doesn't penetrate.

"How long can you last while I tease you?"

I orgasm fine, either by myself or with a partner. "I don't know."

"I can do this all night," he declares. He gathers my wetness and gives my clit the faintest of touches. "Getting you so close you beg."

I whimper at the thought.

"Maybe I have other ideas." He enters me with a finger and I moan. "Fuck, you're so responsive. I love it."

I was soaked already. He slides in and out so easily, adding another finger. He plays for a moment, his thumb on my clit finding a perfect rhythm as his fingers work inside me. I shouldn't trust a stranger like this. I shouldn't be open, but he wrenches it out of me. I can't deny him.

It's not sex I need. It's him. It's Orion.

His other hand plays with my nipple, pinching it harder than I'm used to, but I like it. With the way he has me, I'm completely at his mercy. But all he cares about is making me feel good.

My orgasm builds. I'm almost embarrassed at how fast it happens. Right before I'm pushed over, he removes his hand from me.

"Fuck." I squeeze his arm.

How did he know?

"Not yet." He kisses the side of my neck.

"Why not?" I reach to put his hand back where it was.

"Beg," he commands.

"No." But I want to. This is new for me. Games in bed that are for my pleasure, not his. A challenge about me breaking in ecstasy, rather than how much I can bend for someone else.

If I drag this out a little longer, I'll be rewarded.

He nibbles my earlobe. "Come on, Carina. Be a good girl and beg. I bet you do it perfectly."

I haven't felt such clarity as I do in this moment with him. We're both playing a role with each other. We both want this, and he could thrust into me easily. But he's not getting me ready to take him. He's enjoying giving me pleasure. The game makes everything better.

He's right—I hide from everyone else. I'm terrified of anyone seeing my flaws. I can be perfect for him and give him what he wants. He's already stripped me down. I don't have to be afraid of him.

"Please, Orion. I need you."

He turns my head to face his and kisses my lips. At the same time, his other hand resumes its position in me. "Good girl," he whispers. It only takes a few touches on my clit before I come hard. My entire body tense, and then relaxed, and I feel completely wrapped up in him.

I catch my breath as he holds me against his chest.

"Glad your phone got left behind?" he whispers as he peppers my neck with light kisses.

"I'm starting to wonder if you hid it to get me here."

"I'll manipulate you in bed, but never out of it. I don't have the energy for that."

"Good." I move onto my back and inch away from him slightly. I want a better look at him. He's about to be inside me. I want to memorize his face.

The lights are low in the cabin. It's dark outside, but I see enough. I love the lines of his jaw and his perfect amount of scruff. What I can't wrap my head around is the look he's giving me. Like I matter to him.

This is supposed to be transactional. We both get off and move on. But he's not looking at me like it's a transaction and this doesn't feel empty.

He grabs the condom and pulls his shorts down. The anticipation builds in my stomach.

This could wreck me. I take a deep breath and remind myself of my rules. It's one time. He won't get under my skin if I don't let him.

His cock is out, and I reach to stroke it while he unwraps the condom. It's heavy and thick and suddenly the stretching he did with his fingers feels necessary.

I'm relaxed and feel like I'd do anything to have him. I'll beg again if he asks.

Once he's sheathed himself, I lie back on the bed.

"How are you doing this?" I ask.

He follows me down, his body hovering over mine as he casually tosses one of my legs over his shoulder and then wraps the other around his hip.

He leans down, pushing my knee to my shoulder, somehow knowing it's an easy position for me. "You think you're not an active participant in this?"

I'm not passive in bed. But most men I've been with haven't given me much to work with—we pick one position and ride it out until he orgasms. They take advantage of my flexibility to get a good look at my ass while they're in me and it works for them. I can get myself off.

Orion slowly eases his cock into me. "Fuck." I grab his shoulders as he stretches me past the point I'm used to.

"Breathe through it. You can take it."

"Arrogant bastard," I murmur.

He smiles and then kisses me. "I'm only as good as the woman I'm with."

"Oh fuck off." I laugh. He's fun to be with.

"You want me to go?" He starts to pull out.

"No!" I grab onto his biceps and pull him back until his pelvis hits my clit. I suck in a breath and close my eyes with contentment.

I expect him to start thrusting, but he stills, his hands on my hips.

After a long moment, I open my eyes. "Are you going to do something?"

"I was waiting on you."

"For what?"

"To move. Show me what you got, Carina."

I kind of hate his arrogant, sexy ass, but I love the way he's making me smile. I want to let loose and have fun and he's already balls deep in me. Maybe I suck at sex. If it turns out I do, I'm sure he'll take over and make it good for both of us. This is a man who takes care of the woman he's with.

I swivel my hips and we both moan at the sensation. He answers by thrusting in and out of me like I wanted. He brushes my clit exactly right and he's hitting a place deep inside me everyone else has missed.

"Fuck, just like that. Don't stop," I groan. He thrusts deeper and I swear I see stars. I didn't think I would come again, but it's building, and I don't know if I can handle it.

"Wouldn't dream of it." One of his hands moves from my hip to my breast and lightly rubs my nipple. I expect him to go hard like he did before, but this caress is different. A contrast to his hard thrusts.

This is us. Together. It's not him fucking me or the other way around. We're both making this happen.

"Fuck, Orion. I'm so close!"

"I know, princess. You can do this. Let yourself have this."

When was the last time I let myself have anything?

He licks his finger and places it where our bodies meet and all it takes is a tiny bit of pressure and everything inside me explodes.

My orgasm goes on for ages.

I swear it's a spiritual experience.

I'm barely aware of anything else except the constant pulse of Orion between my legs as he shifts them so they both wrap around his hips, and he lowers himself, until his body is flush with mine. I hold him tight, his face buried in my neck. Every part of me needs to feel him.

His movements become ragged, his breath faster. His muscles tense under my hands. I squeeze his hips with my thighs.

"Fuck!" he growls, and his entire body shakes as he comes.

When we both finally still, I'm aware of the sweat covering us. I could feel self-conscious, but I don't.

He doesn't speak. Instead, he brushes back the hair that's fallen in my face.

"I…" I don't know how to react.

"Yeah…" he agrees.

We pause, taking each other in. I should look away. But I stare into his eyes, their brown waiting for me to tell him how good it was. How I'm changed by it.

Fuck, it was. But I can't say it.

He has to feel it too. I can't risk finding out that was an ordinary fuck to him. I have to take control.

"This was a one-time thing," I say when he's still in me.

"Right." His tone is as cold as I feel when he pulls out.

I grab my clothes and retreat to the bathroom. It's tiny and I barely have room to maneuver, but I don't want to get dressed in front of him. My hands shake. I've never felt anything like that before. It wasn't the orgasm, but the connection I felt with him. I should say something to him, to know if he feels the same. I'll be devastated if I am just another lay to him.

But it doesn't matter anyway. I'm sure I'll see him around. It's not like he wants a relationship. I'm not ready for one that so obviously will end.

I open the door and he's back in his shorts and T-shirt, adjusting the sheets on the bed.

"Is that a sailor thing? Make the bed as soon as you're out of it?"

He smiles, and I'm devastated anyway. "Yeah, old habit. Small space."

"Well, I should go. It's been a long day and I have to be up in the morning."

"I'll walk you home," he offers.

"It's fine. It's not late and the area is safe." I grab my purse from the kitchen and double-check I have my phone. "I'll see you around."

Before he gets the chance to protest, I climb the stairs and am gone.

 five

ORION

I wasn't done with her.

I have no idea what happened. It was supposed to be fun—she'd let loose and I'd break up my dry spell. I hadn't planned on a hookup so soon after arriving in Wendell Beach and starting my new life. I certainly didn't expect to feel connected to her. To need her so much.

I tidy up the galley, washing the glasses we used. Then I make my way to the bow of the boat, with the bottle of rum in my hand. I might as well go full pirate as I think about the way she came apart. The night air is hot and sticky, the breeze off the water barely making it tolerable. I love the feel of it. I love the sound of the water hitting the hulls of the boats around me. Otherwise, it's quiet here. Any nightlife this island has is somewhere else. This has been my life for so long. Me, alone on the *Twisted Rigging*. But it's changing.

I've hooked up with women on my boat before and sailed around with girlfriends. When they left, either for the night or for good, it didn't matter to me. Sure, we'd made memories together. But they hadn't seeped into the construction of the boat. Carina rose to my every challenge. She was free with me and so utterly perfect.

I know, just as I know my own name, she's never uninhibited like she was with me. It was in the way she laughed. The way she looked into my eyes after. She gave me something she's never given anyone else. I don't know what I've done to deserve it. She was bold and brave and so fucking beautiful.

It didn't hurt exactly when she said it would never happen again. But it felt wrong. I don't need a relationship right now. Not with moving and getting everything squared away with the business I just bought. I want her again, and I would've thought she would've been open to the idea after I delivered two mind-blowing orgasms.

But she was out of here so fast, as if it was nothing to her.

She must be as terrified as I should be.

This feels different. I should be scared. I'm familiar with the exciting first days of chemistry with a new flame. When every movement is intense, and it feels like it'll last forever because how could anything this good ever end?

Carina was different. Raw. I am adrift without her.

I want her back here, but I can't chase after her.

Six

I don't normally end up at Paradise at three in the afternoon on a workday, but my week has been so thoroughly fucked that I don't question it.

The street I live on dead-ends at the beach. I have uninterrupted views of the Gulf of Mexico. A few feet from my front door is a path through the beach grass that takes me over the sand dunes and directly to the water. It's quiet for the most part, with people only venturing here if they live on my street or have rented one of the houses as a vacation property. All the houses have the same Key West-style architecture, with pastel paint and wraparound porches, regardless of when they were built. We're supposed to feel transported to a different time and a different island, two hundred miles south of us.

The house next door to me, which mine blocks from having a perfect sea view, was sold six months ago. Since then, it's been through extensive renovations. The noise has been truly terrible at times. It must be almost done because the same SUV has been parked in the driveway the last few days.

I'm sure it's been transformed into a short-term rental property. I miss the former owners. I grew up with the elderly couple

"

watching out for me during our vacations here. Mrs. Lawson always made sure I reapplied sunscreen and refilled my lemonade when my parents were too busy with work to care about me frolicking on the beach. It's a miracle I didn't drown.

The Lawsons were having troubles with the house's narrow staircase, so they moved to a retirement community on the mainland. It's just across a short bridge, but that strip of water makes it seem so much farther than it is. I now need to prepare myself for loud parties and people who don't feel any sense of responsibility for the area.

This morning a truck delivered furniture and I needed to be out of the house for as long as possible. I can't concentrate in my home office with its sliding glass doors facing that house, and every noise breaks my concentration. Then I look at my phone and wonder that while I didn't give Orion my number, I still feel like I'm waiting on him to call.

I have years of experience with mindfulness. I know how to control my thoughts. It's been a week, but I can't get him out of my head.

I've never felt a connection like that with anyone else. Not even Hamilton when we were years into our relationship. Sex never made me feel closer to him. It was a fun thing we did. I live by the lessons my mother instilled in me when I was fifteen: Relationships always end. There is no such thing as a happy ever after. Leave before you get left.

It's cold, but living any other way feels too much like a risk.

Instead of working from home, I walk the mile to the Wendell Beach downtown area and the Nebula Athletics storefront. It's the location of my first-ever store, the yoga studio I opened a few years later, and our corporate office. It's right on the town's main street, surrounded by restaurants, tourist shops, and resort wear boutiques. All of them have the town's same pastel-colored buildings with balconies on their second stories.

It's here I answer emails about supply chain issues, brainstorm new fabrics with the design team, and co-teach a vinyasa class to a group of women from Georgia who traveled to Wendell Beach to visit the studio. I'm incredibly honored their road trip through Florida involved a stop at a place I created. It happens often, but it always means the world to me when I hear it.

I founded the company while I was getting my MBA. My dad wanted me to start as soon as I could. Most first businesses fail. He thought if I got it out of the way young, then I could recover faster and better. I'm determined to prove him wrong. I won't fail at all. My first business is my last. It will continue to succeed.

Unfortunately, he's convinced it will end any day. My sales numbers don't matter, or which celebrities are seen coming out of a spin class in my leggings.

After the yoga class, I'm sweaty and grabbing my things to go home to shower and finish up the rest of my work there, crossing my fingers that the noise has ended. My friend Christian walks into the lobby. He owns Wendell Beach Rum Works which is next door to the studio. We have lunch together frequently. Sometimes he offers to drive me home when it's storming.

"Hey, Carina. Any chance you're done for the day?"

A few of the students from the next class notice him and browse the racks of clothes instead of heading into the studio space. But they aren't paying attention to the clothes, they're watching us.

Christian and I have been friends for years. He's married to a lovely woman named Autumn and has never once flirted with anyone else. But that doesn't change the fact he's one of the most attractive people I've ever met. I beg him to model for me, but he declines. He's an excellent friend and wears my T-shirts with jeans like they're his uniform.

Of course, my mind drifts to what Orion would look like draped in the fabrics and cuts I plan. But I need to refocus on the now and not on the sailor I met a few days ago.

"I can be," I respond. I'll catch up on work later. If he's here, it's probably because he needs something. I'm always happy to help him. "What's up?"

"I'm opening the first bottle of a new batch with Alex at Paradise. Thought you might want to join."

I understand this is a moment he wants to share with Alex. They are close friends. But I don't know why he's reaching out to me. I'm near him, that's all.

I shouldn't take time off in the middle of the afternoon to sample alcohol. But a thought niggles my brain—it's rum. Orion loves rum. Christian will give me an entire history of its origins and how this batch was created. When I see Orion next, I'll have something to discuss with him.

I stopped at the liquor store the other day to grab a bottle of wine. I strolled through the rum aisle, looking for the bottle I shared with Orion. I wanted to remember the way he tasted on my lips. They didn't have it, and I was so disappointed.

But it's a terrible idea. I don't want to hook up with him again. I stick to flings because I know how those end. I set expectations. And with the precautions I take, the biggest risk is it isn't fun. I felt something deeper with Orion. This could turn into something more. I could become invested. He doesn't have any connection to Wendell Beach. He could leave at any time. He lives on a boat. Dreams of sailing around the world. This place won't hold him long. And I'll be left standing on a beach, alone.

He demanded my honesty. No one has wanted that from me before.

Christian asked me to join him for this occasion. He is truly one of the nicest, most caring men I have ever met. He inherited his grandparents' distillery a few years ago and has worked diligently to make it better than it was before. He didn't have any business experience, so I taught him how to keep his books in order and developed a solid marketing plan for him. He took my advice and ran with it. He's a few years younger than me and has done so much with what he has been given.

He probably doesn't have investors breathing down his neck to take his marketing in a different direction.

"Sure. But I'm sweaty," I answer.

"It's Florida. Everyone is always sweaty. Get your water and get over it." He smiles.

I grab my bag, wave goodbye to my staff, and head out the door with him.

I apologize one more time for my scent as I climb into his pickup truck.

"Seriously, Carina. Bristol drives my truck after kayaking. Haley has spilled raw fish in here. You're the least smelly of our friends." He's probably right, but I feel guilty about it. "Plus, isn't your fabric formulated to reduce clingy odors? Or is it a marketing ploy?"

"It's real," I say.

Once we're at Paradise, a place so familiar to us it feels like a second home, we sit at the square bar in the center of the locals' section where Alex greets us. Christian hands him the bottle of rum, while I take a moment to admire and appreciate the view. The main level of the restaurant opens out to the beach, giving us a perfect perspective of the gentle waves. I never get tired of seeing it. Inside is decorated with seashells, driftwood, and palm fronds.

"Anyone else joining, or can I open it?" Alex asks, not bothering to hide his impatience as he taps the bottle with his fingertips.

Christian looks at his phone and frowns. "Go ahead. Haley can't make it. Something about steak marinating."

"Autumn?" I ask after his wife. She should be here supporting him.

He shakes his head. "School's back in for the fall. She has theater club."

I wonder if this moment isn't important enough for him to

wait for her or if something else is happening. They're a great couple, but she doesn't hang out with our group much.

"Shouldn't I get to open it?" Christian's sister Bristol walks up to the bar with a container of limes. "It's my grandparents too." They both have the same sandy blond hair. Hers is tied back in a ponytail. She's growing out her bangs and often complains about being in the awkward stage where she can't put them behind her ears.

"My bar. My rules. My rum," Alex says with a fake stern glare at his bartender. She rolls her eyes and gets out four tulip-shaped glasses.

Christian lifts his after Alex has poured, examining the color in the bright sunlight. "This is our first long-aged rum. My grandfather blended it fifteen years ago. When we were kids, he never let Bristol and me in the distillery. After I turned eighteen, he took me around and pointed to the barrels and told me these were his legacy, even if he'd never get to taste it."

The emotion on his face is obvious. I find myself fighting back tears.

"To Jake Bailey." Alex lifts his glass, knowing Christian will go on about the man, and it will be easier if we have a drink first.

"Jake Bailey," we echo.

I take a sip and appreciate the way it tastes sweet on my tongue. It's different from the rum I had with Orion but I like it all the same. I can't think about it without remembering the way his skin felt under my lips. The way I tasted rum on his.

"It's good." I refocus myself and scan the bottles behind the bar for Orion's preferred blend. It's there on the top shelf, next to another bottle of Wendell Beach Rum.

I smile.

Alex gives me a look as he refills his glass. "I didn't know you ever drank straight liquor."

"Not usually, but Christian asked, and this is good," I say.

That's the downside of having a friend who is also your

bartender—they tend to learn your drinks quickly and how they change with your mood. I drink mojitos and daiquiris at the bar, and wine everywhere else. He knows this and I expect a comment if I stray.

I'm sure if I drank more diversely, he wouldn't comment. Our friend Sienna drinks everything under the moon. She lives in Boston, and when she visits he goes out of his way to create recipes hoping to find her a new favorite.

I ask Christian a few more questions about the rum, something I can tuck away to casually drop into conversation if I run into Orion. *Hey, so good to see you. Small town, right? Wendell Beach Rum Works has a new blend you should try. Oh, you don't know where it is? No worries, I can take you. I'm friends with the owner.*

I shouldn't be thinking this. I'm not planning on beginning a relationship with him. I don't have time to commit to anyone. Even a fling with someone in town feels risky. Those purposefully happen away from home. Then I don't have the chance to get attached. Thinking about Orion like this feels like I'm getting attached. It's too big of a risk. It'll blow up in my face. I've been protecting myself for far too long to let this man under my skin.

If I run into him around town, I'll be pleasant and professional and pretend nothing happened, like we agreed we would. I'm sure it will happen. There are only a few thousand permanent residents, and with school just back in session, the visiting crowds have thinned. If I see him more than in passing, I'll cave to my temptations and sleep with him again. I can't do that right now.

"You should have a launch party for it," I suggest to Christian. "Really get people excited."

Christian shakes his head. "I don't have time to plan anything."

"I could help," I offer. I want to do this. I want something to invite Orion to. Show him off and let him meet everyone I'm friends with.

But I push the thought away. I won't send him mixed messages, even as I send them to myself. I'll do this for Christian. He might pretend this doesn't matter to him, but it does. Someone should promote it. And seeing Orion right now is a distraction I don't need.

"Don't you have enough with Sienna's wedding?" he asks.

I groan. He's right. Her wedding is in two months. Since it's taking place in Wendell Beach and she lives in Boston, a lot of the errand-running has fallen on Haley and me. Her fiancé, Beckett, hasn't helped nearly as much as he promised he would.

"Not a full party then, but something special. This is a big deal, Christian."

"I know." His voice is quieter than I expect.

"Right, I'm headed home. I have marketing research due by the end of the week," I say. I slide from my barstool, grab my bag, and wave goodbye to everyone.

Paradise is so close to my house, it's a given I'll walk, so there's no polite offer from anyone to give me a ride. I put on my sunglasses and head out the beach side of the restaurant. The fine white sand is hot on my bare feet as I carry my flip-flops. I do this short trip so often it's easy to ignore what's around me. But I appreciate the beauty of the beach and the vastness of the gulf. This beach stretches the entire seven miles of the gulf side of the island. The water is relatively still today. It's early enough that I might have time for a paddle before sunset. It's so hot out and I want nothing more than to plunge into the water. I pick up my pace. At least now it doesn't matter how sweaty I am.

I get home, and after grabbing a glass of water, head to my back porch. The neighbor's house is quiet and I didn't see the SUV parked out front. I want to sit for a few moments and see if I can reclaim a little bit of the equilibrium that's been missing over the last week. Then I'll grab my board and head out to the water. Market research can be done after the sun sets. What's the point of owning an athletic wear company if I'm too busy to use the clothing?

I see movement from the corner of my eye in the neighbor's yard and turn.

"No, you can't be here," I gasp. I expected the shirtless form of a stranger.

Instead, I see the beautiful skin and tattoos of the man I can't get out of my head.

SEVEN

ORION

I knew moving to Florida in August would be demanding. The endless heat and humidity drain my existence. But the renovations are done on the house and I'm ready for this new chapter of my life. All the improvements had to be done before I moved in. Otherwise, I'd be tempted to escape rather than deal with the chaos of construction projects.

I don't have a lot of belongings, so the house needs to be filled. Today was delivery day for my furniture. My sister, Brooklynn, told me to hire an interior decorator, but I don't want outside influences on how my house looks or feels. I want my vision to come through. It was risky since I'd never decorated anything before, the boat only ever having the necessities. But I'm happy with the results as I walk from room to room. It feels like home to me.

Now that my bedroom is set up, tonight will be the first night I spend here. I love the *Twisted Rigging*, but my pillow smells like Carina. It made me antsy from wanting her.

I'm hot from the moving, and even with the a/c on, I feel sticky. I had the pool cleaned a few days ago, and I decide to check it out. I step into my backyard and pull off my shirt.

That's when I hear her voice.

"No, you can't be here."

I turn to the house next to me, the one between me and the water. And only a few feet from me, looking perfect, is Carina. The sun dips toward the horizon behind her and the light hits her blond hair, making it look like a halo. She's wearing yoga clothes. *Did she come from the studio?* Her hands rest on her hips like she's angry.

My mind freezes. I genuinely don't know how to react to her. I wasn't expecting to see her. At least not like this.

I'm so fucking happy.

I've been thinking about her constantly, but I'm biding my time. I'd let it happen naturally at Paradise or bring her up casually with Alex. As much as I can't stop replaying the way she came, I didn't think our paths would cross this soon.

The fence between our houses is low enough that I can see straight through to the beach from my raised deck. If I'm in the pool below, I have a little privacy. But right now I'm elevated, and I see her standing on her deck.

She looks mad.

"Sorry?" I let her know I'm confused.

"You can't be here."

"I don't know what to tell you, but I am." Is Carina my next-door neighbor? The thought of having her close to me all the time sends all my blood straight to my dick.

I shift my body away from her, like I'm surveying the land. I can't get hard right now. It'll be too obvious in my shorts. I don't think that will endear me to her.

"No, that's not right," she says.

"Will you come around so we can talk about this like adults?" We both have gates on this side of our houses. She can be here easily and then we're not shouting at each other.

She huffs but does what I ask, while I put my shirt back on.

She's seen me naked, but I can't read her right now. While distracting her with memories of sex might be fun, I should give her the chance to focus. None of this is a game to me. I'm certainly thinking about the future, and not just now—I've thought about pursuing a relationship with her, but I have to be careful. Her living next door gives me too much access to her. It could get dangerous fast.

"What are you doing here?" she asks when she gets close to me.

"I live here," I say.

"No, that's not possible. You live on a boat."

"I moved."

"But I live here."

"No, pretty sure I bought this house."

She rolls her eyes. "I mean, I live there." She points to the house next to me.

"Fascinating." I shove my hands into my pockets. "Well, this makes it easy for you to show me around town."

"No. I can't do this."

"Why?" My annoyance grows. We didn't leave on the best of terms with her flying out of the cabin. I thought that was because everything was more intense than we expected. Not that she never wanted to see me.

"We can't sleep together again."

"I know. You said that. We're neighbors. We're not sharing a bedroom or anything." Eventually, I'll at least convince her that visiting each other's bedrooms is a good idea.

She looks around as if searching for an exit, and I need her attention back on me.

"Let's go inside," I suggest, turning to the door. She nods and follows. I lead us through my living room to the kitchen. It's the first room after my bedroom I unpacked. I can't wait to spread out and cook everything I don't have the space for on the boat. I checked out Haley's blog and I already bought what I need for the famous fish tacos.

Carina's skin is a little pink. I can't tell if it's from the sun or if she was working out. She walked to the marina that day, and now that I know where she lives, I'm not all that surprised. She probably does that a lot. I've checked out her brand—she's genuinely concerned about the environment, focusing on sustainable fabrics and recyclable packaging. Maybe she just got home?

I don't understand why she doesn't wear a hat.

She's removed her sunglasses and holds them in one hand as she plants herself in front of the fridge. I lean back against the counter with my arms crossed, watching her.

"Look, the sex was great, but it won't happen again," she says.

I take a small victory in her admitting that much. "Spell out why for me, exactly. And detailed, please." I need to know what she's thinking. I won't play catch-up.

"I only do flings. Short, casual, we have our fun and then go our separate ways. If we're neighbors, which we are, we can't go our separate ways. It'll get messy."

It might not get messy, but based on my history, she's right.

"What if it doesn't get messy? What if it works?" I counter.

She rolls her eyes. "I'm thirty-two. You're, what?"

"Thirty-five."

"You're single so it clearly hasn't worked for you before. It's never worked out for me," she continues. "No reason to believe after one night this one would be different."

"You're committed to being single forever?" We're both young enough. This isn't the eighteen hundreds. She's not a spinster. Isn't the whole point of dating to find the one that does work?

"I have a fulfilling life. I don't owe you an explanation of my choices. Are *you* even looking to settle down?" Her "you" is full of accusation—she can't imagine I'd want this.

Yes, I want to yell. But she's right, at least for now. I need to get my life in order with moving and the new business before I pursue any type of relationship. I don't know if things would work out with her. But just because I don't know the future doesn't mean I'm willing to completely write us off. I can wait. Get to know her better. Then take a fully informed risk.

I never sail without knowing the weather. This is the same thing.

"Even if I did want to settle down," I muse, testing some waters, "and things went well between us, we'd eventually want to move in together. My place or yours?" She's a thinker and a planner. Let's see how far ahead she plans.

She answers fast. She knows what she wants. "I love my house. It's right on the beach. And as nice as this remodel is"—she gestures to my cabinets with both hands—"I'm not moving farther from the beach." She clearly thinks if we can't move in together, then we're doomed from the start.

And I poured my soul into this house—I'm not giving it up for anything or anyone. Sure, she might be slightly closer to the water, but the exchange isn't worth it for what this place means to me already. "I'm not going anywhere either."

"Really? I thought you'd be gone by the end of winter and list this as a vacation rental."

"Nope, I'm here for good. You're stuck with me," I say.

"You're really not off to the Med or Turks and Caicos?"

I shrug. "For a short trip, sure. But Wendell Beach is my home port from now on."

She looks skeptical. "Right. Well, either way, if it works or if it doesn't between us, we'll both end up miserable. So we shouldn't."

I've learned something about Carina in the last minute I don't think anyone else knows: she says things she doesn't believe. But the truth is easy to pick out.

If our hooking up was only a fling, and was something we are both okay with, then there wouldn't be any risk. We could hook up, it would be great, and then we'd stop and we could live next to each other and everything would be fine.

The only way it would end in catastrophe would be if feelings got involved.

So, she's as wrecked as I am over what happened last week.

She's right. If we hook up again, it won't be enough. We'll consume each other until our world explodes. She's dug in. If she claims she won't move, then she won't.

But I bought this house to be my home. To be a promise of a stable future. Everyone back in Boston might think I'll be bored in a few months and ready to move on. They're wrong.

It's not out of stubbornness or a need to be right. It is about me knowing my mind and knowing even if I was wrong those times before, I'm not wrong now.

This time is different. I need to tread carefully around Carina Webb.

I'm planting here. It's not just that she's next door, but she's also a pillar of the community. I've looked her up since that day. In addition to her polished Instagram feed, she constantly shows up in posts from other small businesses. I also found articles about her advocacy for native wildlife. She might not take revenge on me if I hurt her, but I have a feeling this community would. They know what she's done for them. They will go to bat for her in a way I'm not prepared to cross. If this goes wrong, the way it has with every other woman I've been with, I'll lose everything I'm trying to build. I knew that when we were on my boat. I truly thought it would be just the one time. Before I knew how good it was and wanted more.

What does it mean, that this feels different to me? That she would be different?

But no matter how good the sex is, if she is so against it, I won't risk my home. Not for her and not for anyone.

So I agree with her lie. "You're right. I'm not looking for a relationship. Never had one that lasted more than a few weeks anyway. We should just be neighbors." Anything more than neighbors is taking a risk. I need to be willing to gamble.

I'm not sure I'm ready to yet.

"Good. I'm glad we got that out of the way." She finally looks around her. She'd been so focused on me that she hadn't looked at the house.

She's been next door this whole time, so she must have noticed the contractors. I deeply hope they haven't been a pain for her. I couldn't be around for any of it, so Alex checked on things periodically. He assured me things were moving smoothly and not a bother to the area.

Funny he never mentioned my neighbor.

I practically gutted the place. It hadn't been updated in years, and since I am making this my first home on land since I was a teenager, I wanted the best of everything.

Carina scans the kitchen.

When I bought it, the cabinets were from the eighties and the appliances the nineties. I put in white cabinets and a blue marble countertop. All the appliances are stainless steel and state-of-the-art. I can watch a movie on my fridge if I want to.

She looks down the hall to the living room and slowly walks that way, peeking into the two guest rooms. She's mentally noting every detail and change.

I want to know what she's seeing. Did she know the people who lived here before me? I don't know how long she's been in Wendell Beach, and I honestly don't know anything about the sellers. I did the showing in person, which they were absent for, and the rest was done remotely.

She gets to the living room, to where I have a couch set up with a big-screen TV. Across is a wet bar, already filled with a few bottles of my favorite rum.

"How?" she asks.

I wait for her to finish the question, but she doesn't. "How what?"

"How does it already feel like a home?" Her voice is full of awe.

Her question knocks me on my heels. Does it feel like a home to her? It feels like more to me. It's the exact sensation I want to convey.

I shrug, not wanting to betray how meaningful the comment is.

"I've watched the renovations happen and I thought it would be soulless. But it's not."

"Thanks. I'll be here for a long time. I want the place to reflect that," I say.

"I'll have to get your list of contractors. My place needs a few updates."

"How long have you lived there?" I ask.

She bobs her head. "The math is fuzzy. My parents bought it when they were newlyweds. It's mine now, outright. I moved in full-time about seven years ago."

"I'm sorry for your loss." I don't know anything about her family situation.

She looks at me strangely. "Oh, they're not dead. Just the world's messiest divorce."

"Right." I wonder if that's the reason she's so against relationships.

"So, we're good?" she asks, coming out of whatever surprised her so much.

"We're good." We're good enough for now, anyway.

She moves to leave but turns back to me. "Oh, I was at Paradise this afternoon. It's the beach bar I mentioned to you."

"I do know it." I might as well come clean. "I haven't been yet. I should confess—the owner was the best man at my sister's wedding."

"You know Alex?"

"Yes."

"You didn't tell him about us, did you?"

"No." I narrow my eyes. I told her I wouldn't.

"Oh good. I would rather no one know. I didn't even tell Haley." She sounds relieved.

She hides from her friends and overshares with me. *Great.* "You said that before."

"It's just…you know Alex—he can be a bit meddlesome. And if there was any hint of attraction between us, he'd play matchmaker. It's his thing."

That seems right. He introduced Brooklynn and her husband, Spencer. "Does he know where you live?" I ask.

"Yes, he's been over a million times," she says.

"Strange he's never mentioned you to me, since he knows I bought this place."

She rolls her eyes. "Exactly. No reason to give him more to work with."

If he had told me my charter guest was my neighbor, that night would have gone differently. He had to know.

"Anyway, back to Paradise," she continues. "My friend, Christian, owns Wendell Beach Rum Works. He had me taste his new batch. I think you'd like it."

I look at her and smile. She was drinking rum and thinking about me. I've suspected she says one thing and thinks another. This is the moment when I have absolute proof. "Thanks, I'll check it out."

She smiles at me and then turns to walk out my front door.

"Carina, wait," I say. She turns with a confused look on her beautiful face. Her eyebrows scrunch together, making her nose look adorable. "You know I won't go easy on you."

"What do you mean?"

"I told you I see the hiding you do from everyone. You won't be able to hide from me."

I don't know how things will go with her living next door to me. I will focus a lot of attention on getting to know her. It's probably a terrible idea. I need to focus on other things, but I won't be able to get the feeling of Carina moving beneath me out of my mind for an extremely long time.

"I have no idea what you're talking about," she says.

The slight smile on her face tells me she likes that I see her when no one else does.

eight

CARINA

I wish I could say I was able to handle Orion living next door to me like a reasonable adult, but that would be an absolute lie. It's been three days, and I have his patterns memorized.

He's up early kayaking. After he returns, he drives off wearing a polo shirt with the Lost Craft Charters logo on it. I assume he spends the day captaining charters, and my stomach twists at the thought that he's flirting with other clients. Having personal drinks with them.

I absolutely don't check the website to see if the *Twisted Rigging* is booked.

I do that.

It's gone from their website. It takes a few minutes of investigating to confirm it's out of their inventory and not booked. My charter was a fluke, then. I really should do something to make up for it. Give him a plant or dish to put his keys in. Some thoughtful housewarming gift.

I liked the fantasy of him being around, but it was supposed to be a fantasy. I'm not prepared for him to be in my life. Because even though in my dreams we have a committed, loving relationship, trying for one in real life is too big of a risk, especially with someone who has a history of wandering. I can't imagine he'll be in Wendell Beach for long. He'll get restless and sail off for Bermuda. It's pointless to even imagine.

I need to keep my thoughts on what's important to me. But they always drift, and I hear my father's voice.

"Your mother's and my marriage has failed. We're getting divorced."

"You and Hamilton wouldn't have failed if you tried harder. He's a good partner. You should give him another chance."

"First businesses usually fail. Mine didn't. Yours will. If you stick to my advice, you might be able to minimize the damage."

I push those thoughts away and remind myself his one good piece of advice is that I should focus on my business.

I'm a CEO and I can girlboss my way through this. Even if I hate that attitude and it makes me feel separated from my values and who I am. Orion probably doesn't think about being powerful and fitting into gender stereotypes with his fleet of boats. Fleets.

None of that should be what I'm thinking about at this moment. Now, I need to focus on Haley and only Haley.

We're in my backyard setting up to record a recipe video on the grill. Her large audience follows her every post, cooking alongside her with a devotion I can't fathom. Last year when her cookbook came out, she earned out her advance faster than projected. She does well for herself, seemingly able to be effortlessly stylish and cook everything under the sun.

We both work hard at our jobs, I know that. But a part of me is jealous she makes her efforts appear easy. There's no way she's faking it as much as I am.

A different person would say no when she asked me to take time away from my workday to help her film. But it's part of my duty as a friend and one of her collaboration partners. I'll make up for the work I missed later in the day. We have to get this done early enough in the morning before it gets too hot to function. So I can make it work.

She lives in a condo a few blocks down the island with her sister which is why she uses my kitchen as staging for her videos, plus I have an outdoor setup. My house is big. I've asked her to move in with me multiple times, but she's never wanted to. She didn't come from money, and I think she wants to make sure she earns everything she has.

What I have was given to me. So I should be the first to share.

I can't help but wonder what would have happened if she had lost her phone last week. Orion was looking to get laid; it had nothing to do with me. At least that's what I tell myself.

"Wait, is that the captain?" she asks, setting up a chopping board.

As if thinking about him three times summoned him, he's stepped onto his porch, directly in our line of sight.

"Oh. Yes. I forgot to mention he moved in next door." She won't judge me if I told her I slept with him. I wouldn't judge her if she had. I would've been jealous, but I wouldn't judge.

The whole point of a fling is that no one needs to get involved. No friends are told. Feelings aren't involved. It's been fine so far. Apart from my one relationship, this works for me.

"That's fun. I liked him. We should invite him to Paradise tonight," Haley says, not commenting on the unlikely story that I forgot about him.

"Sure." I convinced Christian to do a small launch for the rum. More like a happy hour than a party. Minimal work. Easy. It's the kind of encounter I wanted in my fantasy, the whole reason I initially thought to do something for Christian. It became a reality and now it feels risky. "He knows Alex, so that would work."

"Weird that Alex never mentioned him," she says. "Have you talked to him much?"

"A little," I say. "I'm not sure he's looking to get attached. He might be around seasonally." He says he's staying but I don't believe it. A quick trip to Antigua could easily turn into him being gone for ages. I need to keep reminding myself why it's a bad idea to get close to him when my body hums at the thought of him.

"You were once only around seasonally."

She's right. It was family trips for years, then breaks from college and graduate school before I was able to make Wendell Beach my home. But I've always had strong friendships here. And I love this island more than any other place I've been.

My mind feels clouded with him. I can't focus on the things I normally do. As if he knows, Orion brings out a speaker and starts playing music.

"Crap, this might be a problem," I say. We only have a few minutes before we need to start filming. Everything is ready and we have a limited window to finish before it's too hot out to properly function.

"It's fine," she says, adjusting the camera settings. "I doubt the microphones are sensitive enough to pick it up. I can always edit it out later."

"I don't want to risk it, especially if it's more work for you."

I exit through my side gate and enter his backyard. He either doesn't hear or is choosing to ignore me. But he will challenge me on my simple request to turn down his music. He said he wouldn't go easy on me, and I feel like this is exactly the thing he'd be difficult about for the sole purpose of being difficult.

"Hey, do you mind turning that down?"

He jumps a little as if I've startled him and I smile smugly.

"What was that?" He points to his ear like he didn't hear me.

He heard me and is screwing with me, he has to be. "Your music. Can you turn it down?"

He blinks. "I'm sure I'm allowed to play music on my property at a reasonable volume during the daytime. Especially when you don't even give me a please."

The way he says "my property" makes me question if I've misjudged him and he's going to talk about his right to do whatever he wants because this is America. I shudder. "It's not a reasonable volume. I can hear it in my yard."

His head tilts to the side. I can't read his expression behind his sunglasses and hat. "I fail to see how that's my problem."

He's right. This isn't his problem. It is my problem so I should fix it on my own. I need him to do something nice for me, out of the goodness of his heart. I don't think I'll get that.

I huff. "I know you don't care about me, but this is for Haley. We're filming a video for her, and we can't have your crappy music screwing up the sound."

He takes off his sunglasses and looks at me with eyes narrowed and arms crossed over his chest. I try hard to not pay attention to his forearms.

It's a few breaths before he responds. "What makes you think I don't care about you?"

"Because our entire relationship is transactional, and you don't have to care about the person you're transacting with."

"That's how you treat people? As if they're a transaction?"

"No, that's not what I..." How did this conversation get derailed? "I have no reason to believe you don't."

He fucked me right after he met me, and that could be common behavior for him. Just because I have my rules about it doesn't mean he does. He's given me no reason to think I mean anything more to him. But he means so much more to me, and a part of me hates him for it. I couldn't keep this in the box I put him in.

His face is impassive, but his eyes flare for less than a second. "Look, Carina, I was always going to turn down the music. You just have to ask. I was giving you a hard time like I told you I would, because no one ever does. But if you're going to jump down my throat and assume the worst of me, then I won't make that mistake again."

"No, I'm sorry...it's..." *Step one is always apologize.* My stomach twists. I try so hard to do the right thing. It kills me when I don't.

"It's fine, Carina." Defeat fills his voice as he shuts off the music and turns his back to me, resuming whatever he was doing before I came out.

He's right and I'm wrong. But I don't want to back down. At least not yet. He is right that no one challenges me. At least not in Wendell Beach. I don't give anyone the chance. If it had been someone else, I would have asked them nicely to turn down the music and probably offered some of Haley's food as incentive.

But it's my father and his team of investors who think they know best about my business—they're the ones giving me a tough time. I can't push back with my dad. I can push back against Orion. He'll meet me halfway because he sees us as equals.

Instead of taking his offering, I've downgraded myself to an elementary school kid—being mean to the person I like.

Fuck.

He started this, and he can take it. As long as I go in a different direction. "Do you give everyone a hard time, or is this treatment exclusive to me?"

He turns to me, his lips lifted on one side. "I like to think I give people what they need."

"And you're so arrogant. You know what I need?" It's bluster. I know he knows. He's proven it at every turn.

He smiles, stepping closer to me and lowering his voice so I can barely hear what he says. "We both know I'm extremely capable of giving you exactly what you need. Twice."

I shrug to play it off, and to let him know I'm not mad. "My vibrator is fully charged so I can take care of myself." I look up at him, his mouth close enough to me that it wouldn't take much movement to kiss him. Like I'm not counting down how long before Haley leaves and I can have some time alone.

His eyebrows rise. "Think of what I could do to you with a vibrator."

I should have known he'd see it as a fun challenge. I let out a breath and cross my arms over my chest, taking a step back. He's likely able to spot my arousal from a mile away. "Fuck off. It's not happening." I laugh, but it sounds forced even to me.

Thankfully he steps back too and throws me a lifeline. "How long will you be filming for? I was about to mow, but I can wait."

"About an hour?" I say. He's being thoughtful and not pushing me harder than I can handle, which I didn't expect. I should have. I shouldn't assume the worst of him. "I can tell you when we're done. I'll bring over some of the food. We won't eat it all."

He pulls out his phone. "Give me your number and I'll text you mine."

It's a good idea. We're neighbors. We should be able to communicate with each other. "A group of us are meeting at Paradise tonight around five. You should come," I add. Nothing has to mean more than what we're saying on the surface.

He nods. "I'll stop by. I have an early morning charter, so I need a good night's sleep."

"I thought the *Twisted Rigging* was out of the inventory?"

He smiles, realizing he's caught me checking up on him. "She is. This is the *Coastal Dragon*. She's a catamaran in the fleet. I'll be captaining her for charters."

"Right. I'll see you later, then." I turn to head back to my place.

"Wait, one more thing." He hesitates for a moment. "I go kayaking by myself a lot." I nod like this is new information to me. "Would you mind if I text you and share my location when I do? Just in case something happens?"

"Of course." It's a safety thing. It doesn't mean anything.

"Thanks. I'll see you later."

"Yep, I'll save you a seat."

When I get back to my yard, Haley is giving me a strange look. "That was weird."

"What?"

"You said you didn't really talk with him, but that looked pretty familiar."

He and I were standing close. I didn't even think she'd see it. "It's nothing."

That's the truth. There's nothing going on with Orion and me. We're neighbors and maybe we'll be friends. The fact that we've slept together once has no bearing on anything.

nine

ORION

Right before five p.m., I head out the door to meet Carina. The walk is only a few minutes down the beach, past houses that are a variation of the style of mine, and then I'm greeted with the world-famous facade of the Paradise Bar and Grill. It's designed to look like a sandcastle, with the entire ground floor open to the beach.

I cross through what would be the patio at any other place, but here the tables are perched in the sand with large umbrellas and palm trees providing some shade. Signs urge patrons to remove their shoes. Inside, the room centers around a large, square bar. Off to one side an area is roped off and a sign proclaims, *Local Residents Only*.

I find Carina quickly, sitting alone at a large table in the locals' section. I'm intercepted by Alex who steps out from behind the bar before I can get to her.

"Hey, man! Glad you finally made it in!" He claps me on the back.

I hide my grimace. It's not that I don't want to catch up with Alex, but I need Carina more. She's calling to me and I feel pulled to her in the way only the sea has ever managed.

"I'm actually meeting Carina Webb. I did that charter with her and to my surprise, and likely not yours, she's my next-door neighbor," I say flatly. I don't know what I expect to accomplish by calling him out, but I do it anyway.

"Carina's great. I'm glad you hit it off without any expectations." He winks.

I need to shut this down. For Carina's sake. I can run interference on Alex all day, but she has enough on her plate. "I just moved here. I'm not looking for any complications." From the corner of my eye, I see a server place glasses of water on the table she's at.

He puts his hands up in surrender. "Right, of course."

We don't know each other well, so he isn't aware of my dating history. Otherwise, he'd keep me far away from Carina if he cares about her.

"Your first appetizer is on the house. I've already made the staff aware you're allowed in the locals' section."

"I appreciate it."

It shouldn't mean much, but being accepted by Alex means the rest of the town will follow. His family has owned this place for generations. It's been a driver of tourism for years. We do a quick one-armed hug before I am free to approach Carina.

She jumps when I pull out the chair next to her. "Sorry, I thought you saw me."

"No, I was focused on the beach," she says softly, pointing.

The table has a clear view of the public beach, and the sea breeze drifts across my skin through the open facade. By our houses, it's been quiet. Here, tons of people play in the water, even this late in the afternoon.

Then her attention turns to me and I realize she's wearing a dress. I'm hit by a wave of lust so strong, I need to take a moment to think of anything but the way the hem wanders up her thighs or how the scoop of her neckline hints at cleavage. Her legs are so strong and her skin so soft. All I want is to bury my head between her thighs and never come up for air. They have quickly become my new obsession.

She's attractive no matter what she's wearing, whether it's shorts or those yoga pants she doesn't wear panties with. I'd never want her to be anything other than strong, but this dress makes it easy for me to see her as the princess everyone thinks of her as.

"I thought you only wore athletic wear." I sit and sip from the water glass nearest me.

She looks down, the end of her ponytail drifting over her shoulder. "This is an athletic dress. It has built-in shorts and stretchy fabric."

I'm guessing the built-in shorts also count for her underwear. "It's one of yours, then?"

"Of course."

"Why don't you wear other brands?" It's a genuine question, but Carina gets defensive.

"Everything I make, I stand by its sustainability and labor practices. I don't know that for many other companies." Her spine straightens when she talks about labor practices. It's so hot.

I respond to her defensiveness with my own snark. "Plus, you look gorgeous so people will buy it in the hopes of looking as good as you."

Her face flushes and her mouth twists. We agreed to be friends. But I can't turn off the fact I find her attractive. If it really bothers her, I'll stop mentioning it. I can't deny Carina deserves to be praised.

"Yes, my body allows me to advertise my products in a way that's in line with conventional beauty standards. But my goal is never to serve as body inspiration."

I've hit a nerve I didn't think about. I don't know what's behind that statement, but I'm concerned she's hurting herself by forcing herself to look a way that isn't healthy. Or she's worried other people will harm themselves trying to look like she does. "Carina, I didn't mean—"

She shakes her head and stands up. I think she's leaving. Instead, she greets a man with sandy blond hair and tattoos poking out of the sleeves of his T-shirt.

"Christian!" she says. "This is the new neighbor I told you about, Orion Edwards. Orion this is my friend, Christian Bailey. He owns Wendell Beach Rum Works."

"It's good to meet you," I say, shaking his hand and refusing to let jealousy take over. They didn't hug. Now that I'm thinking about it, I don't remember her hugging anyone on the boat. The other women were constantly getting close for selfies. She stayed apart.

"Where's Autumn?" she asks him.

I make a mental note to check in with her later about the beauty standards. I'm not done getting into her head. She might think she can distract me but I have more focus than she gives me credit for.

"Teacher drinks," he says, pushing the menu in front of him to the side.

"But this is your launch party." Her face is full of concern.

"It's fine, Carina. I opened a bottle with her last night." He folds his paper napkin.

"Sorry, Autumn is his wife," she tells me.

"I didn't realize it was a special event," I say.

Christian drapes his arm over the back of the chair next to him. "It's not really. I have a new rum on the market. I told Carina it isn't a big deal, but she insisted on going all out."

"This isn't all out," she says. "It's happy hour with a few friends."

"Who else is coming?" Christian asks.

"Haley and Beckett. As soon as they finish a wedding planning session."

"Oh, Haley's engaged?" I ask. I'm not attracted to her, but it would've been nice to know.

Carina glares at me. "She's not getting married. She also doesn't do hookups. Beckett is marrying our friend, Sienna, who lives in Boston. Haley is the maid of honor so she's helping." Her voice is protective and seething. Message received. I won't have any romantic interest in Haley, like I always planned.

"Right," I say.

"You okay?" Christian shifts toward Carina. "You said he was cool, but you snapped."

She freezes in horror. Christian looks like he would hurt anyone who hurts her. I don't know why she glared at me. I need to smooth this out in a way that preserves both our reputations.

"We had a disagreement earlier," I say with a smile. "Don't think she's gotten over my—what was it? Self-centered arrogance?" Thank god this makes her smile. I'll be as self-deprecating as she needs and let Christian know the two of us are fine. I'm a friendly asshole.

"Something like that," she says.

"Okay," Christian says. His eyes soften as he focuses on her. I think he believes us.

Haley arrives wearing a blue sundress, with a man in a polo shirt and khakis. I note the logo on his shirt and it's an expensive brand. He checks his watch, either purposefully showing it off or he needs us to be aware his time is more valuable than ours. I assume this is Beckett.

I own two businesses and bought a house close to the beach, but I've never cared about material things. If it took up space on the boat, it had to earn its keep. I can tell he's concerned about his appearance.

I also note Christian is wearing one of Carina's T-shirts. Haley gives me a hug and thanks me for helping with her cooking shoot earlier. I compliment her food. Beckett's gaze goes from Carina's chest to me as he sizes me up. When the formal introductions are made, I catch his last name, Foley, and some pieces fall into place. His family owns the luxury resort at the south end of the island, Coastline Beach House. The exact resort I would love to have designate Lost Craft Charters as their preferred sailing company.

Alex walks over with a server who he introduces to me as Bristol. She places a bottle of rum on the table and lines up glasses for us. Christian takes a few minutes to describe the process of how this rum came to be. Bristol also mentions how proud she is of her big brother taking what he inherited from their grandparents and building on it. How the community has come to rely on him for jobs and to bring tourists into the area.

I want to reach for Carina's hand under the table and squeeze it. She doesn't realize what it means to me to be included in this. These people have ties to Wendell Beach and to each other. I've been drifting on my own for so long. But this is why I came here —to get away from the cold and find a place where I can build something.

I want to pull Carina in for a kiss and break in my new bed with her. The reasons she had for not hooking up again don't hold up in this moment.

Christian pours the rum, we toast, and I take a sip. It is good. I need a few bottles of this. I look at Carina for her reaction and find her watching me.

"Do you like it?" she asks.

She's so transparent. "I do. Christian, I'd love a tour at some point."

"Any time," he says.

We finish our samples and Bristol takes our drink order. I try to catch Carina's eye when she orders a cocktail made with the rum the two of us shared the other night, but she's fixated on the food menu.

"Haley was telling me you have a boat?" Beckett says, sipping his beer. I'm surprised by the choice since the bar is famous for its cocktails. At least it's from a local brewery.

"Yeah, I own Lost Craft Charters," I say. "We have five boats here total."

"But you do have your own sailboat? One not for charter,'" Beckett asks. "I saw the pictures Carina posted."

I nod without responding because I know where this is headed.

"That would be a lot of fun for the bachelor trip. Don't you think, Alex?" Bristol has returned to the bar, while Alex remains seated since it's slow enough that the bartenders can keep up with the orders.

"You don't have your own?" I ask.

"No, too much work to deal with the maintenance."

"Like you said, I don't offer my boat for charters," I say. "I'm happy to work something out with the fleet. We have a really nice catamaran for groups."

Beckett shakes his head. "No, I looked at the others. They don't go nearly as fast. You made an exception for Carina. You can make an exception for me." He turns to Alex. "You're the best man. You should be organizing this anyway."

To his credit, Alex hesitates when he sees my reaction. "We'll figure something out."

"Where have you sailed around here?" Christian asks, shifting away from Beckett who pulled his phone out. "When Bristol isn't bartending, she does kayak tours around the island. I'm sure she's worked on your boats before you bought the company."

"Not many places yet. I've been busy with the house. I am sailing to a sandbar south of here tomorrow on a day charter, and then I'm taking my boat to Egmont Key on Monday."

"You're going out by yourself?" Carina asks.

"I've sailed alone plenty. It's a popular destination so I need to scout it."

"I've never been," she says.

This is my opportunity. To get her back on my boat. Just the two of us.

"I haven't either," Alex says.

Fuck. Well now I can't invite her without excluding everyone else, making me the asshole. "You should all come," I suggest, not letting my tone betray how much I don't want that.

"Some of us have jobs," Beckett says.

"I can make Monday work," Carina says. Haley and Christian agree, suggesting Bristol come along to help me with the sailing.

It won't be quite the romantic day I had in mind. But I'll make do with what I have.

Beckett's phone vibrates and he smirks. "Sienna wants me to approve ties for the groomsmen." He passes the phone to Carina. "What do you think about this one for Hamilton?"

She tenses. "It looks fine to me."

"That's all you have to say?" Beckett asks.

I don't know who Hamilton is, but I hate seeing her tense.

"Beckett." A fake smile spreads across her face. "Hamilton and I broke up because he didn't want to do long-distance."

I keep my face straight as best I can. Never did it cross my mind the challenge to some kind of future for Carina and me is that she is holding out for someone else.

"Things change, Carina. Weddings are romantic. You never know what you'll agree to."

"We'll see," she says.

I see the gritted teeth, but no one else comes to her rescue.

ten

CARINA

I HATE THAT BECKETT BROUGHT UP HAMILTON IN FRONT OF Orion. We don't owe each other anything, and he's not the type to be jealous, which I don't want him to be. But it's that I have this big relationship in my past that I couldn't make work.

Nothing makes me feel like more of a failure than Hamilton Kane.

It doesn't help that my father made Hamilton his protégé and now they both get to tell me how to run my business. He and I weren't big on feelings with each other, so it's not that I miss him. It was more than a business relationship, but at times it didn't feel like much more. All the same, I should have found a way to care more or to make it work.

At least Christian and Orion hit it off. While I'm discouraging Beckett from his attempts to be a wingman, Christian asks Orion about his favorite rums.

My stomach turns at the thought of Hamilton using the wedding as a chance to get back with me. The part that scares me is I might have let him in. I might have agreed to hook up because he's there and I do eventually want a family. Hamilton and I have history. He's not a risk. We'd talked about marriage before. So maybe I could make it work with him. But even when we lived in the same place, we didn't have the connection I wanted. On paper he was the type of match my father wanted for me, someone who elevates my status. I wasn't unhappy with him.

But he never lit my body on fire with a single glance.

I rope Haley into the wedding discussion when Alex waves over a pretty brunette who walked in from the street side. He introduces her as Kim.

"Oh, your date for the wedding," Haley recalls, having the guest list committed to memory.

"Yes, I'm excited. It should be a lot of fun," Kim replies. They clearly recently started dating. I'm surprised Alex invited her. "And congratulations, Beckett. I'm sure it'll be beautiful."

"It's a bummer you aren't coming," Alex says to Orion.

I look up. Do I want Orion at the wedding? A vision flashes in my head of him in a suit, looking at me with lust in his eyes. It'd be perfectly tailored if I have any voice in the matter. I'd spend the whole night running my hands over the fabric to feel it and the way his muscles move under my touch. He'd lose the jacket at some point and roll up his sleeves. He'd look at me like he's imagining my clothes disappearing.

He shrugs. "I'm sure you'll have fun without me."

"Why don't you go as Carina's date? She has a plus-one she's not using," Alex suggests.

My heart freezes, but I keep my face passive. Alex can't know the thoughts I have about Orion. But he's right—I could take Orion to the wedding. We're friends, and over the next few months he'll get closer to everyone else at the table. By then, it'll be weird if he's not there.

I could make my fantasy real.

He places a hand on my knee where no one can see, warming my skin. I want it to stay there. "It's fine. I'm sure I'll hear about it," he says.

"Alex is right," I tell Orion when he moves his hand away. "I wasn't planning on taking anyone. So you can come with me if you want. It'll be a good networking opportunity anyway." The wedding will be a who's who of everyone on the island and the surrounding area.

Orion holds my gaze like he's trying to see what I'm really thinking. And fuck him, because I think he might be able to. "Nothing more than a professional event?" He's asking if it would be completely business between us, or if there might be something more then.

Before I can answer—and it's for the best, because I wouldn't be able to keep desire out of my voice—Beckett speaks up. "You should come. I'll introduce you to my parents. We control the tourist market in the area. They need to like you for you to get your feet off the ground. And we'll do my bachelor party on your boat."

He should decline. Beckett is great to Sienna, but when he and Hamilton get together, they revert to their college frat bro days.

"Sure, it'll be great," Orion answers.

"That settles it," Alex says, his voice flat like something went wrong in whatever plan he was working on.

I should be annoyed with him. He's being as manipulative as Beckett. But if I tell him to back off, he will. I trust Alex.

"I was just stopping by," Kim says, aware she stepped into something she probably doesn't want to be involved with. "I'll see you around."

"I have to head out too," Beckett says. "Alex, you got my tab?"

They head over to the bar. When they leave, it's Christian, Haley, Orion, and me.

"I like Orion. Don't know why he rubs you the wrong way," Haley whispers to me.

The bar has picked up. It's always crowded on Friday nights. The locals' section usually fills up since it isn't tourist high season —the weather is far too hot—and we feel like this place is ours again.

"I don't know," I say. My insides roll, with Beckett wanting me to hook up with Hamilton, and Alex pushing Orion in front of me. I can't handle Haley tossing her hat in the ring for him. He's also currently sharing with Christian about the months he spent in Tahiti and how much he loved it. I can't imagine he wouldn't want to go back there with how he's talking about it.

"I'm glad we were able to connect with him," she continues. "He was so helpful on the boat trip and he's definitely good-looking."

I feel my last cocktail in my stomach. "I thought you were dating Eric." My voice is sharper than I intend. I want her far away from Orion. I have no claim on him, but the thought of him dating my friend makes me want to vomit.

Which proves my point that I need to stay away from him. I can't keep my emotions in check. I demanded a fling; it ended. I should move on and quit acting like it was anything more.

She gives me a look, telling me she sees more than I want her to. "I am. I wasn't suggesting I date Orion. I thought we were becoming friends."

"You're right. Sorry. I'm jumpy tonight."

"Change is always difficult," she says. "With Sienna getting married, the dynamic of our friend group is shifting, even if we think it won't."

We get a few more rounds and I'm feeling pleasantly buzzed. Bristol knows me well enough that she makes sure I drink a full glass of water between each cocktail, so I don't get hungover. I have my limits. I'm for having fun and trying new things, but I also don't want to do anything reckless or stupid. I am the very definition of *drink responsibly*.

"I'm headed home," Orion says, finishing the last drop from his cocktail.

I shouldn't have been following everything he ordered. I can't remember what Haley had but I know everything Orion drank tonight.

He signals Bristol to bring his check. "I have to be up early."

"I do too," I say. It's not necessarily true. I have an early morning yoga class. I do every day. Saturday isn't an exception. But there's no reason to stay at the bar with Orion gone.

If anyone asks, it's a safety thing, having him walk me home.

We close out our checks as Autumn arrives to join Christian and they move to the bar. We wave goodbye to Haley who heads to the parking lot where her sister picks her up.

Orion and I turn toward our homes, walking along the dark beach. The sun has long set and I'm surprisingly happy with that. I don't need a romantic moment with him, and the sunsets here are gorgeous.

I remove my flip-flops and hold them in my hand. Orion takes a few steps in the sand and does the same. The sand is cool in the night air—a stark contrast to how it felt earlier.

"Thanks for inviting me out," he says.

"Of course." It didn't go exactly the way I planned, but I would've regretted leaving him out. I can't avoid him forever. The more I am around him, the more it won't mean anything, and the thought of not having him around won't make my skin itch. It's exposure therapy.

"I mean it, Carina. I'm glad I got to meet Christian and see Alex. And you should know that Alex purposefully didn't tell us about each other."

I knew it. "He's trying to push us together." He probably thinks Orion is a safe alternative to Hamilton. "He might like the idea of us as a couple. He might also want to spite Hamilton. The two of them never got along. Beckett met Hamilton at college. He moved here for a little bit to work at the resort." I almost add in "until he was poached by my dad to work for his firm" but I don't want Orion to know yet. I have too many complicated feelings about it. "Hamilton isn't from here and was never impressed by Paradise. Plus, Alex actually works behind the bar. Hamilton has never done manual labor in his life."

"I'm assuming lifting golf clubs doesn't count," Orion says.

"He hires people for that." I hope my sarcasm comes through.

Orion chuckles. "I shut it down. Told Alex I'm not interested in dating."

I nod and don't say anything specifically. Whatever feelings I have in my pants, they will pass. This is fine. The alcohol I drank doesn't feel like acid in my stomach.

He stops in the middle of the beach. "Do they even know you?" he asks.

It feels like a question out of nowhere, but it's not. "Of course they know me. I've been friends with Haley and Alex since we were kids, and I met Christian five years ago." My heart breaks a little at how right he is about this. How it's possible for me to be so transparent with him and opaque to everyone else.

"Right, but none of them know you."

"Oh, and you do?" He does and I want to be angry at him for it.

"Maybe not yet. I know better than to act surprised when you express any emotion beyond 'pleasant.' And what is the deal with so many people trying to dictate your love life?"

"Excuse me for trying to be a nice person. You're the one who's letting Beckett have his bachelor party on your boat even if it feels like a dagger to your soul. You're only doing that because it will make you look good to his family."

"We're not talking about me. This is about you." His voice is forceful. "You are a nice person. You're kind and caring and beautiful. You are more than that." I ignore the *beautiful* comment. "Do you think I'm attending this wedding to network?"

"Why did you agree, then? Trust me, if you didn't like the idea of Nebula Athletics on your boat, you'll hate a bachelor party. Especially this group."

He looks at me like I'm completely dense. "Figure it out, Carina."

I huff. I don't have the patience for speculation. "Have you ever thought since I get along with everyone else but can't get along with you, you are the problem?"

"I'm fully aware of my problems. But I'm not your problem."

"I don't care. Whatever. We don't have to be friends. We can be neighbors and have the same friends and we don't have to pretend we are anything more than that." I start walking again. He'll agree it's for the best and I don't want to be looking at him when he does.

"We're going to a wedding together," he says.

I stop. He won't let this go. "We don't have to. I can talk to Sienna. I'm sure the guest list has flexibility. Or one of her sisters will need a date."

"I honestly don't care about Beckett getting married and I don't know Sienna. The only reason for me to go is to be your date."

I can't see his eyes in the dark or read his expression. He sounds sincere. I don't know what any of this means. "There's a networking opportunity," I try.

"For fuck's sake, if you really think that's my motivation, then you don't know me at all."

"I don't need a date," I protest one last time.

"When was the last time you did something for yourself? Something you didn't strictly need?" He steps closer to me.

The water is right there but this man smells like the sea. I want to lose myself in him.

"All the attention will be on Sienna and Beckett, and you'll work so hard to make the day perfect for them. Wouldn't it be nice if someone was there just for you? Someone you don't have to impress or perform for? Someone you can relax around?"

I've never had that. I've never had someone who cares about me first. It's a tempting offer. But I can't let him get too close. In two months, he could already be bored with Florida. "Fine. But only because Sienna won't care and this is too minor of an issue to bring to her attention." It'll be a friend thing. No big deal.

He places his hand over his heart. "You wound me."

I smile. "I get final say on what you wear. You can't embarrass me with cargo shorts."

"Please, I have standards."

"I've seen you wear cargo shorts."

"Yes, on the boat, where I need pockets."

He's currently wearing shorts. They are black and the logo is from a major competitor of mine. I don't take it personally. They are pricey and super soft. I might have some of their women's clothing stashed in a drawer to be pulled out when I will be at the house all day.

He steps close enough so I can see him in the dark. We're almost touching. "The wedding is on the beach, I'm guessing."

"Yes, at the resort." It's a safe guess on his part. Everything important on this island takes place on the beach.

"I have a suit." He looks away from me and at the water.

"Right. I still want to see it. Make sure it fits."

"It's bespoke."

I didn't expect that. He doesn't appear to be the type to have custom clothing. Not when he was living on a boat. "I'll have to trust you, then."

"You should. Trust me. I want to be your friend, Carina. Fuck being friendly neighbors."

I don't know what he means. We stare at each other in the dark and I have a feeling he wants more from me than friendship. I need to find an escape.

"The stars are really bright tonight," I say, pointing up to the sky. My eyes have adjusted, and I can pick out so many constellations.

He steps back. "I've seen better." He sighs, not interested in the fight I want to pick.

* * *

HE DOESN'T WALK me all the way to my door, like I hoped and feared he would. It would have been the worst temptation. Instead, he waits at the end of my driveway until I open the front door. He's making sure I'm safe. It's preservation for my heart. If he came to my door, I'd invite him in and then upstairs. We could be soft in the moonlight as we strip each other down.

"Be safe tomorrow," I say. He's an experienced sailor and has a capable crew. It's silly. But so is making sure nothing happens to me between the sidewalk and the door.

He smiles under the light of the garage, and he knows he matters to me. I care about him, regardless of what I said earlier.

Once inside, I make my way up to my bedroom. My en suite bathroom is massive, with a large soaking tub and a separate shower with two showerheads. I have windows that face the gulf. I can soak in the tub and watch waves crash on the shore. I want to fill it and sink into the water, thinking of Orion. I can't do that. Instead, I will myself to let go of this stupid crush.

I move to my yoga room, telling myself some bedtime stretching will help me unwind. It happens that this window faces his house. Out the panes, I watch as Orion turns the lights on in his house and the waves they travel as he moves. On. Off. On. Off.

Then darkness.

I've been in his house plenty growing up. The Lawsons always had cold lemonade for Haley and me on hot days. The largest bedroom faces the water like mine does.

He's gone to bed, not thinking about me. But I'll be up late, unable to get him off my mind.

Eleven

ORION

It's the crack of dawn on Monday morning and all I want to think about is how when Carina leans forward to reposition a cooler in my SUV's trunk, the gap in her tank top gives me a perfect view of the swell of her breasts. I don't even care that Haley and Alex are standing in my driveway and can probably see me staring.

I've been on edge all weekend and the fact it's taking us forever to even get our gear in my SUV doesn't help any of it. I wanted to spend this day with her, and her alone. Not with all her friends that she'll be performing for.

"No, it would be more efficient if you put that there." Carina points to one of the totes we're taking to Egmont Key. She's dug in her heels on something about optimal legroom for the people in the back seat and I hope to all hell she's frustrated at the situation like I am, and not that she's truly concerned with how much Alex can spread out on a five-minute drive. She's pushing me to my wit's end. So instead of her tits, I'm thinking about how if later today she fell off my boat, in what circumstances would I not jump in to rescue her.

"It's packed fine, Carina." Of course, in this imaginary

scenario we'd be anchored, so it's not like I'd leave her behind. And she's a strong swimmer. There's no reason why she couldn't swim her ass over to the stern and hoist herself up.

Now I'm envisioning water dripping over her breasts as I reach for her hand to help her onto the swim platform.

Frustrated horny is the worst.

Haley decides to help. "Orion, couldn't you—"

I put my hand up to stop her. She's also a capable swimmer and could easily rescue Carina if needed. I wouldn't need to be involved at all.

Alex sips his coffee next to Haley. I'm surprised he's not complaining again about having to be up this early. He's a bartender, he asserted. He doesn't exist before ten a.m. And *he* wouldn't jump in to save Carina if a shark was approaching.

For fuck's sake, if a shark were nearby, I'd jump in to help her. I'm not a monster. But for the fight she's giving me right now, she can flail for a few moments in a controlled environment.

"Look, it's my SUV," I say.

"We should take my hybrid," she counters, one hand on her hip as she points to her house.

Of course, if there was any indication she was injured, I'd be there in a heartbeat.

"Christian just texted," Haley says. "They've already parked."

That's another thing I don't understand. Christian and Bristol can meet us at the marina fine. Why are Haley and Alex here? It's something about efficiency and parking. But the group text planning this moved faster than I was prepared to follow.

"It's less than a mile," I tell Carina. "The gas savings don't matter."

"Every little bit helps."

I don't disagree with her on the gas issue, which is the annoying thing. I rarely disagree with her. "Whatever. If you have a problem with how I've done this, then you can walk to the marina. You don't have to ride with me."

I mean, if there were rocks nearby, or other boats or Jet Skis, or anything that could harm her, I'm there, in the water and reaching her to make sure she's okay. But if it's us and the open ocean and the current isn't strong, yes. Right now, I'd let her figure it out herself.

"Fine. I'll walk, then." She turns around and walks in the direction of the marina.

I run my hand through my hair. This should make things easier for me. The car doesn't need to be packed as tight with fewer people. But I don't feel relief.

Because I know how fast conditions change. Even if the water is still and she has a life jacket on, as frustrated as I am with Carina, there is no scenario where if she falls in the water, I'm not jumping in after her before she has time to surface.

I almost call her back to tell her I'll do whatever she wants. She can pack the car her way. But she'll be fine. I'll see her in a few minutes.

"You two ready?" I ask Alex and Haley. I keep my snark internal. I don't need either of them thinking I'll jump down their throats because I argued with Carina. What they witnessed won't change their opinion of me. They know I didn't start it.

They nod and get in the car.

"What's with you and Carina?" Alex asks.

I don't trust him to not have ulterior motives right now. He might have said he was backing off whatever matchmaking he had attempted, but I don't believe him. "Proximity breeds familiarity."

"I don't know about that," Haley says. "I roomed with her in college. We never argued."

"Yeah?" I look at her through the rearview mirror. "Did she do your dishes for you?"

"Well, I did a lot of the cooking, so she cleaned up. It was only fair." She looks down, embarrassed I pegged her so easily.

"Sure. I'm saying she'll do whatever it takes to keep everyone around her happy and I won't let her do that with me."

"You won't let her make you happy?" Alex repeats.

"I don't need anything from her, and she doesn't know how to respond," I say.

"What does that even mean?" Haley says.

"Huh," Alex says. "Is this your seduction method? Because I'm not sure it's a good one."

I can answer this honestly. "No, I'm not trying to sleep with her. That sounds like it would be fun for no one." Well, that last bit wasn't honest.

"Hey!" Haley says.

"What do you have to say to that?" Alex asks her.

"I don't know. But I don't like people picking on my friend."

"She can take everything I dish out. And if it upsets her, then she can talk to me or ignore me. No one is forcing her to go sailing today. Trust me, I don't want her actually mad."

They both look at each other and I wonder if they think I'm full of shit, but I know Carina. She's strong and she wouldn't be where she is if she couldn't take some shit. The only difference with me is she's finally giving it back. I saw the way her friends treat her. They care about her. But she's been acquiescing for far too long.

We pull into the parking lot at the marina and find Christian and Bristol waiting for us.

"Where's Carina?" Bristol asks.

"She decided to walk," I reply. I hope that's the end of it. If she wants to hide who she is from her friends, that's her business. I won't be the reason for her exposure.

And selfishly, I want this part of her to myself.

We load up the boat. I check the radar, again, and decide which sail to use. Bristol appoints herself my first mate even though it's unnecessary. This boat is rigged for a solo sailor. I don't need any help. But I won't turn down someone calling distances for me. Bristol mentions that when she's not bartending, she leads tours on kayaks or paddleboards and will occasionally go out on chartered vessels. She knows her way around enough to be helpful, especially getting out of the marina.

Haley heads to the galley to organize the food. She packed a picnic lunch and plenty of booze. Christian and Alex follow her, knowing their roles in helping her out.

She has an easy camaraderie with both men. They're in relationships with other people, and I don't pick up any underlying sexual tension between any of them. It was something I noticed the other night at Paradise. It's the same with Carina. The only person I noticed checking her out that night was Beckett.

And Carina looked beautiful. I've been thinking about her in that dress all weekend.

I'm taking off the mainsail cover when I see her walking down the dock. I hope she's burned off whatever frustrations she felt. She gets closer, and from the smirk on her face she's been thinking up some snarky comeback the entire twenty-minute walk over.

The sun has fully risen at this point, and I see a sheen of sweat across her chest. She's wearing a pair of shorts with a white flowy tank top sheer enough for me to see her baby blue bikini top underneath. Until now, I haven't seen her in anything other than her own line of clothes.

I wonder what she'd look like in a cocktail dress, at sunset, at a candlelit table for two.

I stand at the stern as if I will offer her a hand across the gap between the boat and the dock, but that's not all I intend.

She stands in front of me. "Permission to come aboard?" she asks, one eyebrow raised as if daring me to start again. I love the challenge I see in her and how much our relationship has changed since we were last in this position. It's only been a little over a week, and along with the house and the water, Carina has been my constant in Wendell Beach. Not just her physical presence, but the way she's always in my mind. I can't believe it's only been ten days since we first met.

"Not yet. We need to call a truce."

"Why?" Her eyes narrow behind her sunglasses.

"No fighting on the boat. It's a safety thing. I need to know in an emergency you'll listen to me no matter what."

"Your boat. Your rules?" she says.

"Something like that."

"I don't like this."

"I wouldn't expect you to."

"If you're an ass to me, I will take it out on you once we are back on land."

"Sure, no problem. Throw me in the ocean," I say. She'd jump in to save me. I know it.

"Gulf," she corrects.

"Whatever. Do you agree?"

It's clear she doesn't want to, but Alex walks up from below deck and she sees him watching us. Her glare at me turns into a smile that I know is fake. "Won't even be an issue. I'm perfectly pleasant all the time."

"Sure, princess." She doesn't react to my nickname. I'd like to think it's because she's holding back. I'll say it again on land and wait for her to explode.

"You going to help me board?"

"Nope, you're capable. It's not like you'll fall in the ocean."

I turn and continue my work, knowing Carina will be able to get on the boat no problem. But she waits a minute to take the step.

twelve

CARINA

ORION IS INFURIATING. NO ONE SHOULD LOOK AS GOOD AS HE DOES while he navigates a thirty-seven-foot boat out of a marina in the morning light. And how dare Bristol be so helpful.

She's so bright and sunny, and anyone would be lucky to date her. She's usually single—I've only seen her in casual relationships. If she wanted to start something with Orion, I'm sure they would be a good match. It's not hard to notice they are both incredibly fit. Orion thrives on having a partner who can match his strength.

When Orion had mentioned sailing when we were at Paradise, my plan was to remind him it's dangerous to be out on the water alone. I should come along, for safety reasons.

It was complete bullshit. Orion has plenty of experience sailing on his own. I wanted time alone with him. In a platonic way, of course. I was not thinking about navigating him to the cabin when we anchor.

Definitely not.

I'm almost thankful for his insistence that I can't pick a fight with him on the boat. Because I want to. I want to stake my claim on him and let everyone know he is mine. I want to force a reaction out of him because I'm special to him. It's childish and I don't know what about him generates this response from me. But it makes me feel alive.

Once we're in open water and the sails are raised, Bristol shares a long history of Egmont Key State Park. It's primarily a wildlife refuge with clear blue-green water I'm dying to explore. That type of beauty shouldn't faze me since I've lived in Wendell Beach for seven years and came here growing up. But the beauty of the gulf never gets old to me. Haley is the same way.

We reach the island and Orion expertly anchors the boat close enough for us to wade in the shallow water to the beach. I'm surprised by how deserted it all is. There are only a few other boats down the beach, but far enough away that it feels like we're alone. Maybe because it's a weekday and school is in session.

Haley, Bristol, and Christian automatically head toward the beach to fish, and Alex follows, saying something about looking for shells. I didn't know he was interested in shelling. I immediately think about bringing Sienna here. She's a marine biologist who studies seashells. I pull out my phone to text her but don't have service.

A shadow crosses over me, and I realize I'm alone with Orion.

"What are your plans?" he asks. "I can pull out the paddleboards."

I look down at his feet. We're on land. He's being nice to me.

"Um…not sure." I focused on getting here and being with him. I didn't think about how I would pass the time once I got here, except absorbing the stunning nature. "I can paddle at home. Maybe we check out the fort?"

"Sure." He walks toward the structure.

"What's happening here?" I ask, moving briskly to catch up.

"We're exploring the fort," he says.

"Together?"

"Is that a problem?"

"No, I thought you needed to do other work stuff. Like explore the water or something."

He shrugs. "Nope, I know where to anchor. How long it takes to get here. Guests can figure out the rest." It's because I'm the only one doing any exploring. Besides Alex. Maybe Orion doesn't care about shells. I'm sure he'll interrogate everyone else later.

We don't talk. It feels natural and comfortable. I don't need to pick a fight or find something to complain about. We take the red brick path lined with palm trees until we get to the fort. There, we climb up the white stone stairs until we stand on the rampart. From here, we have a clear view of the water for miles. The crumbling walls overlook the sparkling turquoise water and I want to take it in. I can't believe we have all this to ourselves.

"You looking for a spot to pose?" Orion's question brings me out of my thoughts.

"Um. Yes." I wasn't. I was trying to be in the moment. But he's right. This is a great spot.

I know better. Part of my job is always being on. I'm constantly promoting my brand with everything I do. But, fuck, sometimes I just want to look out over the gulf and breathe.

I pull my phone out of my pocket and hand it to him. "You think you can do it?"

"Half my job when I'm captaining is taking pictures of the guests."

"I'm sure taking pictures of women in bikinis is really difficult for you."

"Carina." He drags out my name because he knows he dragged out my jealousy.

It's easier to be mean than to admit I don't want to hear about him with other charter guests.

I bite the inside of my lip and move to the edge of the structure. In my head I run through a few poses that would look good here. Handstands are popular, but the edge is narrow. I'm high up so I don't want to risk it going wrong and falling. Not if my mind wanders to Orion.

His opinion shouldn't matter to me. Because I don't want anything more from him, and he's already gotten everything he wants from me.

I think back to the time in the cabin with him. How he didn't treat me like I was fragile. I've never been one to show off my physical strength, opting instead for balance and flexibility. I was always taught I should be delicate and graceful. He saw through me.

Orion watches me and waits. He's not saying anything, being patient as I decide what I want to do. I'm surprised he's taking this seriously and not treating it as a joke.

But everything Orion does surprises me.

I plant my hands on the ground with a bend in my arms, and balance my right knee above my right elbow. And then I lift my left leg high into the sky. Flying crow. I should focus on what I'm doing, but I'm listening for a reaction from him. I hear the breeze through the trees, but nothing from Orion.

thirteen

ORION

I SHOULDN'T BE SURPRISED BY HOW MUCH I LIKE BEING AROUND her. I should be paying attention to the fort and stopping at every informational sign. But all I care about is her reaction to the fort.

I don't have to play tour guide on charters. The deckhands and other crew know enough. My job is to sail the boat. But going above and beyond helps with tips.

I've clicked to her Instagram often enough to know her primary content is pictures of her demonstrating yoga poses in beautiful locations. In less than two weeks of living here, I've begun to recognize her spots. The section of our beach where it's always empty. The brick wall on the side of the fire station. And of course, Paradise. It's famous itself. Those have the most likes.

This pose isn't one I've seen before. I'm in awe of the strength it must take to balance on her arms and make it look effortless. Her face is passive, as if it wouldn't take one strong gust of wind to knock her over. I'm so mesmerized by her flexibility and strength that I almost forget I'm supposed to be taking a picture. I crouch down, making her look larger than life, and align the horizon with the wall and her body and make sure the proportions are where I want them. Then I tap the camera button several times in quick succession.

"Got it."

She slowly lowers to the ground and jogs over to me.

I'm prepared to go through this multiple times. When I take pictures of guests, inevitably someone blinks and we repeat the process. Carina is a perfectionist, so I expect the same process.

I don't mind. I could stare at her all day.

A smile inches across her face as she stands close, swiping through the photos. "These are great. Thank you." She turns toward me and I forget how to think. "You would make a great Instagram boyfriend." She shakes her head. "For someone else, obviously."

"Obviously," I repeat. I don't feel that way. "I would hate spending all our dates taking pictures of you. The food always getting cold because it takes forever for you to pose perfectly with your wine." *At sunset. In a cocktail dress.*

"Imagine being up at the crack of dawn to beat the crowds for one perfect shot."

"I like sunrises. I wouldn't mind that part."

She smiles as if the idea of me being her boyfriend, following her around like a puppy, isn't a terrible thought. She steps away, putting her phone back in her pocket. "I'll post one later. Do you have a personal Instagram? Or should I tag Lost Craft?"

"Don't worry about it." It hurts that she's not as curious about me and my social media as I am about her. That she so obviously hasn't looked me up until now. But she's not missing much since it's mostly sunrises over water.

"Come on. Let me give you photo credit," she persists.

I give her my handle, wondering if she'll even remember it later.

We wander through the rest of the fort. She walks close to me, her body occasionally brushing mine. Every pore of my skin drips sweat in the heat the sea breeze can't cool. She should keep her distance.

I shouldn't want her so close.

"Do you want me to inflate a paddleboard for you?" I ask as we approach the beach. Her friends wade in the shallows, engrossed in their fishing rods and whatever story Bristol is sharing.

Carina scoffs. "Your inferior boards will probably kick me off on principle." Her voice isn't in the denial.

We hit sand. She pauses, her hand resting on my shoulder for balance while the other pulls her flip-flops off.

"I won't judge you if you fall or whatever you're afraid of. You're a good paddleboarder," I say. I don't mind fighting with her over the last few days. At least I know she feels something for me. And for her, fighting is a risk.

I want her to take all the risks with me.

She lets out a huff. "No, it's not that. It's hot. I want to go for a swim."

It's hotter than hell and the only way to stay even remotely cool is to be in the water. "Sounds like a plan." I pull off my shirt and toss it on the pile of towels and shoes the group assembled. I head for the water, eager to get some relief.

When I turn around, Carina's stripped down to her bikini. I should look away, but I can't. I've seen her completely naked, but I'll never take for granted every inch of skin she shows. My eyes flick toward the constellation tattoo on her side, the tiny stars connected by thin lines to form a shape I know well, and I'm itching to get my hands on it.

"What?" She wades up to me, looking down to her bottoms. "You don't like the design?"

"Nope, it looks good. Functional." I shove my hands into my pockets so she doesn't see me clenching my fists. Anything to distract me. I don't know how she made a swimsuit so sexy and at the same time ready for whatever activity its wearer has in mind.

Everyone is occupied. No one will miss us if we venture back to the boat and to the forward cabin. It's a few feet away. We could be there so fast.

She wades in farther. The water is crystal clear and calm, with gentle waves lapping at us. I'm so used to reading the surface of the water, studying the waves for the wind, comparing it to the wind in my sails. But even as my reflexes tell me to look around, to watch the horizon, to check the radar, to notice everything at once, I can only look at her as her body slowly disappears under the surface.

My body desperately misses hers. I've never craved a woman the way I crave her. Not even after great sex before. It's not that she's rejected me and *that* made her sexier. That would be fucked up, but logical for some people. Instead, this means she's something more to me and there's nothing I can do about it.

I follow, unable to resist her pull. We're the only two not fishing. No one pays attention to us. The water is shallow, so we're able to wade far from the beach. She leads, taking us to the other side of the *Twisted Rigging* so her friends aren't in our direct line of sight. Is she doing it on purpose? Or is she letting the water carry her?

"Better than Boston?" she asks. She turns to face me and does a modified water treading action. She can touch the bottom sometimes but not always.

"Obviously." I bend my knees to match her. Only our heads are above the surface. We're close to each other. I could reach for her under the water and touch her before she reacts. "There is a reason I was only ever there for half the year."

This past winter was the first one I'd spent there in a long time. My parents were moving out of their house, downsizing to a smaller place, and I'd foolishly agreed to help. Then I met Megan and somehow ended up staying at her place too often.

Falling into a relationship that for a moment I thought would be forever.

It was a flash in the pan. If anyone had blinked, they would have missed it, the heat gone before it had a chance to do any damage or build anything lasting.

I crave heat and the humidity. I was done with the cold and ready to build something to last.

I didn't know how much I'd end up craving Carina.

I inch forward. She doesn't retreat. I've seen her a handful of times since I moved in. Every time she's had her guard up. Now she's looking at me like she wants me closer. I wonder if it's the ocean. If the water is her home. If it's here she'll give in to what she wants.

She's a siren calling to me.

The boat blocks us from view of her friends and no one else on the beach is close enough to see what we're up to.

I stand to my full height. The surface barely breaks my shoulders. A large wave hits, and since she's treading water, it pushes her into me.

The ocean is on my side.

With finesse I didn't know I had I lift her up against me. I hold her with one hand on her hip and one on her low back. Her legs open to wrap around my waist.

She'll be able to feel my erection pressed against her.

She doesn't react except to drape her arms over my shoulders as I move into deeper water.

"I got you," I say.

"I know." It's almost a whisper, and I strain to hear her over the waves.

I'm so glad she knows. I hold her tight against me. The space around us is beautiful. But Carina holds all my attention.

Her gaze pours into mine. "We shouldn't do this," she says, squeezing her legs tighter around me.

I shift my hand so I'm gripping her ass. "We're not doing anything."

"We said we wouldn't. It's too complicated."

"There is nothing less complicated than a swim in the ocean."

"Gulf," she corrects.

I inch my fingers closer to the edge of her bikini bottom.

I'm prepared to pull away the second she gives me any indication this isn't what she wants. But she doesn't. She looks so beautiful, with her hair slicked back and wet. If I kiss her, her lips will taste like salt.

I want to stay here forever, unaffected by the waves crashing around us and whatever creatures swim in these waters.

But someone shouts and panic crosses Carina's face. It's rejection of me in the face of the rest of the world.

I do the only thing I can think of—I lift her up and toss her back into the waves.

She surfaces a second later.

"What the fuck was that?" Her expression is shocked and defiant.

I laugh and raise my hands in surrender. "It seemed like a good idea."

"You bastard." The heat is gone from her voice, and it's replaced with something closer to trust and a laugh. She dives under the water and before I'm even able to register where she's gone, her hands grab my ankles, pulling me under.

So this is how she's playing it.

I swim, attempting to catch her, but she's fast and splashes out of the way. I'm almost able to get my arms around her waist again but our game of two-person tag catches the attention of the rest of the group.

"What are you two doing?" Christian asks, moving into view and looking at Carina as if she needs saving. He's a good-looking dude, standing in the shallows, shirtless with his upper arms and chest covered in tattoos. I wasn't jealous of him before, but it's threatening to fester in my mind. He's married, but I've been around him for hours and his wife has only been mentioned in passing by Bristol.

And I might have just had my hands on Carina's ass. But I want everything else she has to give, including her friendship and familiarity.

"We're just messing around," Carina says before splashing me. She has the guilty look of a kid called into the principal's office. It's so fucking precious.

"Uh huh." He's probably never seen her let loose before. "Careful with her."

I splash her back. "She won't fucking break." I want to remind her of how rough I'd been with her and how much breaking she'd done. Next time we're alone, I will. Or maybe she doesn't need reminding.

"Right." Christian returns to the other side of the *Twisted Rigging*. I'm not sure if he believes us, or if he'll trust that we're adults who can figure things out on our own.

"Asshole," Carina says.

"Me or him?"

She looks at me horrified. "Christian is one of the nicest men I have ever met. You should hang out with him more. It might rub off on you."

I get into her space again. "I could rub off on him. Turn him into an asshole." I don't give her the chance to respond. I pick her up and toss her into the water again.

"You'll pay for this!" she yells with a laugh as soon as she surfaces.

"I know. I'm terrible. I got you wet."

"You wish!" She lunges at me and I catch her, pulling us both underwater.

She's holding on to me when we surface again. I keep us low so only our heads are above the water. Our legs are intertwined, and no one can see how she's rubbing against me.

"Don't worry," I whisper. "It can be our little secret."

"I thought you were a big secret," she breathes.

"I'm whatever you need me to be, princess."

She doesn't respond. We hear more shouting. This time she pulls away from me and heads for shallow waters. Bristol caught something, and Christian and Haley help her reel it in.

"We should really get this on ice," Haley says, looking at me.

"I'll help you with it," I respond.

"We'll pack up things here and meet you back at the boat," Carina suggests, already gathering everything we've scattered on the deserted beach.

She's back to being the person she is for all of them. I had her wild and free with me for just a few moments. Haley is already wading back to the boat, making sure to keep the fish out of the water. I nod to Carina, already in a worse mood for being separated from her.

ORION

Once we're at the *Twisted Rigging*, Haley heads for the galley and one of the ice chests she brought. I hand her a roll of plastic wrap and she wraps the fish before placing it in the cooler.

"There's plenty here. I'll be too exhausted to cook when we get back, but how would you feel about having everyone over tomorrow to grill it?" she says while washing her hands.

"Did you just ask me if I want to throw a party at my place?"

"I'd offer my place, but it's tiny. Carina has enough on her plate. She did Christian's party. Plus, we're dying to see what you've done with the house."

"Sure, my place works." My home is my sanctuary, but it's built for entertainment too. I want to fill it with friends. "You've known her forever? You were little kids running around the beach together?" I ask. Carina has told me a little about her friends. I want to know more. Even if we've been getting along today, we haven't talked nearly enough and I'm a little afraid if we do, we'll end up fighting.

"Yep, she used to come every summer and winter break. She was making a sandcastle by herself and I asked if I could help. We were ten. From then on, it was cartwheels in the sand. The

Lawsons—you bought their house—used to let us watch movies at their place when it was raining. They had grandkids so they had an awesome video game setup."

I can't imagine even tiny Carina playing video games or not being productive all the time. "Where were your parents?"

"My mom was glad for me to be out of the house, so she only had to entertain my little brother and sister. Carina's parents were around, I guess. They worked."

The conversation cuts off because we hear everyone else moving around the deck.

"Let me get lunch started." Haley pulls food from the small fridge. Carina comes down and sets the table. We had planned on a beach picnic. But we're sunbaked and need a break.

Haley lays out the food. "This is cold avocado soup, summer melon salad, and fried chicken."

"Fuck me, this is delicious." I moan taking my first sip of the soup.

Haley blushes a little and Carina rolls her eyes. We've gathered around the table in the galley. It's a tight fit with six of us. But I won't complain with Carina pressed up against me.

"Do we have to eat in silence, or can I put on music?" Bristol asks.

No one has the energy to make idle conversation. I want a nap and a beer, but I can't drink if I'm sailing. "Sure. There's a Bluetooth speaker system." I point next to where she is sitting.

She's able to connect her phone, and the familiar piano chords of an Ashley Ferris song play.

"You're just fucking with me now," Christian says to his sister.

Our eyes pass between the two of them. Bristol smiles mischievously and explains. "He promised to get Autumn and me tickets to her concert in Tampa but wasn't online when they went on sale. They sold out."

"I was four minutes late!"

"They sold out in three! Autumn warned you!"

"Hey! No fighting on the boat," I say firmly. If the rule applies to Carina and me, then it applies to everyone. They grumble under their breath in the way only siblings do.

Bristol notices the same books Carina did on her first time here. I answer the same questions. No, I haven't circumnavigated the world. Maybe one day. But today, it's not some hypothetical partner I would do that with. I'm wondering what it would be like to be with Carina that long of a time. But she refuses to meet my eye when I talk about it.

We finish eating and Carina jumps up to help with the dishes, surprising no one. I stare down Alex until he offers to do them instead. She looks a little lost for a moment.

Everyone reapplies sunscreen and heads into the water or back to the beach, leaving Carina and me sitting on the stern with our feet dangling in the water. Again.

"You okay?" I ask her. "You look tired."

"You should know better than to tell someone that," she asserts.

"Normally, yes. But we've been out here all day, and you're a little pink. The cabin is free. Take a nap." I'm annoyed with her and with her friends. When she was spraying sunscreen on her back, she turned down my offer of help and struggled for a full minute before Haley jumped in. I hate that no one thinks to help her.

"I'm sweaty and covered in seawater."

"We do have a shower on board."

"I don't have a spare change of clothing."

Everything is difficult with her. But I refuse to back down. "I do. There are some T-shirts and shorts in the drawers of the main cabin." She looks like she might give in. "But you wouldn't wear that because you only wear Nebula Athletics." Maybe it's a mistake to needle her when I want her to give in. But I can't help myself.

She glares at me, then back at the horizon. "It wouldn't be fair to everyone else if I took up an entire cabin."

"I'd offer to share, but I know how you feel about that." Why won't she admit that rest is an option? "Have you ever once put yourself above anyone else? Isn't self-care important?"

"I've done things for myself," she says.

"Yeah, once. And you bolted out of here like you were on fire," I blurt.

"Please, you didn't want me to stay."

We said it was a one-time thing—but that didn't mean we couldn't linger. I won't argue about it anymore. "Whatever, Carina. We're on the boat. Let's not fight."

"Right. I'm going for a swim." She stands abruptly, and for once I don't watch as she removes her cover-up.

I shake my head and join the others on the beach.

An hour later, she's a little redder when we finally pack everything up and head back to Wendell Beach.

Bristol helped me sail on the way out, but as we sail back, Carina steps up. I don't know if she's trying to prove something to me or if she's genuinely curious and wants to learn. I explain everything as I do it, and she doesn't fight me once. Not even when I correct her and say they aren't ropes, but lines or sheets.

"The saying is 'showing the ropes,'" Carina says out of genuine curiosity.

"I don't know what to tell you, princess. English is weird."

"I don't get you two," Alex says.

"What do you mean?" Carina asks. She looks up at the mainsail with a little bit of pride, having helped me raise it.

"You're the calmest person ever, and then he shows up and you're a raging ball of fire. Now, you're back to your usual self."

Her eyes flare at the suggestion she is the calmest person ever.

I don't know what to tell them. She thinks she needs to hide herself from her closest friends. The risk of exposure too great for even them.

At the same time, I'm confused about how I get this piece of her no one else does. I haven't done anything to deserve it, but I'll do everything to protect it.

I like her when she's on fire, and I have no doubt if I protect that flame, even when it's flickering and faint, it will turn into a raging bonfire. I want to see her alight.

I attempt to catch Carina's eye, but she won't look at me.

"I need more sunscreen," she says and heads down to the cabins.

"What's her problem?" Alex asks.

I look to Haley for an answer. They've known her longer than I have. They should be the ones to fix this. I'm already frustrated enough with them.

Christian answers. "She's under a lot of pressure right now. It can't be fun for you to also expect her to behave exactly one way."

"Are you saying I hurt her feelings? She could have said something," Alex says. "She's never gotten upset before."

"Christian's right," Haley says. "But she doesn't make it easy or let anyone in."

I can't believe they talk about her like this. They're good people and I'm sure they're great friends, but they only see what they want to see. They see the perfect version of Carina and engage with that.

Alex rolls his eyes. "I'll apologize if it makes you feel better. Maybe she should get laid. It might unwind some of her tension. I don't think it's happened for her since Hamilton."

"Would you know?" I ask. "When was the last time you asked her about her life?"

He opens his mouth but quickly shuts it. This is the same man who would have banned me from his restaurant for a perceived slight of her, but doesn't know her well enough to know what a real one is.

Bristol is contemplative. "She lets me talk and talk about the other customers and my trips. By the time I'm done sharing, she's done with her drink or food. I don't ask about her."

"We'll do better," Haley promises. Her eyes narrow as she looks down and then at me.

"I'll go talk to her." Alex heads below deck after Carina.

"I thought yoga helped with stress," Christian says.

"She can't be everything all at once." I want to follow Alex to make sure he properly grovels and doesn't give a half apology.

"Is there something going on with you two?" Haley asks.

"No, it's nothing," I answer, wishing I was confident in my ability to lie to them.

"She's different around you."

"Maybe it's you she's different around," I suggest.

"What's that supposed to mean?"

"I don't know." I remove my hat and run my hands through my hair before replacing it. "She's overly concerned about what you think of her. She doesn't care what I think of her." I could spend a lifetime figuring out Carina Webb and it wouldn't be enough.

A few minutes later, Carina and Alex come up, a fake smile on her face. It takes all my restraint to not pull her into a hug. I want to be alone with her and get the honest check-in she won't give her friends.

God, I miss the way she feels against me.

We get back to the marina without any more drama, the sailing easy as I demonstrate to Carina a few maneuvers I don't necessarily need to do. The sun is heading toward the horizon and we're exhausted. If I wasn't responsible for driving people, I'd hang back here and sleep. It would be one more night in the bed I shared, however briefly, with Carina.

"I'll help you," Carina says.

"It's fine. I'll be a minute." I turn to Alex and Haley. I have to take care of the sails before I can leave. "If you wait five minutes, I'll be ready to drive back."

"I have space," Christian says to them. "I can swing by your cars. It'll be a little faster." They agree and walk down the dock to the marina's parking lot.

"I'll just walk," Carina says. "It'll be cramped enough without another sweaty body."

"Carina, wait five fucking minutes and I'll drive you." I'm not letting her go. I want five minutes alone with her. Even if we don't talk, I want to be around her.

"You don't—"

"For fuck's sake, I will tie you to this boat. You're already sunburned. You don't need any more UV exposure. Why didn't you wear a hat anyway?"

"I don't make them."

"Are you fucking kidding me?" I murmur. "You're exhausted. Let me do this. It doesn't have to be hard."

"I'm not exhausted."

She's such a little liar. "Well, I am, and I don't want to fight with you."

"Fine." She looks defeated, like she didn't want to lose this argument on its principle but has nothing left to fight me with.

Five minutes later, we walk to my SUV in silence, arms brushing like they did earlier. I open the passenger door for her.

"Carina," I say weakly. I'm not sure what more I have to say other than her name.

"I'm fine," she says, the mask she wore for her friends gone. She buckles her seat belt and then looks at me, clearly wondering why I'm standing with the door open. "If you're going to stand there, can you at least turn the a/c on?"

I want to reach for her, to touch her, to kiss her. To convince her to finish what we almost started in the water. I stand there, frozen.

"Orion."

The firm way she says my name jolts me back to the moment.

Right, it's hot and she's melting into my seats. I close the door and make my way to the driver's side.

At my house, I pull into my garage and turn the car off. We sit in the silence for a moment, knowing it'll be hot as fuck in no time. But I'm not ready for this to be over.

"So," I start. "Today was interesting."

"In what way?"

I turn to face her as she keeps her eyes forward. I look at the wall of the garage to see if there is something for her to complain about, but it's just a wall. "I learned three things."

"Really?" It kills me that there is no fight in her voice.

"First, we can get along."

"We already knew that," she says.

"Nope, we have been fighting since you left that night. And please don't argue with me about that. Second, we definitely want to fuck each other again."

"That doesn't mean it will happen."

"Right. You have lots of reasons why it's a bad idea."

"You agree with those reasons."

Our lives are intertwined. Neither one of us is looking for a relationship. For me, at least not before I feel settled. I remember this was important to me. Having her in my arms again makes me want to reconsider. Not everything is as catastrophic as she thinks.

"Third, you like fighting with me," I state.

"Excuse me?" She finally turns her head to face me.

"You like fighting me. You like that I fight back. You like that I don't expect you to be the perfect ideal you'll never live up to."

"I'm not perfect," she whispers. I can't tell if she's speaking to herself or to me.

"I know."

"I'm supposed to be. They think I am."

"Perfect is boring. You're not. You like that I've seen you. That you don't have to hide from me."

"I like fighting with you," she finally admits with a long exhale.

"Well, I'm right next door whenever you need some verbal sparring."

"You mean that?"

"Why not? You clearly have tension to work through, and you don't want to fuck it out."

She suppresses a laugh. She probably does want to fuck it out. "So, we're what, frenemies?"

"That's a dumb word, but sure." I unbuckle. "It's better this way. No chance of misunderstanding each other."

She gets out of the car and grabs her bag. "Whatever. I'm sure this is a momentary blip on my part anyway."

Something tells me she doesn't want to believe that.

fifteen

CARINA

I SPEND THE DAY AFTER THE BOAT TRIP GETTING CAUGHT UP ON what I missed the day before. As the head of a company, I pride myself on a work culture that supports work/life balance. I minimally check emails on my days off and don't expect anyone else to. But even with boundaries and a fantastic executive team, the tasks don't disappear when I'm out.

I work from home often. Remote work has been great for my employees, and I embraced it for their sake. It also helps me focus. Too many people require my attention when I'm physically at the office.

It's late in the afternoon, and while I'm up getting a cup of tea, I notice Haley's car is in Orion's driveway.

My heart catches in my throat. *No. This can't be happening.*

All I think is *mine*.

But he's not. We're friends who yell at each other. I have no claim on him. It doesn't matter what almost happened in the water yesterday, or what we did two weeks ago. I made it clear to him—I don't want anything more.

And it's not like Haley knows any better. I could tell her, and she wouldn't go near him. She'd never break the friend code stating you don't hook up with the same guy your friend did. Even if I told her it was okay.

This is ridiculous anyway. She's dating Eric. It's casual, but she doesn't stray.

I'm staring at my teakettle, trying to get my thoughts under control, when there is a knock on the sliding glass door in my office. My kitchen has a clear view so when I turn, I see Orion standing on my wraparound porch.

"I have a front door, you know," I say when I open it.

"Yes, but it's on the other side of the house. Why would I walk around when I can come in here?"

This part of my porch isn't in the backyard. I understand it's more convenient for him without being truly invasive. But I don't respond because I'm trying to come up with something clever to say. I can't because he smells like sunscreen and charcoal, and I love it.

"You going to stand there with the door open, letting the a/c out?" He smirks.

I haven't given him permission to enter my house. I debate for half a second about stepping outside. But it's hot and I've already showered once today. I don't need to get sweaty and add another thing to my to-do list. I don't have to let him past the doormat. "What can I do for you?" I step back just enough so he has room to stand. We're close. Too close.

"As you can see, Haley is over. Everyone else will be by in about thirty minutes."

"For what?" I ask.

"The orgy."

He says it with such a straight face that I almost believe him.

My first thought is *Fuck that. I'm not sharing you.*

My second thought is *My laptop could survive being thrown on the floor so we can fuck on my desk.* Who cares if the blinds are open and people could see?

But he's fucking with me. "Ha ha. What's really happening?" I take one step back.

He shakes his head, annoyed he didn't get a rise out of me. "Haley is putting the fish they caught on the grill. Everyone is bringing side dishes and drinks. You just need to show up."

"What? When did this happen?"

"Yesterday, when you were bringing things in before lunch."

"Fuck, Orion. You could have given me some warning. I need to get something together. I have ingredients for dip." I rush to my pantry to see if I have an unopened bag of chips. I usually have basic charcuterie for unexpected guests. I'm usually prepared, but he could have told me earlier. He drove me home yesterday and could have said something then.

He was out on a charter all day. I waved to him this morning as he drove past me while I was walking. He could've texted.

He steps in front of me, having followed me into the kitchen, and places a hand on each of my shoulders. "Carina, we have everything under control."

"I need to contribute. You said we were bringing sides. I have to get a side."

"I have hummus and fresh guac from a local shop. One of my captains recommended it. I have enough for it to come from both of us."

What? "I should at least bring chips."

"I have plenty. Carina, you only need to bring your beautiful face."

I look around my kitchen. "Plates. And silverware." I should make a list for this. I start sweating as I think of everything that needs to be done.

"Haley brought reusable plastic ones."

"I can at least bring a bottle of wine." I point to my living room where I have a wet bar. I'm sure I have something already chilled.

"I doubt anyone will argue against that, but both Alex and

Christian said something about enough rum punch to drown an army."

"You talked to them?" This wasn't planned with only Haley. This was a coordinated effort. I strain to take control of the situation as he follows me around, then steps in front of me to get my full attention.

"Yep, group text and everything."

My phone is at my desk. Did I miss a notification? Can texts go to spam? My stomach turns in knots.

He intercepts me. "We didn't include you on purpose."

I knew it. My friends hate me. It's fine. I'll make new ones. Orion can leave, and I'll head upstairs and cry in the shower.

I don't move. His hand gently lifts my chin so I'm looking at him. "It's a casual get-together. You didn't need to be involved in planning. I thought it would be a fun surprise for you. All you need to do is show up."

"I don't understand."

"You're an over-planner. You would have made a spreadsheet—"

"Then we would have everything we need."

"We have everything. If we're missing something, we'll go to the store. It's a few blocks away."

"So, you don't hate me?"

He rolls his eyes. "I might have to spank you for even thinking that."

Don't threaten me with a good time.

I don't know how to respond to this. In the past, my friends have loved the effort I put into planning events. They would have jumped at the chance to let me take over.

And I probably would've neglected some work to squeeze it into my day, and then worked late into the night while someone comments on how effortless it was for me.

I walk to my living room and pick up an orange tree seedling I have on a windowsill.

He follows me, because of course he did. I hand him the pot. "Here. It's a housewarming gift."

He laughs, a sound so warm I want to drown in it. "Thank you." He sets the pot on my coffee table and pulls me in for a hug. I inhale his scent.

"It's the neighborly thing to do," I say, clinging to his T-shirt.

"Of course. I'll see you in a few minutes." He releases me. I hate it.

As soon as he leaves, I run upstairs to my home yoga studio. It was the first space I renovated when the house passed to me. I replaced the bedroom carpet with hardwood, and mounted mirrors over an entire wall. I keep the lights off, letting the filtered sunlight from the window fill the room as I unroll my mat.

It's been years since my anxiety has run away like this. I need to push it down and push it away. Orion came into my life like a storm. I have no preparations completed. I need to throw my shutters closed and keep him out.

* * *

I'VE LEARNED a few things in the last twenty-four hours.

I might actually like Orion. I'm attracted to him. That was never in doubt. But for a brief period, he was mine. Sure, he'd met Haley during our charter, and knew Alex from before. But we had a special relationship. I was the one he shared rum with on his boat. I was the one he messed with because he knows I can take it. I don't know how he figured it out, when everyone treats me like I am breakable and need protection. Something nice and pretty to look at but never to engage with. I was the calming presence. Never the life of the party, even if I was the one who planned it.

Now he knows everyone, and they smile at him. And he and Haley have some kind of code they speak.

Okay, maybe she's explaining the recipe she's making.

I'm polite and drink my rum punch out of my tumbler and pretend I haven't fucked him and then rejected him and now want to throw myself at him. Damn the consequence and the ultimate dismissal and heartache I would face.

Why did he have to bring up orgies?

All I could think about was his sweat and my sweat, and he smelled so good standing in my office, and I wanted to reach for him and pull him close.

Haley sits down on the chair next to me. "You okay?" she asks.

"Yes."

"Come on, I know that face. Are you mad we planned this without you? It was Orion's idea and I have to admit it was a good one."

"No, it's not that."

"Then what is it?"

"It's nothing. Adding a new person to the group changes the dynamics. I'm working on it." After yesterday and feeling like I had to do everything even around fully functioning adults, I can admit it's nice to have the burden lifted. I can't remember the last time someone did something for me. I look to Orion, who's laughing with Autumn and Christian.

"Uh huh." Haley doesn't appear convinced but doesn't want to push more.

Orion would. He's figured out what buttons to push for a reaction and I don't know how that happened. But Haley doesn't push. She lets me stay hidden.

I've already shared more of myself with Orion than I have with her, beyond the sex. He knows all my fears. If I had known it would be like this, would I have changed anything?

He looks at me and I want to look away. For anyone else, I would look away. Instead, I hold his gaze. He's reading me. *What does he see?*

"Sorry, everyone. I would play some music, but my neighbor doesn't like it when I'm loud," he proclaims.

"Oh lordy," Haley mumbles. "Here we go."

"Why would I complain about it now?" I ask. "I'm right here."

"I don't know," he says. "You're notoriously difficult to deal with."

"Hey! She was perfectly pleasant when we chartered your yacht." Haley might be Team Orion at times, but the second he picks on me, she's ready to fight.

"It's fine," I tell her. I almost reach to touch her arm but pull back. "If everyone thinks I'm easy to deal with except you, maybe you're the problem," I say.

"You wound me." He fakes an arrow to the heart.

"You have weird vibes," Autumn says. She's an elementary school teacher and doesn't hang out with us often. I've never really understood it. She and Christian are beautiful people. But I've never met two people with less chemistry.

I've often wondered if they hide it until they are home.

"I should grow my hedges taller, so I don't ever have to look at your yard." It's my turn to watch him struggle to maintain composure. We haven't been suggestive in front of others, and he's thinking about a trimmed bush.

It's comforting that we have this shared communication, and he's proved I can trust him with a secret. I feel warm and protected, regardless of the look on my face.

"I don't care what you do with your bushes as long as you two don't bring it into the bar," Alex says. "The locals' section must stay conflict free."

"Scout's honor," Orion says before winking at me and turning back to the grill.

The food is good, as it always is when Haley cooks. Orion helps her, and I watch for flirting. It's not there. If he does stay in Wendell Beach longer than the winter, he'll find someone else to date, since I told him it won't be me. He's too good of a man to be single for long. It's a possibility I'll prepare for, even if it might have broken me to watch it happen the day after he had his arms around me.

I should have let his hands continue their journey into my swimsuit bottom.

I should have pulled him into the cabin and helped him out of his wet shorts.

We could have watched the sunset from my bedroom.

But I can't have a fling with my next-door neighbor. There's no outcome that doesn't end awkward or with heartbreak or with one of us giving up something that matters to our very souls. I see how much this house means to him. How proud he is to share it with our friends. I see the vision he has for it.

His gaze finds mine again, and I wonder if it's obvious what I'm thinking.

* * *

AFTER FOOD and drinks and a glorious sunset, everyone says their goodbyes.

"You don't have to help me clean up," he says. It's the two of us in his backyard, lit magically with string lights that almost look like stars overhead.

"It's no problem. You've been up all day."

"So have you," he replies.

"Look, I know you want to say something about me being a people pleaser and helping you clean up because it's the 'right thing to do.' Seriously, you're being stubborn. And not letting me help to prove a point about me is just as dumb."

"So, you don't want to fight about who does the dishes?"

"No, I want the dishes to get done. We can fight about how you load the dishwasher or something."

"I'll definitely have issues with your rinsing technique."

"Wonderful." I usher him into his house, and I'm once again

hit by the sense this is a home. Orion has left his mark on this space. My place doesn't feel like me as much as this feels like Orion.

The tiny orange tree has a prominent place on his kitchen counter. I smile.

The kitchen is large so it's easy for us to move around each other. I don't have any reason to casually bump into him as much as I do. He doesn't need me to touch his triceps as I reach past him for a lid.

He also doesn't react.

I can't help myself. I don't remember the last time someone else touched me. My friends don't give me hugs, and I don't offer them.

I'm processing this realization when he pulls his phone out of his pocket. "Shit, I should take this." He moves down the hallway to answer the call.

I don't think anything of it so I go outside to grab the remaining condiments. When I'm back inside, he's in the kitchen again.

"No, the house is unpacked. Just had some friends over." Pause. "Yeah, of course. If you're ever in the area… Bye." He has a concerned look on his face when he turns around and sees me.

"Everything okay?" I ask.

"Yes." He leans back against the counter and crosses his arms. He's still for a few breaths. "That was an ex."

"Oh." My stomach twists. We haven't talked much about past relationships, other than when he mentioned he'd been tested after his last girlfriend. I have no idea when that was. It could have been the week before we hooked up. And he knows about Hamilton. But I have no right to ask about anyone he's been with. I've made a lot of assumptions about what he's done in the past. Most of it is probably unfair.

He raises an eyebrow as he waits for further comment.

"I didn't know you were the committing type," I reply. I'd

imagined he'd meet someone, but I don't know what that looks like for him. Does he do relationships?

He runs a hand through his hair. "It's complicated."

His brown eyes hold mine. I wish I could trap all their color at once. If I found a dye that was all that sunshine and warmth, I'd sell out of every pair of leggings.

But he doesn't owe me an explanation of what he's done in the past. We're not together. We're not moving toward anything except friendship. Despite that, I find myself wanting to know every fact about him. I want to know his scars and his tattoos and every person who's broken his heart.

What I've seen of him is the surface, and he has depths I can't imagine. I want to explore them all.

He doesn't say anything, so I break the silence. "Let me guess. She wants you back? Pregnant with your child?"

"Definitely not the latter, maybe the former." He shifts and rests his forearms on the opposite counter. "We hadn't been together long when I decided to move to Florida. She was coming with me at first but thought it was a temporary thing. We'd sail down, spend a few weeks in the Keys, head back to Boston. Then I bought a house. She wasn't upending her life for someone she just met."

The thought of someone else in bed with him on the *Twisted Rigging* turns my stomach. I know it's happened, but I want the boat to be our spot. I want to be special to him.

"Why did you take the call, then? If it's clearly over for you?" I hope it's over for him.

The possessiveness I feel toward him doesn't help anything.

"We very briefly lived together. Sort of. It wasn't anything official. I don't like other people on my boat for extended periods." He waves his hand in the air. "Not important. It was winter. Anyway, I had her place as my shipping address on a couple of websites. I placed an order and didn't realize until it was too late. I've been trying to coordinate with her to get it to my sister."

"Oh, that's logical," I say. Because it is. "Were you together long?" It's possible I was a rebound fuck to him.

"A couple of months," he says.

They lived together? I don't voice the thought because I don't want to sound like I'm judging him. I'm not, but that's a level of seriousness I've never achieved in a relationship. The goal was to marry Hamilton and I still couldn't bring myself to live with him. I didn't think Orion was the committing type. None of this makes sense to me.

He grabs a dish and loads the dishwasher. "I tend to burn hot and then burn out. I meet someone, convince myself she's the one. Then a couple weeks later, it's done."

My gut absolutely clenches, a feeling so awful it might be permanent. I can't imagine a future where it won't toss and turn. This conversation will wreck me.

I'm right to keep my distance from him. I won't survive this man deciding to walk away from me. It would be so much more. He would dismiss me and move on without a second thought.

I want to say something, but I'm frozen.

He finishes with the dishwasher and then stares at me. I lean against the counter because I need it to hold me up.

"Anyway, she wanted to hold my package until I go back to Boston. I told her my sister will swing by this weekend."

"Good. It's good to get your stuff." I wipe the counter with a cloth he had out.

"Carina." His voice is a plea.

"What?" I say, giving him my full attention.

He doesn't answer—his eyes beg me to understand. I wish I couldn't read him so well, because while I know what he wants from me, I don't know what I want him to say. That I'm right and we have no future. Or he's changed and we're different.

I let the moment pass and return to cleaning up the kitchen.

<h1 style="text-align:center">sixteen</h1>

ORION

I DON'T GO OUT ON THE WATER THE NEXT DAY. I'VE SPENT SO MUCH of my life on a boat that the ground feels rocky beneath my feet.

Instead, I have the pleasant task of reviewing administrative work for the business here in Florida and the one in Boston. I have capable managers at both locations, but someone is required to sign off on certain things and that person is me. When I've traveled before I didn't micromanage, and it never bit me in the ass. I want to be hands-on now.

I have plans for the company here. I want to expand. I've never lacked ambition, even if it doesn't show the way people are used to. We currently cater to families on vacation, but I want to offer more. Luxury day trips with personalized menus and service. Overnight trips for a once-in-a-lifetime adventure. So I need more boats. I need to be constantly coming up with new ways to get repeat guests and always offer the best experience.

I could advertise to brands and social media influencers. I should reach out to the Foleys to get placement at Coastline Beach House. But I'm hesitant. It would be a terrific opportunity, but I'm not sold on working with Beckett. I'll see if I can get more information from Carina or someone familiar with how the resort works. It would change my calculations if they referred guests who want to do sailing trips directly to Lost Craft Charters.

I'm doing market research and reviewing invoices for the boat repairs we always need when I get a text from Christian inviting me to the tasting room at his distillery. It's three in the afternoon. I've been here since six in the morning, so I can leave. I wave goodbye to the office staff and drive the short distance to the address he gave me.

I didn't know what to expect when I get there, but it wasn't discovering Wendell Beach Rum Works is next door to Nebula Athletics Studio and Store.

I wonder if she's here or if she's working from home. I like having her close to me. It's already begun to feel natural when I'm home to know she's near me.

All day, I've thought about the way Carina's expression changed when I told her about Megan and my dating history. I confirmed her worst fears about me. She's wary I'll do to her what I've done in relationships before. That what we're feeling right now is just me being hot, and we'll burn out before hurricane season ends. She doesn't understand that I always want to commit. But it's never been right, as hard as I've tried.

Carina feels right. I need her to see through what I was saying, like she always has. I don't avoid feelings. I collapse into them. It's never worked in the past but it could with her.

It's the little things throughout the day that make me think of her. I wasn't an "out of sight, out of mind" guy before. But reminders of her are everywhere. If I see someone in yoga pants, I wonder if they're Nebula Athletics. If I see oranges, I think of orange blossoms and the orange sapling she gave me. I'm out on a boat and I'll remember Carina likes the water.

She could only be a few feet away, but I walk into the distillery instead of to her.

The tasting room at Wendell Beach Rum Works is brightly lit, with big windows facing the town's main street. It's a great spot for tourists to wander in when they're looking to cool down. Signs advertise *Free Yoga at the Distillery* and *Outside Food Welcome*.

I'm not surprised it's quiet since it's the middle of the afternoon. A few people watch a sports recap show on the TVs. The Orlando Sorcerers football team is doing well this year. Christian stands behind the bar, reviewing a tablet next to a woman.

He looks up when I walk in. "Hey, Orion. Glad you came by. This is the tasting room manager, Natasha. Natasha, this is Orion. He just moved to town and owns Lost Craft Charters."

We make small talk for a few minutes until he gestures for me to sit at the end of the bar.

"Anything you want to sample? You've already had our long-aged, so you'll probably like this blend." He grabs a bottle off the shelf and pours it into a tulip-shaped glass.

It's good, and I take the glass with me as he gives me a tour of the place. He's working on expanding operations, and truth be told, I'm already impressed with the place. We settle back in the tasting room, which has nearly emptied.

"What's going on with you and Carina?" he asks.

A wave hits me at the sound of her name.

I shake my head. "Nothing. We're friends."

I don't know if he believes me. "She's special. To this town. And to me," he says. I raise an eyebrow. "Not like that. When I inherited the distillery, I didn't know what I was doing business-wise. A chemistry degree doesn't help with financial statements. She took me under her wing. Answered my questions for years. I couldn't have expanded without her."

I wonder if this is leading to an explicit "hurt her, I hurt you" threat.

"I have no intention of fucking with her." It's not a lie. "She did build a multimillion-dollar company. She can handle herself."

"Right, you're right." He looks a little put out. Like he'd imagined how the conversation would go, and it wasn't with me standing up to him and for her. "She is a little closed off."

I laugh. "That she is. And she'd hate it if she knew we were talking about her like this."

"You have her figured out faster than anyone else. Maybe that's a good thing," he says.

"We understand each other. We communicate better than it appears." I might as well give him the promise he's looking for. "I care about belonging in this town, and that means protecting Carina Webb. It was the first lesson I got when I docked here. Don't worry, I'm on your side." Neither she nor I have any plans to go anywhere.

He doesn't need to know I'm completely infatuated with her.

* * *

I'm INCREDIBLY careful about driving, and even though I've only had one drink, I want a little bit of time before I hop behind the wheel. That's exactly what I'll tell Carina if she asks. Not that I'm dying to see inside her store and office. And definitely not that I've missed her. She won't say anything, but I also need to know if she'll treat me differently now that I've told her about my dating past. Will she push me away?

No one stops me as I enter the office suite at Nebula Athletics. The assistant desk in front of her door is empty, and Carina doesn't notice when I stand in the doorway.

"Your security is terrible."

She jumps, then smiles. "Only because you ignored the *Employees Only* sign."

I shrug. She's wearing a maroon tank underneath a white cardigan I haven't seen before. I wonder how soft it is. I want to reach for it and feel it. And I hate it at the same time because it's between me and Carina's skin.

"What are you doing here?" She's surprised, and maybe I'm not welcome.

"Christian gave me a distillery tour." Her office smells like orange blossoms like her house does. One of the ubiquitous trees sits in the corner.

"Right, no reason for you to drop by for yoga." She's disappointed. I see her, wanting me to herself the way I want her.

I look around, still standing in the doorframe, and make sure we're alone. "You know firsthand I'm not flexible enough to do any of that." I know yoga is more than flexibility. But I can make her hot and bothered and angry at the same time.

She rolls her eyes. I want to trace the neckline of her cardigan along her collarbones. "I promise you, unless you sign up for advanced arm balances, you'll be fine in any of our classes."

"When do you teach?" I ask. She shakes her head and pulls a sheet of paper from her desk drawer. She scribbles something before handing it to me.

Orion Edwards is entitled to one month VIP membership, authorized by Carina Webb.

"I teach an all-levels class Wednesdays at six a.m. Reserve your spot online. It fills up."

I laugh. I couldn't handle her teaching me anything. I'd have a competence boner no compression shorts could hide. "I'll see if it fits my schedule. You want a ride home?" It's nearing five. We could eat dinner together and watch the sunset.

She looks at her watch. "I have to get numbers to my investors before close of business Chicago time. But thanks for the offer."

"Next time. I'll see you around." I keep disappointment out of my voice, wondering how many times I'll say "next time" to her before I really get one.

seventeen

CARINA

IF I THINK OF THE CALL I HAD AS BEING WITH MY INVESTORS, THEN it feels like less of a gut punch. If Jeffrey Webb and Hamilton Kane are strangers, and I can pretend they shouldn't know my values and my passions, then I won't be so angry. But they're my father and ex-boyfriend. They should, so the thought experiment is short.

I pour myself a glass of wine because I need a moment to myself. I realize I'm so defensive, I'm talking myself into doing something I don't need permission for—I'm an adult. I can have wine.

The business portion of the call was grueling enough. Normal Webb Group patronizing for sure. But after an hour, my father kicked everyone off to have a "father/daughter" chat. I braced myself because I knew what was coming.

My mother was making a fool out of herself running around with younger men. I should settle down with someone stable. Don't I realize how good Hamilton is doing at the firm?

The same Hamilton who spent the first thirty minutes of the meeting pointing out everything wrong with what I was doing.

It's the same lecture over and over. My dad thinks I need a

partner. The way he describes his vision for me, it's more like he thinks I would benefit from someone corralling me. Someone to guide my business career. Otherwise, dating and relationships are a waste of time. My father believes in me. But he believes in the patriarchy more.

"You could have tried a little harder with Hamilton. I think you gave up too soon. You don't want those years you spent with him to go to waste, do you?"

As if instead of dates with Hamilton, I could have been working on my business.

My phone vibrates and I see a text from Orion.

ORION

Back

It's accompanied by a selfie of him and his kayak with my house in the background. His version of proof of life.

I clench my jaw and look out the window behind me. From here, I see him hosing off the kayak in his driveway. He's gone out every day this week. Sometimes early in the morning or late in the afternoon. It varies depending on if he's in the office or has a charter. As he said he would, he texts me every time. And every time I think I'm fine knowing he's out on the water. Thinking it doesn't bother me. Every time, I relax a little when he's back safe. The tension I hold in my shoulders releases.

I'm used to paddleboarding on my own. The first time I went out after he moved in, I'd considered making a big show of not telling him. Letting him know I'm experienced and not worried. But as I got my board down from its rack, I realized how smart it is to have someone watching out for me.

I could have texted Haley. She would care. She might even have joined me. But Orion is closer, and it makes so much sense. It has nothing to do with wanting him. So I'd texted him I was headed south and shared my location with him.

Temporarily, of course.

He crawled his way into my life, and I don't think he's trying or even realizes it. It's not that we're watching for each other. It's that we use the same grocery store, we hang out at the same bar, and that was nothing compared to the shock of seeing him in my office two days ago. Of course he'd be hanging out with Christian. I'd wondered if he'd take me up on the yoga offer, so I checked our class rosters. Sure enough, he took power flow with Vanessa yesterday. I was tempted to ask her what he was like, but it felt like an invasion of his privacy. If he's not coming to my class, then he doesn't want me involved in his yoga practice.

Which I didn't even know he had.

I want to know everything about him.

A few times a day, I see him in passing, or I see him get out of his SUV. Every time, my heart skips a beat.

Today, he's wearing a long-sleeve sun shirt and shorts. He clearly jumped in the water because everything clings to him, and his hair falls in waves that should come with a warning message.

And none of it is helping me with my anger toward my dad and Hamilton.

The last straw comes when Orion turns on his speaker and starts playing fucking country music. Again. I storm out of my office and onto my porch overlooking his garage.

"Hey fuckhead, can you turn that down?" This is a huge escalation in temper. I need some kind of outlet, not just from work, but from Orion. I already went for a run, yoga won't help, and there is only so much my vibrator can do. The wine was my last-ditch effort.

He looks at me with pretend confusion and then to the hose in his hand. I can feel him thinking it. I'm wearing light blue leggings and a white cardigan over a matching blue crop top. I make quality clothing, so getting it wet won't make it see-through. But I don't want to encourage him.

"I didn't know it was your nap time. I'm so sorry, princess," he says.

I glare at him, but my anger eases. "It's common courtesy to not inflict your music tastes on others." He knows I'm bullshitting. We live on the beach. We can hear at least three other speakers from where we stand. It'll be so much worse when we get to spring break.

He marches over to his speaker and makes a demonstration of turning it off. "Happy now?"

"Delighted."

"See, I think you're lying. You won't be happy until I turn my place into a private meditation retreat center. Even though you've benefited from my loud music and party-hosting capabilities."

I grind my teeth. *I'm more than that,* I want to yell. *I'm more than the calm person everyone thinks I am.* Of course, my father did tell me to calm down today when I spoke up to counter an idea.

"It doesn't matter," I call back. "I'll wait you out. You'll be bored of Florida and sailing away in no time. Your house listed on Airbnb." The thought of his place becoming a vacation rental is more upsetting than it should be.

Something flashes in his eyes, and somehow I've struck a nerve.

He told me this is what he does. He convinces himself he wants something and tires of it in no time. It doesn't matter that he's made his house feel like a sanctuary I could weather any storm in. He won't stay. I'm sure of it.

"You want me gone so you're not tempted every day," he says.

"No!" I protest too much.

"Admit you'd miss me if I left." He pulls off his wet shirt and tosses it onto a pile of towels. My eyes widen at the muscle on display. I've seen it before. I'm used to being around strong bodies all the time. It shouldn't affect me.

I turn away to stop myself from staring. It's him that affects me.

"Carina." He says my name like a song. "Look at me."

I don't.

"Last warning."

"Last warning for what?" I barely have the question out of my mouth before a spray of water hits me, completely drenching my side. "Oh, for fuck's sake! That was unnecessary!"

I hear him laugh as I move toward the back of my house. I have towels stored on the pool deck. I have no desire for him to learn if my nipples poke through the fabric. But he follows me, and as soon as I grab a towel I turn, prepared to counter whatever attack he has coming for me.

He stops me with a kiss.

All thought leaves my brain.

My hands rest against his chest and I almost push him away. Instead, I wrap my arms around his waist and pull him closer. He effortlessly moves us against the side of the house. His hands cradle my head. His lips are soft, and he tastes like the sea. It shouldn't be good. But it's uniquely him and exactly what I need.

He breaks the kiss.

I almost whine at the separation, but I catch myself. "You kissed me," I say.

"Water didn't get you to stop thinking. Had to change tactics. Do you want to talk about it?" His face is full of concern as he steps out of my reach.

"Talk about the kiss?" *Can we do it again?*

"No, whatever's on your mind."

The fight falls out of me. Of course he knows I'm upset about something else and not his music.

"No, that's not part of the deal." I lean against the porch railing and close my eyes. I let the music from someone else's yard disappear until all I hear are waves crashing on the beach. Orion stands next to me, not touching. But close enough to feel the heat radiating off his skin and the smell of sea salt.

Fuck, I love it so much. I want nothing more than to completely collapse in on him and let him take away my frustration. He might be my friend and clearly thinks it's okay to kiss his friends. But he didn't sign up to take on my emotional needs.

Though it couldn't hurt to share some of my problems.

"Fine." I cave. "I had a strategy session with one of my investors. His team thinks if I downplay the sustainability aspect of the clothing, it will reach a wider audience."

"Do they think people specifically not buy because it's sustainable? Like people think, 'Fabric's soft. Looks nice. Too bad it's not harming the planet as much as those other pants.'"

"Exactly. For some it's a selling point. Others a bonus. No one treats it as a deterrent. But he thinks environmental concerns are a niche market."

"Sounds dumb."

"And then. *Then*. They had the audacity to tell me since their approach is guaranteed to sell more, I am actually hurting the environment by not doing things their way."

"Carina, they're gaslighting you."

I'm not prepared for the ferocity with which he comes to my defense. "I know. What am I supposed to do? He's my biggest investor."

Orion's eyes wander to my backyard. I expect him to offer some advice about standing up for myself or to mansplain environmentally conscientious living, but he doesn't.

"You said you got the house in your parents' divorce?"

"Yes. They kept arguing over who would get it, so they put it in a trust for me when I turned eighteen." I'm thankful for the change in topic. It's an old wound. It doesn't hurt as much.

"So, you came here a lot as a kid?"

I nod. "Met Haley collecting seashells on the beach. Alex used to chase me out of the locals' section. She'd yell at him since it wasn't fair. I would've lived in Wendell Beach then if I could."

"You had to stay then, to spite him."

"I'm sure he feels that way." I smile.

"And your parents? Do they visit?"

It occurs to me that this conversation was an odd segue. He doesn't know the bad marketing advice is coming from the man who raised me.

"Not often. They're busy," I say. I wait for the follow-up about me visiting home.

"Did you ever think about selling and getting a smaller place?"

"No," I blurt out. It's more house than I need, and I purposefully avoid thinking about its carbon footprint. It's an indulgence. "My parents might have made terrible memories here, but I have good ones. I want to pass that on to my children."

"Your children?" he questions.

My barriers have fallen around him. I don't know how to rebuild them. "You surprised I want kids?" I search his eyes for a reaction.

"No, just hard when you don't date."

Any other person I would smile and comment on my schedule and timing. But I can't stand judgment from him. "Fuck off." I push away from the railing. "Why did you move here, then? If you didn't know anyone besides Alex and clearly aren't close to him."

"I like sweating," he says as if that's an answer.

"What?"

"I like sweating, so I decided to move to a swamp."

I shake my head. My eyes burn. It's not fucking fair that I open my soul to him repeatedly and then he gives me that bullshit. He pushes me to open up. He's the one who made me come undone, and he gives me nothing.

He sighs, then looks at me with serious eyes. "Last fall, a wave knocked over my kayak and my paddle hit me in the head. I was unconscious when I hit the water."

"Oh my god." He could have died.

"I came to quick enough and was able to flip upright. I took a hard look at my life. I'd been drifting my entire adult life. I wanted to settle down."

"So, you came to Florida to go wife hunting? A state that denies the existence of queer people and forces people to give birth?"

"You're here too, princess."

"I am trying to make the world a better place."

"So don't let your investors talk you into downplaying the part of your business you care most about!"

"What?" How the hell did we get back here?

"You care about your home and the environment. You wouldn't give this house up for anything. You love this island, and I love how much you love it. Even though you know how bad Florida gets hit with extreme weather. So don't back down with them. Especially not when it matters," he shouts.

"It's not that simple." But he's right, and he cares, and I need this so bad.

"I can play my music loudly every day at this time if you need to yell at me."

I smile. "What are we doing?" I ask, even more exhausted than I was before.

"We're being friends. I'm guessing you don't complain to anyone."

"I have Haley and Sienna."

"You didn't reach out to either one to vent."

"To be honest, you were closer."

He sighs heavily. "It's always nice to be chosen for proximity reasons."

"Oh please. Don't pretend your interest in me is more than geography based."

"Come on, Carina. If I didn't want to be around you, I wouldn't be around you. Please tell me you have enough self-esteem to know that."

I want to be around him. No matter what he told me about wanting to settle down, he's a flight risk. I feel raw. I need to get away from him. I reach for the door handle, but he grabs me from behind. I expect to be spun around and for him to kiss me. Instead, he tosses me over his shoulder and walks us toward my pool.

"Put me down!" I don't know if I mean it.

"Don't worry, I will."

I wiggle, trying to escape his grasp, but he's strong. For my effort, there's nothing I can do. I feel momentarily weightless and then I'm underwater. He holds me while he does it. Cradling my head so I'm safe, and then immediately releases me so I can surface on my own.

"You bastard!" I swim to the shallow end, and he laughs behind me as he follows. We're both standing in my pool, water dripping down our skin, my cardigan clinging to my chest, staring at each other.

It wouldn't take much effort to close the distance between us so I could run my fingers through his hair. I remember how good he feels. I want it again.

It's a terrible idea.

The heat falls out of me. "I should go." I need him to know I'm not mad at him. I just don't want to fight anymore. "I have to send some emails."

I get out of the pool and he follows. I grab us both towels. Instead of taking his, he pulls me in for a hug. It would be a friendly hug if he wasn't shirtless. I accept, pressing my face into his neck because he's warm and he's here and he's the only person to have touched me in weeks.

Any reasons beyond that can't matter.

ORION

Labor Day weekend was hell for me. All our charters were booked solid. All boats were at capacity. We do private tours and group excursions. Both types are demanding and there is something about the holiday weekend that brings out the worst in people. I was up before dawn each day and I didn't make it back to my house until late into the night. We had so many last-minute requests my staff suggested we open up the *Twisted Rigging* for charter.

I said no.

It would've been a good business decision. We have the staff to handle it. But I don't want strangers on my boat. I did it once and it brought me Carina. I don't want anything to taint the memory. Now that Carina's been there, I can't bring anyone to that space, unless it's with her.

I spend the Tuesday after the long weekend running through paperwork at the office and making sure everything is functional on the business side. Now that summer is officially over, we need to pivot our marketing. We'll go from families on vacation to the snowbirds visiting for the winter. They are harder to impress since they return year after year and have fixed incomes, so we need to justify why we're worth it for them.

When five o'clock hits and the afternoon storms have passed, I head home and pull out my kayak. I need some alone time with the water. No one asking for a drink or flirting with me or getting in my way when I'm trying to get the lines out.

ME

I'm headed out.

You started sharing location with Princess Carina.

I don't wait for a response from her. Sometimes she acknowledges. Most of the time she doesn't. The point is someone is watching out for me if something were to happen.

It doesn't take much effort to launch from the beach, and I quickly lose myself in the movement. The water is almost flat for once, the wind minimal.

"Ahoy!" I hear her voice from the direction of the shore.

I turn and see Carina paddling in my direction. She's in shorts and a long-sleeved sun shirt. My eyes instantly go to the way her powerful legs support her as she gets closer to me.

"Hey," I respond.

"Hope you don't mind some company. It's a big gulf. I can go somewhere else."

"I won't stop you." I want her here with me. I want her close enough to smell her sweat and her sunscreen. I'll settle for her cruising along next to me.

We find a rhythm and don't talk. It's relaxing to have her with me. I've never known what it's like to simply share space with another person. Yes, I want Carina naked under me. But more than that, I want little moments with her. I want her to be a part of my day.

The wind picks up, and while that doesn't bother me, it

affects Carina more. She kneels on her board and adjusts the length of her paddle.

"It doesn't count if you're sitting," I say. "It's called 'stand-up paddleboarding.'" I don't mean this. I want to push her, because I want her, and I'm frustrated that she doesn't want me.

She shrugs. "I'm out on the water. That's the point of the activity. I've stood plenty."

She's not fighting me. She's not proving my limited knowledge of paddleboarding wrong or arguing it's superior to kayaking. She's enjoying the moment the same as I am. I let it go.

The sun sets behind us as we glide back to the beach. I normally don't bother with towels and instead drag myself home, showering the sweat and salt off as fast as possible. But Carina's left two towels on the beach, knowing no one would mess with her things on our quiet section of sand. She lays them out.

"Sit for a moment and watch the sunset with me," she says.

I don't hesitate. I'll give anything for a few moments with her.

We watch the sky darken from light blue to black, as the colors on the horizon remain vibrantly orange.

I thought living on the beach in a tourist town would be loud, and some days it is. Tonight, it's quiet. It's Carina and me, the water and the sand.

"I got samples for next year's fall line," she says. "The colors are gorgeous."

I freeze. She's sharing without any prompting, and even in the dark I can tell she's smiling. She was happy, and she reached for me.

"Yeah? Brown and yellow?" I ask, thinking of the changing leaves in New England.

"No, we tried a brown once. It kind of looked like poop. This is dusty rose and hunter green."

I love the sound of her voice when she's talking about her work, soft and wistful. It's clear to me she loves what she does and has a passion for it.

She's so close to me now. Our legs brush each other. If she keeps her attention ahead on the water, we won't be in any trouble. If she looks my way, I'll kiss her.

Because sitting on the beach, watching the sun set with the person you care about, is the most romantic thing in the world. She turns to me, her face in a slight smile that comes from being relaxed. I hope she says something about the look on my face, because there is no way I can hide how badly I want her right now.

She doesn't. She studies me and I wonder what she sees. She leans in and presses her lips to mine.

I don't hold back. I can't. Not when she tastes like salt and the sea. My hand goes immediately to the nape of her neck, pulling her in close.

I'm tired of pretending I don't want this. That somehow this is a terrible idea, when it feels so good to have her in my arms.

She ends the kiss but doesn't pull away from me. I rest my forehead on hers. We need to take care of her board and my kayak. Then I need her in my bed.

Or really, the shower, because we're both covered in sweat and sunscreen. Every time I see Carina wet, every time I've got her in the water with me, all I think about is sleeping with her. Shower sex is my perfect fantasy.

But Carina is skittish. I can't scare her away with how much I want her.

She doesn't speak. I feel her breath on my lips.

"You are—" I start.

She jerks away. "I shouldn't have done that."

"*We* did that," I correct. "It doesn't have to be a big deal." Though this is a big deal to me. She's all I want.

She shakes her head and stands up. "As fun as it would be, a fling is a bad idea. We don't want you to burn out when you're stuck with me forever."

"Right." She's wrong. She's afraid feelings will get involved but it hurts even if we don't have sex. I can't deny to myself that I have feelings for her. We would be great together. It would be worth it if we worked out. I want to risk everything for her. Risk the house. Risk Wendell Beach.

She is worth it.

She reached out to me when she was having a good day.

She shakes the sand out of the towel.

"I'm surprised you even use a towel," I say, falling back on the one thing she accepts from me. "Since you don't make them."

I've earned myself a glare. "This towel is made from organic cotton, and a portion of the proceeds from every purchase go toward marine conservation."

"Are they union made?"

A deeper glare follows. "They are the most sustainable and employee-friendly towel company out there. I did my research."

I wonder how long that took her. If she spent weeks comparing towels until she found one to her exacting standards. I look at the label and make a note to buy some for myself.

She throws it over her shoulder and picks up her board.

"Let me help you." I reach for her paddle for her, but she beats me to it.

"I got it," she says.

I expect her to walk away and leave me behind, but she doesn't. She waits for me to pick up my kayak and together we cross the sand.

nineteen

ORION

She ignores me for a week after the kiss on the beach. She's re-finding her equilibrium, and I understand that even if it annoys the fuck out of me. She doesn't realize how quickly she's become the center of my everything. The way she's depriving me of her presence makes me feel like I'm collapsing in on myself.

We had a problem with the catamaran today—the engine wouldn't start. It was a fucking nightmare to explain to the clients that yes, sailboats have engines and no, we couldn't leave the dock without it. It's technically possible, but it's much more difficult to get in and out of the marina with just the wind. I can do it, of course, but the wind can change at any moment and it's not worth it for a charter. I booked the group with another company. That didn't save me from a woman yelling at me for thirty minutes about how I ruined her vacation.

I sprawl on my couch because I don't want to move, don't want to think. The doorbell rings. Instead of answering it, I open the app on my phone to see who it is. It's Carina. I shouldn't be surprised. I still don't want to get off the couch but she's the only person I would for. I'm tempted to text her the code. In the future, if I go out of town for a few days, I'll give it to her so she can watch the place. She wouldn't overwater the little orange tree.

"Fuck," I say, getting up.

She blows past me into my kitchen before I say anything. I take in her outfit—loose joggers and my favorite cardigan. She was probably working from home.

"Your hedges are overgrown," she declares.

They're not. But that isn't the point. I'm too tired to fight. Some days it gives me life and energy. Today I don't want this.

I just want her.

But I'll play along because it's what she wants. "As long as they're on my side of the property line, then it's not your problem." If I give this to her, she'll realize she needs to let me in. I'm sure Carina would love it if I told her I could solve her problems.

"They're putting pressure on the fence and the fence is mine."

"What would you like me to do about it, princess?"

Her eyes flicker. I hope she can tell my heart isn't in this today. I hope she'll back down.

"I would like for you to give a shit about your property."

That's not backing down. She knows what this house means to me. She's out for blood today, and I can't give it to her the way she wants it. "I'd like for you to stop assuming the world revolves around you and that everyone will drop everything to do your bidding."

"I don't think that," she says.

"You don't? It's always about what you want. Your fence. Your quiet time. Your rules for whatever the fuck we're doing." A part of me is angry. I'm annoyed at how much I depend on her, and I can't have her the way I want her.

She's staring at me as if trying to figure out if I'm saying the truth or if I'm fake fighting with her. "I wouldn't need to be on your case if you weren't so selfish all the time."

I don't know what she's talking about anymore. I don't want

to play games. Fuck it. I'll tell her what I really want. I run my hands through my hair. I'll give her what I think she needs.

"I'm not fighting with you today. You can either get naked in my bed and wait for me to have the energy to fuck this attitude out of you or we can go out on the boat for a relaxing sail. Those are your options if you want to involve me."

She freezes.

The boat is filled with memories of us fucking so it's not safe anyway.

"Well. What's your answer?" I command. She could walk away. I'm prepared for her to walk away.

"The boat."

"Fine, give me thirty minutes. Bring food since we'll be out over dinner." I'm disappointed. I want her in my bed. Even if we didn't have sex. I want her there.

She nods and turns away before saying anything else.

Exactly thirty minutes later, Carina reappears in my driveway in shorts and a tank top, holding a small cooler. "I hope sandwiches are okay," she says.

"Perfect." The buzzing in my chest won't go away until I'm on the boat.

Does she realize my bad mood isn't her? That I've had a terrible day and I'm letting her see my full range of emotions, something she isn't aware is an option for herself. I open the garage door and unlock my car. We don't speak as she puts the cooler in the back and slides into the passenger seat.

As we're waiting for the light at the top of our neighborhood, I feel the tension radiating off her. "I'm not mad at you," I say.

"But you are mad?" she asks.

"No, it's been a rough day. I'm assuming same for you?"

"Yes." She struggles to admit it. Like she's never been able to admit she's not okay.

"The water makes it better." I reach for her hand and give it a quick squeeze, some assurance everything will be all right.

We arrive at the marina, and it doesn't take us long to ready the boat for departure. She helps me where she can, and I comment that I'll turn her into a sailor in no time.

She visibly relaxes. I don't ask what was on her mind. I want to know, but I want her to stay this way. That has always been my goal, I think. Just to make her feel better. If that's all I can have, I'll take it.

I don't want to talk about what's on my mind. I might have started out annoyed at my clients. Now I'm aching that I can't have her.

Once we make it out into the gulf, she disappears below for a moment. I don't think anything of it. When she comes out to the deck again, she's wearing one of the shirts I store on the boat. It's a white short-sleeve polo shirt. It reaches down past her shorts, so it looks like she's not wearing any. She's also holding the collar and looking so content and satisfied, I almost wonder if she masturbated while she was changing.

"What are you doing?" I growl.

"Wearing clothes that don't have my name on them."

"Oh no, what if someone sees you?" I say in mock horror.

"Aren't we in international waters or something? It doesn't count."

"No." I should lecture her about international waters, but I don't.

"It's just you and me out here. I can relax," she says.

That shouldn't mean so much to me. I want to deny my world revolves around her. But I couldn't even if I tried. Every part of my life here has been through her. I get how important it is that we stay in each other's good graces. If this falls apart, I have far more to lose than she does.

A part of me doesn't care. I'm fine with her being the center of my everything. It won't be me that ruins it. I'll do anything to hold on to her—I want to take the risk.

We pull out the sandwiches she packed, and eat while the sun sets behind us. She sits on the bench directly in front of the helm, like she did on that first sail. I watch her and the sails and the waves while I wait for her to tell me what's on her mind, as patient as I can be. She's come to me before and she's here now. I hope I've proved to her that I am someone she can confide in.

I'm so much calmer now. The tightness in my chest is gone. No more racing heartbeat. It might be that I'm at sea, or it might be her. I think it's both. She's calmer too. Maybe this could be something we share—we both love the water. So this boat could be *our* safe place.

"I had an investor call today," she starts unexpectedly. "The same one as before. And even though I have ten years of data to show him, and an MBA, he shot down every idea I had."

"Did he call you 'little lady'?" I ask.

"No. He did call me 'kid.' He's been investing longer than I have been working, but he doesn't have any experience in clothing. Especially not athletic or athleisure. It doesn't occur to him that I might be competent."

People think owning a company means you don't have a boss. It's much more complicated. She reports to people as with any regular job.

"Will he force changes?" I ask.

"Not yet. He wants me to work closer with his protégé." The way her face scrunches tells me she doesn't like the person.

I want to ask about other investors, brainstorm ways she could cut this guy loose and survive. But she doesn't need my help. She needs me to listen. So I take the opportunity to ask about something else.

"Do you do branded gear, by any chance?" She looks confused at my question. "My crew's sun shirts and polos are terrible. I want to outfit them with new ones. I thought it could be your shirts and get them printed with our logo."

"It would be expensive," she says.

I shrug. "We can sell them in the gift shop too. People get to the dock all the time and realize they've forgotten something. Or they think they'll use them back home."

"I mean it, Orion. My margins are slim. I can't give you a discount." But she looks at me like she wants to. Or she wants something I can't pinpoint.

"I wasn't expecting you to. Okay, fine. If not yours, what's another brand you'd recommend?" I ask.

She glares at me, and I have her. If another brand made good enough sun shirts, she wouldn't make them herself. "Fine, I'll draft a proposal. Would you want to be a regular wholesale dealer as well? Sell some leggings while you're at it?"

"Sure, why not?" I don't tell her I now recognize when people wear her clothes out on my boats, or the people who mention seeing her at the yoga studio the day before. She's famous, and people like her. She deserves all the praise for the work she's done.

But we're out on my boat and none of that matters to me. Not when I have her undivided attention. "Can I ask you a question at the risk of upsetting you?" It's something that's been bugging me for days, and I want an answer.

"When has that ever stopped you?"

"You're right. The thing you said at Paradise about being 'body inspiration.' What do you mean by that?"

She looks at me thoughtfully. I hope she's not about to filter her response. I want the whole truth. "The fitness industry can be incredibly toxic and harmful. For as much as we promote a, quote, unquote, 'healthy lifestyle,' people will shame anyone who's new or doesn't fit conventional beauty standards. I have immense privilege because I'm white and skinny." She pauses for a moment. "I want a better message for the future."

I nod. I can see that in Nebula Athletics' marketing and the models they choose. Only a few look like her in the ads I've seen. As much as I applaud her taking care of everyone else, I'm worried she's trying to undo all society's flaws at once. It's too much for one person.

But I support every fight she takes up.

An hour later, after the sun has set, we pull into the marina and her tension returns. I assume it's because she's never done this at night before, but I've done it a thousand times and the wind is calm, so it's an easy docking. Which I tell her in a slightly taunting way. We have a "no fighting on the boat" rule. I thought she'd loosen up. She smiles but doesn't take my bait.

She's constantly touching me when we're close to each other. I've never met another person so tactile.

"Give me a second to change," she says when we've docked and everything has been stowed. I almost tell her to keep the shirt. But I know better than to suggest she wear something that isn't hers in town. Even for the short drive to our houses.

I gather the rest of our things and am ready to head to my SUV. But Carina hasn't appeared. I almost yell for her, but I've enjoyed the quiet we've shared. I head to the cabin where I'm sure she is.

The door is ajar. I push it open.

twenty

CARINA

I THOUGHT I WOULD CHICKEN OUT. SO, I WAITED. KNOWING eventually he would get impatient and come looking for me, or he would yell for me to get my ass up so we could leave. Maybe even threaten to leave me behind.

I want him to look for me.

My back is to him as he opens the door.

"Hey, I'm ready to go." He's calm as he says it. He's not irritated or angry that I thoroughly fucked up his evening. I appreciate him for that. For giving me the chance to relax and forget about the hell that was my day.

My father never thinks my success is of my own making. He insists on taking credit for my sales growth even when I do the opposite of what he suggests. I couldn't have done any of it without his investment. But that doesn't mean I haven't worked hard to get where I am. Or that I don't deserve credit for my success.

Of course, I wouldn't be so stressed if I hadn't also decided to plan a last-minute celebration this weekend for Haley, complete with a wedding planning extravaganza with Sienna.

I thought picking the boat would relax me. It did. I feel calm on the water and in Orion's presence. Being around him, venting my feelings to him and having him listen without trying to micromanage me, makes me feel safe. But he's a risk. I could lose my heart to him and still be forced to see him constantly.

Right now, in his cabin, I feel safe. I want to hold on to that for a little longer.

I face Orion and step closer. I don't want to talk or discuss this. I don't want to fight. I simply move into his space and wait for him to react.

We know what happened the last time we were alone in this cabin. The air is warm between us.

"It was either bed or boat. It wasn't both," he says. He tucks a strand of hair behind my ear and cups my cheek. I place a kiss on the palm of his hand. "Carina, we—"

I lift on my toes and press my lips to his. "Stop talking."

He does as I ask and pulls me close, taking over command of the kiss. His tongue invades my mouth, and I let go.

This will end poorly, but I'm tired of seeking the right answers to everything. I want to rebel and do something I might regret. We've already done this once, and it wrecked me. I didn't even know him then. Now I do, and I trust him to keep my secrets and to keep this in the little box we'll put *us* in. He'll wreck me again the way no one else has. But I can handle it.

The boat is *our* safe space.

He breaks the kiss and rests his forehead on mine. "I'll stop talking in a minute. But I need to know, is this just tonight?"

"Just tonight. We need to get the tension out of our systems." Boundaries are good for both of us. We'll fuck and that will be it. Then everything will go back to the way it was. It doesn't have to be complicated.

"Tonight is good," he says, but doesn't resume the kiss.

My heart is telling me to stop this now because I'll end up wanting more. But this is what we agree is best. It's not like I'm waiting for table scraps from him. I know exactly what's happening here.

One of his hands cradles the back of my head and the other is on my hip. I place one hand on each of his and take a step back, pulling us to the bed. He might be the one to strip me down, but it's only because I let him.

His lips find mine and it's different somehow. Soft and gentle, like he's trying to savor me. Last time, Orion said he wouldn't treat me like a princess. Like I was something glass that could be broken. He didn't, and I was sore for days and loved every second of it. He somehow knew that before him, sex was something that happened to me, rather than something I was an active participant in.

That's not what Orion is doing now. His gentleness is throwing me for a loop. I don't need it rough; I just need him. I thought he'd fight me all the way down, but he's not.

The back of my knees hit the bed. The jolt sends me to my back, and I prop myself up on my elbows. A second later Orion is on top of me, his hands bracing himself on either side of my head and his knees outside of my hips.

He's strong and powerful and so fucking attractive I can barely look at him. I'm stuck in his trap. I try to wiggle away, enjoying the little bit of fighting. He grabs me and sets my head on the pillows.

"No fighting on the boat," he whispers with a gentle nip of my earlobe and then trails kisses down my neck.

I close my eyes and focus on the feeling of his lips and the way his muscles move under my hands. I lose myself in it as I remove his T-shirt and he removes the polo I'm wearing. Neither one of us pauses to appreciate each other's body. Not like last time. His hand moves to my breast, and I gasp at the sensation as his thumb rubs the fabric over my nipple.

"This isn't a win for you," I say. He must be keeping score. He hasn't been secretive about wanting to sleep with me again. But this isn't me caving in to him. This is me finding peace with him.

"This is a win for us," he responds. He struggles with my sports bra, so I take over. If there is one skill I have, it's getting out of a sweaty sports bra.

I grab a condom out of my shorts before he pulls them down.

"Do you always carry protection in your pocket?"

"In my bag. I grabbed it when I came in here," I admit. He resumes his position on top of me and reaches a hand between my legs, finding my already drenched core. "Preparation allows for spontaneity."

I expect him to say something sarcastic, but he doesn't. Instead, he moves down my body, and before I can process what he's doing, his mouth is on my clit.

I can't think about anything else. I only feel. My entire awareness is reduced to his fingers and his tongue and the scruff of his beard on my thighs. He teases me with one finger, and then two, curling until I see stars. It's unfair that he knows my body so well this fast.

The rest of the world falls away. I tangle my hands in his hair so he knows he's exactly where I want him. His strands are soft and a mess from blowing in the wind all evening. I need to focus on a different sensation, or I'll fall into this storm too quickly. So I hold back. I can't endure his smugness at how fast he makes me come. He doesn't know how long it's been since I've even had the time to masturbate. The last time I did, I thought of him. And I need this, badly.

But I can't keep any of my pleasure a secret or hide from those spots that drive me wild. He knows. He's always known. I cry out as I come, biting my lip to stop his name from escaping me.

He's over me when I come down from the high, more relaxed than I have been in ages. I want more. He strokes my cheek and kisses me. I taste so good on him.

He's quiet, which surprises me.

I reach for his shorts. He opens the condom and quickly sheathes himself. He places himself at my entrance. "You ready for this?"

"Yes," I say, and he presses in.

"Fuck, you feel amazing." He pushes in a little farther. "I'm taking this slow. You're going to feel every inch of my cock. You'll come again because you deserve it. And you'll know it's me giving you everything you need."

Now he's getting chatty? My instincts are to fight him, but I shouldn't on this.

Not when sex with him feels so much like home.

I want this between us. I want him to be the only one who can make me feel good. And fuck, I want to be the only one he does this with.

He does as promised, moving slowly within my body, drawing out every movement so I feel everything intensely. His head rests against my neck and he's kissing me or whispering something I can't hear.

My orgasm builds slowly. A few times I think I'm about to lose it, but he keeps going, slowly testing my endurance. His hand finds mine and he intertwines our fingers and I fall over the edge. I come and my moan is silent. A few seconds later, he shudders, and I hear my name.

I'm back to reality much faster than I want. I wait as he pulls out and disposes of the condom. I wait for him to dismiss us. To claim this doesn't mean anything.

He doesn't.

I move to get up. He reaches for my hand. "Not yet."

"What?"

"Don't run away this time," he pleads.

I want this to mean more than it does. "Let me clean up first."

He nods.

When I return from the bathroom, he gestures for me to

climb back into bed with him. I didn't realize cuddling is an option. Still, I need a few minutes before my equilibrium resets.

I crawl under the covers and rest my head on his chest. I pay attention to his heartbeat. It starts fast. Over the next few moments, it slows until he is as relaxed as I am. His fingertips trace my side as I trace the anchor over his heart. It takes me a moment to realize he's also lingering on my tattoo.

"Clever way to tattoo your name," he comments.

I still my hand, surprised he recognized it. "Did you look it up?" I get asked about it a lot. Most assume it's the Big or Little Dipper. One guy at a yoga retreat asked if it was Orion's Belt. It was probably the only constellation he could name.

"I'm a sailor. I know the stars. And Carina is the keel of the Argo. You expect me to not know when you have a ship on you?" His voice is soft and reverent. Like my skin is a temple he is called to worship at.

My fingers slide to his waist and his compass tattoo. "Have you seen it?"

"I have." He kisses my forehead. "I worked on charter yachts in Australia. You?"

"No." The Carina constellation is only visible in the Southern Hemisphere.

"We could leave now. Sail south until we hit ice."

It sounds sweet, like we have a future. We could do something fun and drastic together. But what I hear is: *I'm only in Wendell Beach temporarily. I'm going to leave.*

I tense. "We should head back." I don't need to drag this out.

He holds me tighter. "Let's stay the night. It doesn't count if we're on the boat."

It's a tempting offer. We could hide here for a few more hours. I'm sure round two would be as good. He likely has a bottle of rum we could share. He could be my escape.

"I can't," I say. "I have an early morning yoga class."

He examines my face for a moment and I hold his gaze.

He kisses my forehead. "I know when you're not telling the truth."

"It is the truth. Tomorrow is Wednesday," I say. The one morning I teach.

"It's not the reason you don't want to stay."

He has me there. Neither of us says what I'm thinking.

I slip out of his arms and find the clothes I discarded. He does the same. Once we're back on the stern, I grab my bag as he steps onto the dock.

I freeze.

"What's wrong?" he asks.

"Will we start fighting as soon as we're both off the boat?" I like the peace we've found, even if I believe it's temporary.

He tilts his head at me. "Not unless you want to fight."

"I don't want to fight," I admit.

"Then we won't fight." He reaches his hand out for mine. "Come on, let's go home."

I reach for him and then disentangle myself the second I can. He's reluctant to let me go.

The ride home is silent.

"This doesn't change anything," I say when we pull into his garage. "And it won't happen again. We needed to get it out of our systems."

"Got it." He exits the car.

He doesn't care that I dismissed him. It's wrong of me, but I want him to. *I* care. I'm pushing him away because I don't think he does, and I'm afraid this will blow up in my face.

"That doesn't bother you?" I chase him out of the vehicle.

"You've been clear about where I stand with you. Don't worry, princess. Things can stay exactly where they have been," he says without looking at me, his voice flat.

My preparations against him were useless. He was always going to get in.

twenty-one

ORION

PRINCESS CARINA

Can you come to Paradise tonight?

ME

I have a sunset charter.

PRINCESS CARINA

What time will you be back?

ME

About 9.

Why?

PRINCESS CARINA

It's a secret.

ME

I'm not playing games.

PRINCESS CARINA

Fine. Haley hit 1 million subscribers (it's a big deal).

I'm throwing her a surprise party at Paradise.

ME

Warning would have been nice. Someone else
could have done this charter.

PRINCESS CARINA

It's fine. Don't worry if you can't come. It's my
fault. I was trying to keep it as quiet as possible
so she wouldn't find out.

ME

Will it be on when I'm back?

PRINCESS CARINA

It should. This is a big deal for her. It sounds silly
if you're not focused on content creation. But
this is a major step in her career.

ME

I believed you the first time you said it. If you say
it matters, then it matters. I will do what I can to
be there. I'll text you when I get to the marina.

My body aches with how much I miss Carina.

I feel like I fucked up in the end with her. I should have
pushed a little more, told her I wanted her again. Not anyone,
just her.

I think I see what's happening with her, but I'm missing a
piece of the puzzle. Something she hasn't told me that will
make this skittishness understandable. It's been two days since
I've been inside her, and the short text exchanges aren't
enough. We're coexisting in the same space but not sharing
anything.

I make it back to the marina on the *Coastal Dragon* on schedule. It's full dark at this point, and the charter guests are a little
tipsy and looking for a bar to continue their night. I point them
in the direction of a seafood place by the pier. I haven't been, but
it's a go-to recommendation from the rest of the crew. It also
happens to be in the opposite direction of Paradise. Carina's

party will be in the locals' section, but I've encountered guests after charters enough to avoid it at all costs.

I text Carina to tell her I'm on my way and hop in my car before I get a response. I have a spare T-shirt in my passenger seat and change quickly. I drop off my car at my place without bothering to go inside and walk down the beach to Paradise, the few lights from the houses guiding me.

It's never worth it to drive there. Parking is terrible, and I don't get to drink as much as I want. Not that I'll be drinking much tonight since I have an early morning fishing charter. I understand this is important for Haley, and I want to be a supportive friend. I'm not solely going because I miss Carina like I miss the sea when I'm landlocked.

When I enter Paradise, the locals' section is taken over for the party. A band plays and a few people dance. Usually that's reserved for the upstairs level. A server I haven't seen before passes out plates. Carina sits at a table with her head close to another woman I don't recognize. She doesn't see me until Haley taps the table in front of Carina, and she looks up.

The other woman says something I'd bet is, "Is that him?"

"You made it," Carina says when I'm close. Her shoulders drop down like she's relaxed after clenching them for hours.

Was she waiting for me?

She's so beautiful. Her hair falls in waves around her shoulders. She's wearing more makeup than I've seen before. And I want to wrap my arms around her and kiss her.

She's wearing a dress. It has flowers and ruffles, and I don't think there's a built-in anything holding her in place. "You're wearing clothes," I say, ignoring everyone because none of them matter when Carina is wearing a dress.

Carina blushes and adjusts her skirt. "I'm always wearing clothes."

We both know that's not true. "Maybe. Can you do yoga in it?"

"It's vintage, so it's an exception to me only wearing Nebula," she says. "I can do yoga in anything."

I don't think she's drunk, but she's a little tipsy. She's happy. So I'll take her fighting spirit and match it.

"Handstand, now," I demand, pointing to a spare bit of floor where she might have enough space.

"Oh, fuck off." She laughs and takes a sip of her drink.

The other woman shares a look with Haley. "I'm Sienna, by the way. You must be Orion."

I shake her hand. This is Beckett's fiancée. "I am. I've heard a lot about you. I didn't know you were in town." I should ask her about Boston. We can talk about the neighborhoods we frequent, but I'm still so focused on Carina, I can't think about anything else.

"All part of the surprise," Carina says, a pleased smile on her face.

"Right, congratulations, Haley." I turn to her.

She waves me off. "Really, no one needed to make a big deal of this."

The other women launch into a clearly repeated argument of how awesome she is. I flag a server to get a drink.

"You should try the Southern Captain Potion," Carina says.

"The what?" I ask.

"It's the special for the night," Sienna says. "I'm pretty sure Alex uses a random name generator."

The name is nonsense. The server lists the ingredients and I pass, opting for what has become my usual.

I shouldn't be annoyed, but I am. I don't understand how Carina will let me into her body but won't share anything else with me. Not this party and not that her friend is visiting. I know how much work she does for her business. These side projects must be killing her. When does she get to rest?

She must be barely holding herself together.

"How long are you in town?" I ask Sienna. After my sister's

wedding I know better than to ask a bride about wedding planning. If she wants to talk about it, I'll give her the opportunity and smile along with everything she says. If it's a source of stress for her, then I don't want to bring it up and kill the mood.

"I leave Sunday night to be back at the university on Monday morning," she answers. "Any chance you have time for a boat trip?" Carina elbows her. "What? He's coming to my wedding. I can ask him for a sail."

"I'm fully booked," I say. "If I had known in advance you were coming…" I give Carina a bit of side-eye. I shouldn't be so pleased that I did come up in conversation with Sienna, since Carina had been adamant I wasn't worth bothering her.

Sienna laughs. "Carina barely told me I was coming for this. She's the absolute best person at keeping secrets."

I notice the blush across her cheeks. Do her friends notice it? Do they think it's the alcohol?

"We don't really have time," Haley says. "We've almost scheduled every minute of the next three days."

"We'll be inseparable," Carina says. "Oh! We should have a sleepover at my place! Like in college."

"Yes! It'll be fun!" Haley agrees.

Sienna grimaces. "As fun as that sounds, I haven't slept in the same bed as my fiancé in weeks."

I look around the bar for Beckett. He's in a corner booth sharing a scorpion bowl with people I don't know. He looks like he's trying to drink the whole punch himself. I can't tell if him giving Sienna space with her girlfriends is noble of him or if he's wasting his chance to be with his fiancée. If I'm ever able to convince Carina to be with me, I'll need to be pried away from her side with a crowbar.

"We'll do it the week before the wedding," Carina suggests. "One last girls' night."

I wonder if she has feelings about her friend getting married and her perpetual single status. She's always insisted she's not concerned about finding someone to date. But everything she says is filled with layers of the lies she tells herself.

"Are you taking him suit shopping?" Sienna asks, nodding toward me.

I could be intruding on friend time. Maybe I should have said hi and congratulations and moved on. But they've made space for me around the high top and the server has dropped off my raspberry and rum cocktail.

"No," Carina says. "He claims to have a bespoke suit that can be worn on the beach."

Sienna and Haley look me up and down.

I answer their unspoken question. "I never know when I have to fit in with rich people."

"Interesting," Sienna states. "So have you two been hanging out a lot?"

I'm saved from whatever explanation of half-truths Carina wants to tell by Christian clapping me on the back. He pulls me away to introduce me to some other locals. I expect the conversation to turn to boats since that's what it usually is around me. People asking if they can come out on my sailboat or wanting to compare boats. As if the size of one's boat is some sign of the size of one's masculinity.

I've put that toxicity behind me. I'm more than happy to discuss the mechanics of sailing or destinations with someone who is interested. Usually in these situations, people only want something from me. I didn't mind Sienna asking. She's one of Carina's best friends. And since I'd do almost anything for Carina, I'll take her friends out for a sail if it will make her happy.

The conversation touches on boats for a second before turning to rum. According to Christian, I have a refined palate and can tell these guys exactly what is wrong with their opinions. A fair amount of pirate jokes are tossed in, and Christian gives me a side-eye. I get the feeling he doesn't like these guys any more than I do, and only brought me over so he didn't have to talk to them by himself while they complain about a whiskey brand they think is too politically active. He ends the conversation by informing them he's friends with the owner.

We join Autumn chatting with some of her teaching coworkers. It looks like Carina invited everyone on the island.

I am thoroughly impressed with everything she has done. Everyone is entertained and celebrating what Haley has accomplished. Truly, no one knew what was happening until they absolutely needed to. I haven't seen much of Carina in the past week, except for the time we spent on my boat. I would have thought I would have noticed her planning this.

That hits me too—I want to have noticed she was planning this. I want her in my space as she does it. I have a home office I haven't used yet. It faces the sea. She could work from there in her lounge pants and crop tops, planning her shenanigans. I could simply exist around her.

I keep an eye on her and who she's talking with, and I can't pretend I don't see her walls up around these people. The people she gathered to celebrate her friend. They should know everything about her. Not me. I just got here.

I watch Beckett steal Sienna away. I expect them to make an exit, but he leads her to another corner. They look cozy together. She's smiling, so I dismiss some of the skepticism I've had about him. Eric, the fisherman Haley is dating, pulls her to the dance floor. I met him earlier and almost asked about the good fishing spots. But something about him made me stop.

"Is he good for her?" I ask, sliding up next to Carina.

"What do you mean?" she replies, her straw resting on the corner of her mouth.

I want to wrap my arms around her and shout to everyone about how amazing she is. As if they aren't fully aware.

"I don't know." I can't put my finger on what rubbed me wrong about him.

"It's not serious. Why? You want to make a move on her?" She pushes back from the table, crossing her arms and pouting.

Fucking hell. I should take it as bait. Pretend she's trying to get a rise out of me. She was so happy a second ago, and now she's hurt.

"No, I wouldn't do that to you," I say.

"It's a small island. Everyone is someone's ex. And we never hooked up so it's not even an issue."

The outright lie to my face is new. I roll my eyes. "If I'm going to date anyone, which I've told you is not something I'm looking for right now, it would be someone who gives me shit as good as I give to them." It's a lie that I'm not looking to date right now. I don't really want to date Carina. I want to settle down with her. Anchor with her. Build a home with her.

"Haley never gives me shit," Carina says.

My watch vibrates with an alert reminding me to leave. I want to stay and figure out what's in Carina's head right now, but I can't and still be fresh for the morning fishing charter I have. I want to take care of her and get her to stop taking care of everyone around her, just for once. She'll be the absolute last person to leave this bar tonight. If she's not, I'll fucking give her my house.

"Good night, princess," I say, standing up to close out my tab at the bar. I should ask her to come home with me. She looks at me like she might want me to, but I can't.

She'd say no anyway.

twenty-two

CARINA

I TRIED TO PUT ORION OUT OF MY MIND WHEN HE LEFT PARADISE on Thursday night. And Haley and Sienna are my priorities, as much as I want to follow Orion.

Sleeping with him again wasn't a mistake. I don't think that. But it's not going anywhere and I shouldn't get in any deeper than I am already.

Not that I wanted to do it again. Absolutely not. He can keep his attentive penis to himself.

That's at least what I'm telling myself.

He's a distraction from work and a distraction from the wedding planning. Beckett isn't much help, claiming he doesn't have any opinions on floral arrangements. *"Sienna can do whatever she wants. It's important to me that it's her vision."* So we're packing as much in-person planning as we can into this one weekend, all the things Sienna can't do from a distance. We go to her first dress fitting. Both her mom and Beckett's break into tears when she walks out. We all smile. She looks so happy and ready to be married.

Then we're shopping for her undergarments and choosing the table settings.

By the time Friday night rolls around, I'm so fucking exhausted. I don't want to move.

We end up at Paradise because Sienna loves the food, and we won't have to make any decisions since we know the menu like the backs of our hands.

Orion sits at the bar, and I've never been so relieved to see someone. He's an oasis in my energy desert. The barstool next to him is empty. He rests his foot on the bottom rung. We're on our way to a booth at the back when I stop next to him, letting Haley and Sienna continue without me for a moment.

I try to move the stool. Not because I need it, but to start a fight with him. His foot presses down.

"I mean, Cancun would be fun. Just a lot of open water between here and there," he says to Bristol. I can't listen to what he's saying.

"Can you move your foot so I can sit?" I say in an even voice. Bristol rolls her eyes and shifts to the other side of the bar.

He knows what I'm doing. Knows I'm not sitting next to him. "Plenty of other seats."

It's true. I want to fight with him because it feels like the only safe way to connect.

"I want *this* one." My hands grip the backrest.

He raises an eyebrow. "If you can move it, you can have it."

It's performance. I pretend like I can't move it. He pretends like he's putting in some resistance. I call him a selfish asshole. He calls me a cold princess.

I head to my table and pretend I wasn't thinking about warming everything up for him.

* * *

On Saturday, I decide if I get married, I won't have the over-the-top event Sienna's planning.

She doesn't even want this. But her in-laws want to make it a big deal, and they're paying for everything. I'm sure Sienna would be pulling her hair out if she wasn't concerned about how it'd look in a few weeks. Beckett's mom, Lisa, is wonderful and more than happy to help with planning and doting on Sienna while she's home.

His parents own Coastline Beach House, a luxury resort at the southern end of the island. The family has been an institution for generations. I have always been surprised by their kindness and the responsibility they feel for their property and the surrounding environment. They were the first to give me a job teaching yoga when I was in college and had gotten my certification. I loved starting my days with sunrise yoga on the beach with their guests.

I'm a little jealous of the bond Sienna and Beckett's mom share. I'm not close with my mother, and I can't imagine being close with a mother-in-law.

I fight the urge to text Orion and ask about his mom.

I will not spend the day imagining what my and Orion's wedding would be like. It's a terrible idea to even have these thoughts, and I don't know why my mind goes there. I want to believe there is a chance for a future together. But no matter what happened between us on the boat the other day, this is only temporary. It won't happen again. We said it was a one-time thing.

With my mother's negative attitude toward commitment, it was a surprise to her that I even bothered to be serious with Hamilton. I was trying to make my father proud, trying to do something that would make good business sense and open doors for me.

Neither parent thought a partner would be responsible for my emotions or feelings.

Sienna, Haley, and I have dinner reservations, but I have a little bit of time to unwind first. I head home, grateful Sienna isn't staying with me. I need some time to decompress and rest before I can deal with people again. And I feel fucking terrible for wanting that. I should appreciate the people around me more. I believe life is fleeting and we should take advantage of every moment. But I just want to drink a glass of wine alone and watch reality TV.

I scroll through my streaming services but my attention is torn when Orion plays music loudly in his backyard. *Does he have people over? Why didn't he invite me?* Panic creeps into my thoughts. But I don't hear any other voices outside.

Maybe I missed something. Did he text me he was kayaking, and I never acknowledged, and something happened? Did I drive over one of his plants?

I flip through our texts. He's been silent since Thursday.

He might have been sailing the last two days. Would it be weird if I asked for his schedule? I watch out for him when he kayaks. It should be the same when he's sailing. Someone should always be waiting for him to come home.

I stop avoiding it and look out my window. He's sitting in his backyard with a drink in his hand.

He's provoking me. This is bait. I should let it go. But maybe he needs me like I need him.

I want to be the person he turns to when he needs something, at least for now. He'll eventually move on. But I'll hold on to him for as long as I can.

I want to see where this is headed.

I storm out of my house. Our back fence is low and it's easy to see across each property from the porch. I'm in his line of sight but he doesn't react.

"Does it have to be so loud?" I yell.

"I can't hear you," he says.

I let out a breath and go around so I'm in his yard. He has a smug grin on his face, and I notice the drink in his hand isn't a beer like I assumed.

"Now you're blocking my view," he declares.

"Does your music have to be so loud?"

"It does when I'm trying to distract myself," he says.

"Have you heard of headphones?"

"Then I couldn't hear the ocean."

"It's not the ocean. It's the gulf," I say.

He shrugs. "Does it matter?"

"Of course it matters. You're a sailor. Doesn't it mean something to you? What if I called your boat a canoe?"

He stands and narrows his eyes. "Don't ever call her a canoe."

"It's basically a life raft."

I can't quite tell if he's annoyed with me or if he's playing our game. I can't imagine he would be upset with me. But I don't know him well enough. I need more.

He turns and heads into his house.

I follow. This is a game. He wants to yell at me and maybe he realizes he can't yell in public. Or at least as public as our yards are, where sound carries over the waves. All the houses around us are rented out and I can smell something cooking on a grill nearby.

"You can't just come in here," he says.

"Fine, I'll leave." I turn. If I can't figure out what's happening, then I won't play. Not when I don't know the rules.

They changed when we slept together the other night. We agreed it's temporary. We did it before and had a friendship afterward and we can go right back to where we were. That was the point: we got it out of our system.

He's not out of my system.

But I can't tell him. Not now and maybe not ever. Not when it's admitting a weakness.

"No, wait." I catch a hint of vulnerability in his voice.

Something inside me breaks. This has always been about me —he's always been the strong one. I don't know how to be if he isn't strong. Something was off with him the other day too. He didn't tell me, and I didn't even ask.

Fuck, I'm so selfish with him.

My back is to the door as he strides toward me. He places his hand on the door above my head. As if that little bit of resistance traps me in the house.

I trust him. If I want out, I can get out.

He's not even touching me. I feel the heat off his body and his breath on my neck. I feel him everywhere, and the memory of his skin on mine goes straight between my legs.

If he asks what I'm thinking about, I'll deny it. We'd both know I'm lying.

Of course I'm not wearing underwear, and I feel myself getting ridiculously wet.

I know where this is headed for him. What he needs.

Am I ready to give it to him, knowing I'm in too deep to be a fling?

I lift my face to his. His brown eyes pierce mine, and I do what I can to make myself smaller. He needs me, and I'm too willing to give myself to him.

This will dissipate for him. Our passion will become remnants. While I don't know how not to be caught up in him.

"You can't keep ordering me around," I say.

"I haven't ordered you to do anything," he replies.

"You basically summoned me here," I say.

"I don't think you take orders from anyone. You're here because you can't stand that something fell out of your control. You couldn't control me, or my music, and you had to end it."

"There are plenty of things I can't control. I know better than to attempt to control you because you are a fucking storm."

His lips find mine and his body presses me against the door. His hands reach for my back and pull me closer to him, as if the air between us is offensive to him.

"Boat?" I manage to moan as his kisses travel down my neck. I don't know what this means if we have sex here. On the boat, it doesn't count. We have a truce on the boat. This isn't that. This is his house and presumably his bed and none of the rules apply. It doesn't matter that he's a storm and I was perfectly happy before he blew into my life and made a natural disaster of everything.

This house is his space. It means so much to him, and I don't know if I can look at it every day for the rest of my life knowing I had sex here and then lost him. I could move, but my house means too much to me.

"No. Either bed, or you go home," he says.

I don't want to go home. "Bed." I'll deal with the fallout later.

He looks me in the eye. "Can I be a little caveman with you?"

I nod. I don't know what he means but I trust him. He picks me up, throwing me over his shoulder.

"Oh fuck no. This is not happening," I squeal.

"You don't know where you're going, and as much as I would love to race you to the bedroom, this is faster."

I could struggle but I don't. I have complete faith that he has a firm grip on me. There is nothing I can do that would cause me to fall. He would never put me in danger.

He climbs the stairs to the second story and passes two doors before he tosses me onto his bed. Like mine, his wide windows face the water, and the curtains are open. It's early enough in the evening that I'll experience this in the light. I'm so excited for what happens next.

twenty-three

ORION

SHE LOOKS UP AT ME FROM MY BED AND I'M STRUCK BY HOW MUCH I like having her there.

I hated the distance between us over the last few days, even though it's completely understandable. She's been busy with Sienna and wedding planning. I've had sail tours.

The other day might have meant nothing to her, but it meant a hell of a lot to me.

My hands ache for her.

I need to know she's at least with me part of the way. That these feelings I'm developing aren't just on my side. It's not just the sex, but her friendship and her smile and the way she'll never let me get away with anything.

I need to clear the air. I stand a few feet away from the bed. "You can leave at any time." I carried her up here and she protested the whole way. But I need her to feel safe.

"I know."

"If you stay, I won't be gentle with you." I can't be right now.

She presses her thighs together. "I don't want you to be gentle."

I step closer and wrench her knees apart. "Good. You want this?"

"Yes," she breathes as I claim her mouth in a kiss.

I push her onto the bed so my body hovers over hers. Her hands roam down my side. I want to be consumed by her.

She pushes back on me.

"We're still fighting. This isn't a truce," she says.

I understand what she's thinking. If we're fighting, then this isn't a real connection. It's bullshit, but it's what I'll let her believe. She can lie to herself. She can't lie to me.

"I know. I'm counting on it." I can't tell her the truth—that I'll stop fighting with her at any moment. If all she'll give me is the fight, then I'll take it. I've never been this desperate with any other woman.

It'll take time with her. I'll break her out of her cage.

She kneels on the bed and works me out of my T-shirt. If she notices it's one of hers, she doesn't react.

I missed her so much; I'd do anything to feel closer to her.

I yank off her tank and she wiggles out of her sports bra. I run my fingers across the indents it left. Even in this moment, I want to treasure her. But she doesn't let me linger. She pulls down her leggings. I'm not surprised to find she's not wearing any underwear.

I swear my mind goes blank, even though I was expecting it.

I pick her up and flip her to her stomach, pressing her into the bed. I reach for her pussy and am delighted to find her wet. "I knew fighting with me gets you horny."

"Stop messing around, then," she cries as I press a finger into her and she moans.

"I want to play a game," I whisper into her ear. "First one to come loses." I need chaos in bed with her because my feelings are settling.

"That's not fair to me! If I get you off, what's to stop you from leaving me high and dry?" she asks, her hips pressing into my erection through my shorts, seeking friction.

I kiss her shoulder. "If I come first, I'll lick you until you come twice and then my cock should be ready to go again."

Her pussy clenches around my fingers.

"And if I come first?"

"I'll make you come again. Either way, you're coming at least twice."

I want to rip her open and see her insides. If she won't let me into her heart, I can at least give her orgasms.

"Deal." She pushes back with more force and leverages me off her. She's reaching for my shorts before I can react. "You have condoms, right?" she asks.

I grab one from my nightstand. I stocked up a few days ago, because regardless of what we said, I want this to continue.

She removes my shorts and then takes the condom from me.

"You can't skip straight to fucking," I protest. I want to taste her because it's the best chance I have of winning this game. She comes so easily; it's really unfair of me to suggest this.

"What are you so afraid of? You think you can't handle my pussy?"

I groan as she puts the condom on me, her soft hand squeezing me. How does she know exactly how I like it? I don't know where this version of her came from but I love it. Once I'm sheathed, she leans over the bed, shoving her ass in the air. She's ready and waiting. I thrust in.

She's so tight and feels so good. I love that I'm fucking her on my bed—my last sanctuary from her. This is only temporary, but I'll never get her out of my spaces. She's invaded my boat and now my bed and I want her to grow her vines into my whole life.

It's slow, so I don't notice at first. She lifts her left leg up and presses it against my chest. I realize she's doing the splits against me, and my cock is buried in her, and she is the sexiest being on the planet.

I'm so lucky I'm the man she's doing this with.

I kiss her calf and focus on the sounds she is making.

She's given me easy access to her clit, and I brush it gently, the way she likes it, knowing it won't take her much to come. She clenches tighter around me as I pump into her.

Fuck, she feels amazing. The challenge is she knows this—she's going to make me come.

I pull out of her and she falls to the bed without my support. She quickly recovers and flips to her back.

She knows she almost won. But I'm on top of her and inside her again before she has the chance to get the upper hand. I kiss her as if she's the very air I need to breathe.

The next few minutes pass in a blur. Any advantage I have disappears when she rolls me onto my back and does things with her hips that have pleasure radiating down my spine.

I can't let this woman go.

I do my best to rub her clit. I'm out of my depths. I use everything I have to get her under me again. I hold her close to me and her hands grip my shoulders. I give the last few thrusts I have. I'm about to lose the game. But as I come, I feel her clench around me and her entire body shakes.

I don't want to collapse on top of her, but I don't have any strength left. I pull out and roll to my side.

"What happens with a tie?" she asks, out of breath.

I shake my head. "Multiple orgasms…in a…moment."

She laughs. "I broke you."

I get up to remove the condom on shaky legs, and when I return, she's in bed. I expected her to cut and run. But she hasn't.

I lie down in bed next to her. She snuggles me and rests her head on my chest.

"Do you want to talk about it?" she asks.

"Talk about what?"

"Whatever drove you to this?"

You did. You're the reason I picked a fight. Work was fine. I just need you.

I kiss her forehead. "No. This was enough. Can you stay?" She's a siren calling to me.

"No, I came home to shower and unwind a moment. We're doing a girls' night at the Lucky Oyster."

I don't know what that is. I haven't been to many places besides Paradise.

She lifts away from me and gathers her clothes. Then she picks up my shirt and realizes it's one of hers. "When did you get this?"

"Recently." I try to sound cool about it. I could tell her I got it when I visited her office. I did buy a few things that day, but I bought this online. I got it because I needed more of her.

"You should have told me. I'll give you a discount code."

"Next time," I say. "Mostly I bought it so I had an article of clothing you wouldn't steal."

"Very funny." She throws it at me.

I pull it on and find my boxers and shorts. I want her to stay. Or to come back after her night with her friends. I want this to be a thing. Where we have sex and hang out and she sleeps next to me. But she'll decline in the name of keeping this casual.

While walking downstairs, I notice a slight twinge in my back.

"This was fun," she says.

"It's never happening again?"

She hesitates. "I don't think it should be a regular thing. It's too complicated for us to be together. We really should stay friends."

"Sure. That's a good idea. We'll be friends."

I don't believe her. There is nothing simpler in the world than us being together.

twenty-four

CARINA

WE PACKED SIENNA'S LAST DAY WITH AS MUCH WEDDING PLANNING as possible while nursing our slight hangovers. We've been partying together since we were eighteen, but I should've learned by now I can't do it the way I used to. Hangovers feel like I've failed at holding my alcohol.

I try hard to stay in control. When I was younger, I'd let loose. I have enough regret about the stupid things I did to not make those mistakes anymore. I couldn't risk drunk texting Orion and asking for a repeat.

I shake off the feeling that my life has drastically changed, and I can't do anything about it.

Haley and Sienna kept asking me about the flush on my cheeks. I swore to them it was the heat. I wasn't about to admit I'm sleeping with Orion...if twice in a week counts as an ongoing thing. It's not going anywhere. So they don't need to know.

We dropped Sienna off at the Sarasota airport since Beckett had to deal with a resort emergency. I waited for her to say something negative about him, for her to be bummed he couldn't get out of work, even for the hour round-trip drive. But she doesn't. Instead, we get a wink and a nudge about the amazing morning they had together. I won't judge if she's happy.

I'm finally feeling better, cleaning up after dinner, when I hear a knock at my exterior office door. After last night, I figured Orion would go cold again. He agreed with me that we aren't hooking up again. Even if it was my idea, and I didn't like it.

He pushes past me into the kitchen before I can react. He's limping and grimacing. "You broke me. You need to fix me." He leans against my counter.

"What's wrong?" I reach for him but I don't know where to put my hands. I can't cause him more pain.

"You did something to my back and now I can't walk properly."

"You walked fine yesterday."

"It didn't start until later," he answers.

"Did you call a doctor?"

"It's Sunday. The only places open are urgent cares on the mainland. I have an appointment tomorrow morning. I'm your problem until then." He complains about the mainland being such an inconvenience the way we all do. It's just a ten-minute drive over the bridge if there's no traffic. But on a Sunday evening, it'll be backed up for ages with people headed home from their weekend stay here.

I can't help it. I laugh.

"You think this is funny?"

"It kind of is. You have a sex injury."

"Which I'm very excited to tell a stranger about." His eyes crease like he's trying to hold back a laugh.

"If it helps, I'm also quite sore." It's not a lie. I thought I could handle him. But no amount of yoga push-ups can match him.

Orion glares at me. But his smile threatens to break his mask. He likes knowing he wore me out.

"Where does it hurt?" I ask.

"Right above my hip on the left side." He turns and shows me, lifting the hem of his shirt so I can see his tanned skin.

I run my hand over his muscle. I know a lot of anatomy but I'm not a doctor. If I was teaching yoga and someone came to me with this, I'd tell them to see a medical professional. "I'm not qualified to treat injuries."

"Don't care. I'm your problem."

"How does a hot bath sound? I have some bath salts to help you relax."

He faces me. I'm close to him. In his space. We've obviously been closer. This feels more intimate. This won't lead to sex. It isn't a challenge. It's need.

He nods. "Any chance you have a tub on this floor?"

"I do. But it's a small one. The primary is much bigger. It's worth it, I promise."

He nods, resting his forehead on mine for a second before turning toward the stairs. He hasn't been anywhere except my office and kitchen. But it feels like he belongs here. He stops and considers the stairs like climbing them is Everest. They are steep and narrow, and I go slow when I carry my laundry down because I'm afraid I'll trip.

"I got you." I place my hand on the center of his back. I can't carry him up, but I'll make sure he knows I'm here.

The fabric of his shirt is soft. I smile, realizing it's one of mine.

We make it up the stairs. I point to my bedroom at the end of the hallway. He scoffs when we enter it.

"What?" I ask.

"It looks exactly like I pictured."

I keep it neat and tidy. My bed is made with white linens and my laundry is tucked away in the closet. He pauses before we enter the bathroom, staring at a picture hanging on the wall. It's me doing a handstand in front of a waterfall.

"You remember my favorite yoga retreat was Thailand," I say.

It's risky bringing up the game we played on his boat. But he stays silent.

He whistles when we enter my bathroom. "This is home remodeling porn," he says.

My house needs updating. I'm doing it slowly, room by room. After the yoga space, I did my bathroom. I need an oasis at home. I turn on the taps for the soaking tub and adjust the temperature. I find a eucalyptus bath bomb in my cabinet and place it on the side. "You can get in whenever. Once it's full, drop this in. It should help ease any muscle soreness. Those towels are clean. I'll be downstairs if you need anything."

He stares at me. "I'm not doing this alone."

"What?"

"You're getting in with me."

"No I'm not. Friends don't take baths with each other."

"Friends don't let friends recover from sex injuries by themselves. Especially when the friend caused the injury."

I bite my lip, which I'm sure doesn't help because I'm absolutely thinking about his naked body against mine and what would happen if I kissed him. "Fine, let me grab my wine. I'll be right back." My will is weak.

"Get me one too," he calls after me.

I run downstairs before he can ask for anything else and gather my nerves. I want this. I want to spend time with him. I want to know his moods better than anyone else.

I'm so happy he's here and he needs me.

This is temporary, I remind myself. I'll enjoy him a little longer and I'll end it before he does. My mother was humiliated when my father served her divorce papers. She complained about it for years. That won't happen to me.

I refill my chardonnay and grab a glass of water for him.

When I get upstairs, he's lounging in the filling tub. God, his naked body is something to be admired. He's tanned from the hours he spends in the sun, somehow avoiding any lines or pale spots. His chest and arms are defined by the hard work he does.

"No mixing alcohol and painkillers." I hand him the water. I strip my clothes out of sight and take a deep breath. He's seen me naked before. But this is different. He's not consuming my body this time.

He looks up at me as I approach the side of the tub. I see hunger and lust in his eyes. I've never doubted he's attracted to me, but it's humbling to see it so evident.

He reaches for my hand, helping me step into the water. I turn off the taps and drop the bath bomb in. He touches my shoulder and pulls me against him. I'm between his legs and my back rests on his chest. He wraps his arms around me and holds me tight.

The lights are on and he's in pain and this isn't romantic. But it's caring and intimate and so very trusting. His lips brush my temple and I close my eyes.

"Thank you," Orion whispers.

I hum a response. This feels amazing. I'm taking care of him. We're both stripped raw. It was never like this with Hamilton. But this isn't even a relationship. It's not heading anywhere.

We lie like this for a long time. The water fades to warm, then cool. I finish my wine and he drinks his water. I tell him about my day. About the prep work we did for the wedding. He tells me about the repairs they have to do on the boats.

"It's late," I say when we're drying off and the tub is draining. "You should stay."

I hope he doesn't notice the quiver in my voice, giving away how scared I am he'll decline. I'm not ready for the calm between us to end. It's a risk letting him this close. But I'll take it this one time.

He cocks his head to the side. The bath must have helped because his attitude has returned. He knows I only have one bed on this floor. I'm asking him to sleep with me. In my bed. For him to invade my space further.

"Yeah, I don't think I can make it down those stairs." It sounds like a lie. I'm sure he does this often—says one thing but thinks another.

He puts on his boxers while I retrieve a clean men's shirt from my pile of samples. "That's a rare shirt. I didn't like the color so only a few exist."

He puts it on anyway. "I would judge you if you did sell this," he says. "It's poop brown."

"It's chocolate. But yes. That was why we went with a different shade."

He settles into my bed like he belongs, using the spare phone charger I dug up for him. I wash my face and prepare for bed like this is normal, this is fine. Like I'm having a sleepover with a friend. He'll stay on his side. I'll stay on mine, and that's all it is.

I climb into bed under his watchful eye and brace for a comment about my pajamas, but nothing comes. So I turn off the lights and cherish the fantasy that this could last.

ORION

I WAKE UP IN THE MORNING TO THE SOUND OF AN ALARM THAT isn't mine. It takes a second for me to register I'm not in my bed. I'm in Carina's. And I never want to leave. Partially because she's with me, and partially because her sheets are softer than mine.

Would it be creepy if I buy a similar set? She's so sure she won't be visiting my bed again. She'd never know.

I check my watch and see it's five a.m. "Why are you up this early?" I ask after she silences the alarm.

"I have six a.m. yoga." She sounds as tired as I feel.

I roll over, bracing for pain in my back, but I feel fine. I wrap my arm around her stomach, expecting her to push me away. To tell me this is a friend sleepover, and friends don't spoon. I don't care. I'm risking it anyway. I thought I was dreaming when she asked me to stay. I don't know what's happening between us, but I'll take every moment I get with her.

"You're not teaching today," I say.

She leans into me as she looks at her phone. It's too early for morning wood, but I love her body against mine and the scent of orange blossoms that follows her everywhere.

"No, but I still practice at the studio. You don't have to get up. You can go back to sleep if you want," she says.

I kiss her shoulder. "You trust me to be alone in your house while you're gone?"

"You won't find anything interesting, except my vibrator."

This woman has secrets on secrets. The fact she thinks I won't find anything means she's hiding from herself. "You could stay in bed. I could find it now."

She locks her phone and falls back on her pillow. "You're a bad influence on me."

"I know. You like it."

"I do. But it's Monday, and I need an early start."

She's already checked her email. I'd assumed she wouldn't do that until after her morning routine. Wasn't that a thing mindful people did—no phones in the bedroom? I don't comment and risk triggering her defensiveness. I don't want that, not when she's so soft in my arms.

"When do you have to be in the office?" she asks.

"Soon enough. I'm not sailing today, but I need to work on payroll," I answer. "Maybe after my doctor's appointment we can take the boat out."

"I'd like that." She smiles. "How is your back?"

"Much better. Thank you."

"Of course. That's what friends are for."

"Friends sleep in the same bed as their friends?" My hand rests on the inside of her leg in a way that feels very not-friendly.

"Friends help friends deal with their problems. Like back pain and stress."

"Sure." I kiss her forehead.

"I should get up." She doesn't move. She wants me to remove her shorts and my shirt and remind her how good I can make her feel. She can pretend this is simply sex or friendship, but she took care of me and kept me close all night. She feels more than she is willing to let on.

I can wait until the boat tonight to get her naked again.

I roll away from her and let her sit up. We take turns in the bathroom, and I put on my shorts. I move to give her back the T-shirt, but she tells me to keep it.

* * *

THE BOAT that night goes about the same as before. The doctor cleared me for activity if it isn't high intensity. I overextended some muscles, so rest and stretching my hips will fix the problem. Once we are on the boat, Carina insists on doing the heavy lifting, and I'm happy to let her. She is stronger than she appears.

I wait patiently for some indication this trip will take a turn. That the two of us will end up below deck again. She looks relaxed. Happy, even. Her face is turned to the sun. She doesn't take one of my shirts when I offer.

"Can we anchor here?" she asks as Wendell Beach drifts out of sight. The water is only about thirty feet deep, so it's not a problem.

"Any particular reason?" I'll make her say it.

She steps in close to me. "I thought you might benefit from a massage."

I lift my eyebrows. "I foam rolled before I left the house."

"You're difficult." The wind blows her hair into her face. I brush it behind her ear. It'll escape in a moment but I need a reason to touch her.

"We're on the boat," I say. "Things don't have to be difficult. Just honest."

She looks around at the emptiness of the sea. I want her to decide that here we can have each other. I don't need her to pretend she's perfect. I want her to want me the way I want her: raw, vulnerable, and free.

"I…" She closes her eyes. "I like sleeping with you."

"Good. Because I like fucking you."

She smiles. "It's just sex. We're friends. It's a fling and no feelings are involved."

"Sure." My feelings already run deep. This isn't like any relationship I've had before. Hers do too. She just won't admit it.

"And we're not telling anyone."

I blink a few times, trying to convince myself I heard something different. "Why not?" I didn't expect her to put out a press release but telling no one is restrictive.

I can already feel the thousand ways this woman will hurt me.

She breathes out and adjusts her shirt, not looking me in the eye. "We know what this is. We know what we're doing. I don't need anyone projecting more than friends with benefits."

"Frenemies with benefits," I correct as a defense.

"Whatever. You're trying to find your footing here. When we get bored with each other, at least this way we can minimize the fallout."

"What if there is something more here? What if we could be more than friends? We can't keep that a secret forever."

She looks skeptical. "Then let's figure it out without any interference from others."

She's making excuses to keep me hidden. But I'm so desperate for her that I don't care. I'll be her secret if I get to keep and hold on to the things she hides from everyone else. I won't get bored with her. I might have thought I felt this way with others, but this is different.

She's mine, even if she doesn't know it yet.

I should push for more concessions. I should ask for fidelity. But I don't. I don't want to spook her, and here on my boat, there is no one else. I am the only one who matters.

Instead, I cup her cheek and tilt her face up to meet mine. I kiss her, and in this kiss I promise her I'll protect her secrets.

Then I lead her to my cabin, strip her down, and expose them all.

ORION

I HATE HOW THE NEXT FEW DAYS PLAY OUT IN PUBLIC. MY BACK feels fine so I'm captaining as much as I can. Now that it's fall, we're slower and a few of our crew members have gone back to college or moved on to other jobs. If I can be the one sailing, then we don't have to hire more staff. But I can't keep up this schedule forever.

On my one day off a week later, Haley invites me grocery shopping. I thought it was an odd suggestion for a hangout. But since her life revolves around food, it makes sense for her.

We stop at a farmers market for fresh produce, and she introduces me to the local vendors. I buy what I need and wonder if she notices I'm buying enough for two. Carina and I may keep our distance in public, but we eat together almost every night I'm not on a sunset sail. She claims it's a waste of effort for both of us to cook separately.

I buy blueberry jam, hoping we'll share breakfast together soon.

I don't know what Haley suspects about Carina and me. I hope she'll open up to her friends at some point, but it hasn't happened yet. Haley doesn't flirt with me though. This doesn't feel like a date or like she's angling for more.

When we get into her vehicle after the market, she cranks the a/c and rests her head on the steering wheel. "I have a confession," she says.

"Okay." I draw the syllables out. I can't imagine what she could possibly confess.

"The next stop is Eric." She pauses as if the name means something to me. "He's the fisherman I was seeing."

"*Was* seeing?" I repeat. They were at Paradise together the other day.

"I ended it. It wasn't anything. But this will be the first time I've seen him since. I don't want things to be awkward."

"So you brought me to make him jealous."

"No." She sits upright. "No. I want company, and Carina's too self-assured. The guys have too much history. He supplies Paradise, and they've always been close. You're a neutral third party."

I want to roll my eyes at the comment about Carina. Under the surface she's a bundle of nerves. But Haley is her best friend. Shouldn't she know that?

I wonder how Carina would handle Eric. She'd probably turn into a protective mama bear for her friend.

"What do you need from me? Should I flex a bunch? Puff out my chest? Brag about how big my boat is compared to his?"

"Your boat is nicer even if his is bigger," Haley says. I give her a sideways look. "Just remind me it wasn't worth everything smelling like fish all the time."

I can accept this. She needs a friend, and I can be that for her. It's simple repayment for introducing me to a lot of people at the market, so they know I belong here. Even without that, I like Haley. I want to have her back when she needs me.

But the whole encounter is awkward. I stand to the side, glaring with my arms crossed over my chest. Eric stands close to her, peering down her dress when she bends over to get a better look in his icebox. My initial reaction to him was correct—he's not good enough for her. He doesn't treat her with the respect she deserves.

He probably wants her because she can cook better than anyone on the island.

He asks her to come over that evening. She declines. She doesn't even need to look at me to do it.

"Thanks for doing that," she says when we settle into her SUV.

"Would you have agreed to meet him tonight if I wasn't there?"

"Maybe. I don't know. It wasn't like he was bad to me. But I was bored, and if I stay with him, I won't grow."

I swear the only thing I can do is grunt in response.

"What's that supposed to mean?" she asks.

"He clearly sees you as an object and not a whole person."

If she wasn't focused on the road, she would have gaped at me with her mouth open. "What?"

"He stared down your dress the entire time. If he cared about you, he wouldn't leer."

"So you've never checked out a woman you were interested in?"

"Of course I have. But my eyes do eventually make it to her face."

It's her turn to glare at me. "You're right. I deserve more."

"Exactly."

"Are you seeing anyone?"

I pause, wondering if it's a test as she merges into traffic. "No. Trying to get settled first."

"Right. I thought you and Carina might hook up, but I feel like that would level the island." She says it without any guile.

"Why do you think that?" I ask.

She shrugs. "You're like oil and water. You don't mix."

I should correct her. Oil and water might not mix, but they

don't cause explosions. "Don't worry. I wouldn't inflict that on anyone, especially not me."

Carina and I aren't oil and water. We mix together well. But we are like the ocean—a raging storm one minute and calm the next.

* * *

THAT AFTERNOON, I drive to the Nebula Athletics studio. I've been to a few classes since dropping in on Carina. After my back injury, the doctor recommended I stretch more and recommended I add in yoga more frequently. Carina had the smuggest *I told you so* face I'd ever seen. I kissed it right off her.

The space itself is beautiful, and I feel Carina's presence in it. It's welcoming. I might be fit from the other physical activities I do, but I've never been flexible. No matter which class I attend, the instructors set me and everyone else up to succeed.

I step into the studio. She is at the front of the room talking to the instructor.

Carina turns when I enter. I wish she sensed me the way I feel her, instead of her merely reacting to movement. I wave and she smiles back like I'm any other student. Her hands remain on her hips. I'm sure it's the only acknowledgment I'll get. I unroll my mat at the back of the room and gather the props I need for this yin-style class. The whole time I watch her.

Her skin has a light sheen of sweat. She must have just taught a class. I know she jumps in to help occasionally. The sweat reminds me of the times I've tasted salt on her skin over the past few weeks. When we're at one of our houses, it's rough and fast and we never stop competing. I swear she has an endless list of positions and we've ended up on the floor more than once. One of us will get hurt again. But I don't care if she kills me because it would be an honor to die with my dick in her.

On the boat, we're gentle. She's relaxed first and we focus on saving our strength. I take my time, making her come with my mouth. When I press into her, I hold her close, burying my head in her neck and imagining with every thrust I tell her how much I need her and how perfect she is to me.

I shut those thoughts down. I can't get an erection at the beginning of class.

Carina says goodbye to the instructor and I watch her walk out of the room. Or at least part of the way. I keep my head forward as she passes me. If she won't acknowledge me in public, then I'll keep my head down and not acknowledge her further.

While I'm feeling petty and jealous, a mat unrolls next to mine. The class is filling up, but there is plenty of space around the room. I look up and see Carina standing next to me.

"This spot taken?"

"No. I thought you already practiced today."

She shrugs and sits down. "I did a high-intensity class. I could use a restorative session."

I shake my head. I don't know what she's doing right now but I can't ask her and risk a fight here. I love that she's here with me. That for all the space in the class, she's next to me.

"You kayaked this morning and then trudged around the markets with Haley. I've done that before—it's an adventure. There's no way I've been more active today than you," she counters.

I look at her sideways. I know her endurance because I've pushed it in the bedroom as much as possible. I run her into exhaustion for two reasons: it feels amazing, and I want her to stay the night with me. If I can tire her out enough, she won't make the effort to go home.

We haven't literally slept together since the night my back hurt. I don't ask even though I want it. I want her next to me as I sleep.

"You don't have to justify yourself to me," I say instead of everything I'm thinking.

She smiles, but before she responds, the instructor dims the lights and class starts.

I thought having her next to me would be distracting, but she's on my mind when I'm here anyway. She's always a part of me. So practicing yoga together feels natural.

At the end, when we're both on our backs, lying down in corpse pose with our arms relaxed by our sides, I realize how close our mats lie. Her fingers graze the back of my hand. I'm sure she will adjust and move away. But she rests her hand against mine.

Class ends and she surprises me again by facing me.

"Um…did you drive?" She's so completely relaxed and beautiful.

"Yes," I answer.

"Can I get a ride?"

She never asks. She takes one when offered and I was going to offer, but she has never asked me.

"Sure." I'll take any extra time with her.

We exit the studio. It's not a quick process with so many people stopping to talk with her. But she sees me waiting and extracts herself. I wonder if she's trying to keep me from being annoyed, but I'm too relaxed to gather the energy needed for that.

Once we're in my SUV, she speaks first. "I'm grilling chicken tonight. Do you want to come over? We can relax in the pool a little."

"Sure," I say again. I don't have any other specific plans for the evening. Alex is working and I have been hanging out at Paradise most weekend nights when I'm not with Carina. It's a continuation of what we've already been doing. It doesn't have to be more.

But fuck, I hope it's more.

twenty-seven

CARINA

I HAVE A VOICEMAIL WHEN I CHECK MY PHONE AFTER MY BACK-TO-back classes. I expected it, which was why I did an extra class. I wanted the extra hour without being told I am a failure.

The fact I got to spend it next to Orion was a bonus. I practice with friends all the time—almost everyone I know tries yoga at some point. But it's different with Orion. I turned off my teaching brain and didn't worry what he was doing. I practiced next to him and shared the moment with him.

I unlock my exterior office door so he can enter from the side of the house closest to him. I connect my headphones and press play on the voicemail as I wait for him.

"Carina, I got lunch with Hamilton today. I shared your most recent proposal. The one about manufacturing in the U.S. He thought it shows potential but needs work. He's agreed to give it a punch-up if you call him back. Do that today." I clench my teeth, but the message is only half over. "Also, we discussed your most recent posts on social media. He agrees with me that you shouldn't be posting pictures in swimsuits. It diminishes you in the eyes of investors. You want them to take you seriously, don't you? Call me back."

I rip the headphones out of my ears and throw them across the room.

That happens to be the second Orion walks into my office.

"What's—" But he doesn't finish the sentence.

He crosses the room and gathers me into his arms. I don't know what it was exactly—the message where my father thinks my ex-boyfriend has better ideas than I do and not so subtly conspiring to get us back together, or that they both thought they could control what I wear or post on the internet.

Then I wondered if they were right.

I attempt to hold back a sob, but I'm with Orion and my good intentions fall away.

He kisses the top of my head. "Tell me what's wrong."

I wipe my tears. "It's nothing. I'm overreacting."

"I highly doubt that." My phone is still lit up. He takes it from me.

The voicemail app is open and has provided a full transcription of the message along with the name of the caller, Jeffrey Webb. I watch his eyes move across the screen.

"Those investor calls you have? The ones that piss you off every time?"

"Yes, it's my dad. The Webb Group is my biggest funder."

"And the protégé who's gaslighting you…"

"My ex."

"Carina, you could have told me." His free hand cups my face as he examines me, concern flooding his eyes.

I don't know how to explain this to Orion. How I constantly strive to be better every day so my dad will finally approve of my business and of me. But I'm not there yet. I'm not ready to let Orion see the weakest part of me.

I kiss him. I can save this. He doesn't need to think about me crying over my father and asshole ex. I can make him think of something else. We'll kiss our way to my bedroom and take off my clothes. He likes it when I'm naked. Then we don't have to talk about my inadequacies.

He presses me against the desk, holding me flush against him. He can lift me up from here. He's strong enough. I reach under his shirt and touch his damp skin. He didn't even fully dry off from his shower before coming over.

He pulls away. "Carina." His voice is breathy, the way I like it. "Let's pick this up later."

Oh.

Fuck.

"Right. I'm a mess. You don't want…"

"That's not it." He holds me tight—his hand gently presses me into his chest, protectively. "You're thinking about them and not about us. I'll fuck you when I have your full attention."

How does he not know he always has my full attention?

I unravel myself from him. "Whatever. We should eat. I have chicken marinating in the fridge." He looks at me like I'm deliberately missing the point. But if I take these words at face value, then I have to take everything he says that way.

I feel raw and vulnerable and stripped. I want him to help me forget.

"Carina." He runs his fingers down my arm. "Don't take those pictures down." I can't read the expression on his face.

"I won't," I promise. I don't believe what my father said. I should post pictures of how it's possible to move in my products. If my existence is too much for some of my investors, then I'm not sure I want them anyway, as much as I'm afraid I need them.

Orion cares because I look hot and he took some of the pictures on his boat. We went out right before sunset. I brought my paddleboard and attempted to teach him how to stand. He was adamant there was no point in standing when he could sit perfectly fine in his kayak.

The lines I drew made sense before. We were friends who yelled at each other and we had sex once. Nothing was happening again because I didn't want a messy life around my home. Or maybe because it was doomed since he was always leaving. But it kept happening.

But then he held me when we woke up and I want him so bad. Not only for the sex, but for the moments in between.

I've tried to keep him at arm's length but it's not working anymore—I want him to be here when I'm sad and tell me to stick up to my father and tell me I'm enough as I am. But I'm not sure I would believe him because no one's taken care of me before. The people who were supposed to stopped, figuring I could make it on my own.

"I got some things for us at the market. Let me make you a salad," he says, moving us to the kitchen.

"That would be great." I'm dying to ask how shopping went but I don't want to sound clingy. I don't think Haley's interested in him, even with her recent breakup, but she always likes a guy who cooks, and Orion does. She wasn't serious with Eric, so she could've moved on already.

He washes some vegetables while I head outside to preheat the grill and start the chicken. A few moments later, he comes out with the salad while I'm finishing setting the table. Orion takes off his shirt so he's only in his swim shorts and wades into the pool.

He's so fucking handsome I can't handle it.

"You coming in?" he asks.

"I have to watch the chicken," I say.

"Set a timer. It takes twenty minutes. That's plenty of time."

I don't ask for what. My backyard faces the beach on the side, but the fence is high enough no one can directly see in. On the other side is Orion's place. We can see into each other's yards from our porches, but he's not there to spy on me. The house behind me is blocked from viewing anything by the lush plant growth on both sides of our fences.

I take my dress off, revealing my bikini, and step into the

water. I see the way his eyes track my body and I wonder what's changed for him in the last few minutes.

But he's reaching for me, and suddenly I don't care about anything else.

His mouth finds mine in a familiar way, but I won't take it for granted. His arms envelop me and he lifts me, my legs naturally wrapping around his waist. I press hard into the long and thick length of him.

The pool isn't deep, but he carries us to the deepest part so I'm dependent on him. I loved him holding me like this when our friends were around and we weren't supposed to cling to each other.

His fingers trace the edge of my bikini bottom, and he'll find me wet for him. Fuck, I've been ready for him since he walked into my yoga studio. We don't need much foreplay. We don't have time. As the sun sets, I want him here and now.

His head is in the same place as mine. "I have a condom in my shirt pocket," he says.

I don't want to leave the water yet. "Wait, I...um...I have an IUD and I got checked a few months ago and I'm healthy. You said you are too, so I'm fine to skip, if I'm the only person you're sleeping with."

He smiles and brushes my hair behind my ear like he always does. "Yes, you're the only person I'm sleeping with. I better be the only person you're sleeping with."

"Of course." I laugh. I want to play it off like it's a time thing—why would I sleep with someone else when I have a perfectly hot sailor next door? But I can't imagine anyone else. "You'll tell me if it changes?"

He nods and kisses me. It's not a request for fidelity, it's a request for honesty. I can always count on him for that.

He removes my bikini bottom and I reach for the tie on his swim trunks and we both grab his cock.

He presses fully into me and fuck he feels so good as he kisses down my neck. I'm so close to him, and it's not the lack of a condom. It's him in my space and he's somehow invaded so many aspects of my life and I want him to stay.

He walks me to the side of the pool so we have something to move against. He sets me on the step at the edge. It's high enough in the water for leverage but we're both under the surface. I hear the waves from where we are, but I can't see the beach. I'm safe in this tiny cocoon we've made.

I don't try to flip him or taunt him or find some other game to play. I'm here, moving with him and loving the way he gently whispers my name into my neck. I may be hidden from the world, but I'm never hidden from him.

I let my orgasm build the way it only ever does with him.

We come together as we so frequently do, and I'm left panting into his chest.

I brace myself for him to say something dismissive. Something that reminds me this is only for fun and it's convenient for both of us to skip condoms because it's one less step and this doesn't mean anything to him.

Instead, he kisses my temple.

"How much time do you think we have left on the timer?" he asks.

"Not much," I say.

"See, I told you it was long enough."

"Bragging about how fast you are isn't the flex you think it is." I can't keep from smiling.

He responds by flexing his abs and his still-hard cock moves inside me. I gasp in pleasure. "It doesn't matter how long I last as long as you come," he says.

"Quite the gamble then since we came at the same time."

He looks me deep in the eyes in the fading light. "We've done this enough. I know how you feel when you're close."

I bite my lip. "I should check on the chicken."

"Stay here. I'll grab you a towel and check it while you clean up." He pulls out of me and tucks himself back into his swim trunks. He hops out of the pool and grabs us both towels from the basket on the porch. He tosses me one, and I rush inside to clean myself up.

When I'm back outside, he's at the grill, poking the chicken with a meat thermometer.

"Should be ready in about a minute," he says. I stand next to him to verify, and he takes it as an invitation to kiss me. "You can trust me to not burn dinner." He speaks into my lips.

I want to be annoyed that he knows exactly what I'm doing, annoyed he knows my body so well. But I want this. I do. I want to have dinner with him and cuddle on the couch and I want to fall asleep with him.

But this won't last. Relationships never do, even when I try.

He'll walk away with a vital part of me and I'll be left with nothing but memories of the way he feels. I want to pick a fight and make this night something less. I'm sure I could say something to push him so far away he'll leave before we even finish eating.

But I don't, because I want this one perfect evening. One great memory to hold on to.

I smile my way through dinner, and even though he doesn't comment on it, Orion knows something is wrong.

"What if I stay over?" he asks as we're washing dishes.

"I get up earlier than you do," I argue, putting a plate in the dishwasher.

"Not much earlier most days. And tomorrow I have an early morning charter."

"It's better this way," I say. "We'll both sleep better alone." I didn't like sleeping in the same bed as Hamilton. I couldn't relax with another person there, hearing his breathing and the tiny movements he made while he slept. I assumed Orion would be the same. But the one night we spent together, I slept like a rock. I took a risk when I asked him to stay that night. I didn't realize how close I had let him in. But now I can't risk it again.

He turns off the sink and crosses to where I'm standing against the counter. He cradles my face in his hands and presses gentle kisses to my lips. None of them last long, but each one is soft and perfect.

"Okay, I'll see you tomorrow, then." He gives me one long, final kiss.

I might be the only woman he's with, but this is temporary. We can't burn this hot for long.

* * *

A WEEK LATER, I'm exhausted from too many nights staying up late with Orion. Logically, if he stayed over, I could drift off a bit between rounds and it wouldn't be so bad. But I kick him out or leave before he can bring it up again. I'm afraid my boundary will push him away, but it hasn't yet.

Today I couldn't focus at the office the way I needed to. I curse Orion for being a distraction I can't control. I head home and find a car parked between our homes. It has the generic look of a rental and I wonder if someone got lost trying to find their vacation house.

A man and a woman stand in Orion's driveway. "Hi," I call. "Can I help you find something?" It's the neighborly thing to help, and I'm feeling a little territorial over his house.

"Hi," the woman responds, stepping toward me. Her shoulder-length curly hair is rapidly frizzing in the humidity. "This is my brother's place. We're trying to surprise him but he's not home or answering his phone."

I freeze. I only know Orion has a sister because Alex was the best man in her wedding. Which means the man next to her is close friends with Alex. They are complete strangers to me. I might cross paths from time to time with them in the future, but they won't be fixtures in my life. It's not like Orion will ever bring me home to meet his family. I don't have to be anything to them. I can be me. Or at least the me I am with Orion.

This could be fun.

"His name is Orion. Do you know him?" she continues. I must have stared at her in silence for long enough that she kept talking.

"Arrogant face? Likes to talk about his boat?"

She looks to her husband. "Sure, sounds like him."

"He's kayaking. He'll be back soon. Want to wait at my place for him?" I gesture to my house

"Oh, we don't want to impose."

"We can head to Paradise." Her husband holds up his phone, indicating he figured out how close the bar is to us.

"Don't worry about it. Like I said, he'll be back soon and this way you can experience for yourself how cheerful he is when he's back from the water. I'm Carina," I say, already walking toward my house. I'm thinking too much about the sweat on her brother's body and can't look at her.

"I'm Brooklynn," she says. "This is my husband, Spencer."

"Nice to meet you both." I open the door and we're immediately greeted by the cool air.

I'm used to this feeling. I walk to so many places instead of driving because it's better for the environment. But sometimes I wonder if the trade-off is worthwhile considering the number of showers I take or how much laundry I do. Someone has to have done the math. No, I tell myself—I've made my choices and I can't spend forever recalculating them. As tempting as it may be.

"Can I get you anything to drink?" I offer. "I have water, tea, and I can make some lemonade if you want."

"Water would be great. I'm sure Orion will take care of us when he gets back," Brooklynn says. "I don't want to keep you from your day."

"Oh, it's fine. I'm working from home today. I am offering this in exchange for embarrassing stories about Orion." I hand her a glass of water with a look I hope conveys I will help if she does.

She looks at me and then at her husband. "How do you know him again?" she asks. "Apart from being neighbors?"

I doubt he's said anything to her about me. That is our bargain. I asked for silence, and so far he has given me everything I want.

My face remains neutral. Something I've practiced from years of keeping my thoughts to myself and teaching yoga. I don't even know why this hurts. It's not like I've told my family about him. But it's a reminder I mean nothing to him.

"We're friends," I declare. "And he texts me when he's on the water in case something happens." I offer my phone as a demonstration. Thankfully, the text before this morning's was the two of us coordinating meeting at Paradise. It's not like there is any incriminating evidence anyway. We text only as it relates to our friendship. He would never tell me he needs me and would never put it in writing.

"Right, of course," Brooklynn says.

Spencer's attention is still on his phone. "Alex knows her. Says we should ask her to give us a tour around town."

Alex continues to try to set Orion and me up. I should be annoyed. I specifically didn't want to have someone else's opinion interfering with our relationship. But then I think of him when we're alone, and I don't care enough about anyone else to be annoyed.

I tell them I'll have to work eventually, but I'm more than happy to let Brooklynn take her pick from my sample pile.

In exchange, I get embarrassing stories of Orion as a kid.

ORION

I MAKE IT BACK TO SHORE AND REMEMBER WHY I NORMALLY DO this early in the morning—the sun is beating down and I'm drenched in sweat. I want nothing more than to submerge myself in the ocean again.

But my shower will do.

I pull my phone out of my bag to let Carina know I'm back. She's the reason I didn't go out earlier. She kept me awake most of the night, claiming that since she didn't have any meetings and I didn't have any charters, we could sleep in. Of course, we slept in separate beds, but I spent a lot of time in hers.

I look at the screen in the glare and see I have several missed calls from my sister and a text. I tap the screen and see a selfie of her and Spencer in front of my house.

What are they doing here?

I don't bother to call her. I drag my kayak across the beach and down the path through the dunes to see a rental car parked on the street next to my driveway. But they are nowhere in sight. I'm not surprised she's made the trip without telling me. She's not a big planner. The second she gets an idea in her head, she acts on it. I wouldn't be surprised if she decided to come last night and booked the next flight out.

I'm about to call as I open my garage, when I hear Carina's front door open and I turn, expecting her to step out. But Brooklynn and Spencer emerge.

"Orion!" She sprints toward me, crossing both our driveways, and hugs me, not caring how sweaty I am.

"Brooklynn, I didn't know you were coming," I say, embracing her in return.

"I know!" She steps back to look at me, basically bouncing with excitement. "We wanted to surprise you. This might not be great timing and I don't know what your schedule is like. But we have time off. We can hang out with Alex or explore on our own. You don't have to entertain us."

"And I'm more than happy to show them around."

I hadn't noticed Carina stepping out of her house. She looks awfully smug. I shake hands with Spencer, but my attention stays on Carina. "What did you do?"

"I gave your sister leggings," she says innocently.

"And?"

"Now I know about kindergarten."

I look back at my sister.

"They are very nice leggings." Brooklynn looks a little sheepish.

"I know they are." I'm slightly horrified at how quickly these two have become friends. My sister will see right through to my feelings for Carina, and I don't want to spook her. I wanted us to be out in the open before she met my family.

But she's smiling at me and so I accept she now knows about the glue-eating incident.

"It's fine. Let me shower and then I'll show you around." I indicate they can go inside. "There's a guest room to the left, across from the stairs." I have a lot of charters this weekend but I should be able to manage time with my sister between them. Or offer to let someone else captain. I hired some qualified help for the company, but they haven't been out as much as I would like before turning them out on their own.

I wait until Spencer and Brooklynn are inside before giving Carina my attention. "You'll pay for this," I threaten. Her eyes go wide, catching my tone. I've made her pay before, and she's always been left melty and unable to move.

"I look forward to it." She smiles and lifts her shoulder before turning in an almost twirl to go inside.

The annoying part is it'll be a few days before I get her in my arms again. I don't know how she's reacting to my sister being around. Her nonchalance is more tied to our frenemies game and not us having sex on a near daily basis. I doubt I can convince her I'm an expert at sneaking out of my house without my sister knowing.

In the past, I've brought too many women home to meet my family. I'd convinced myself *this one was different*, no matter how many times I'd been wrong before. But things *are* different with Carina. The fact that I want to protect what we have is enough evidence. She wants to keep us quiet and has reasons I don't agree with. But I have enjoyed the chance to be with her without any interference from anyone else.

We said we'd explore each other and see if there is something here. But I don't need to learn anything more—I'm committed. I'll find the right time to tell her soon. Sometime when we're rested. So she won't be able to find an excuse for why it's not real.

Back in my house, I take a quick shower after telling Spencer and Brooklynn to help themselves to whatever's in the fridge. When I come out, they both lounge in my living room with iced tea.

"This is really beautiful," Brooklynn says. "The pictures you sent don't do it justice."

"Thanks."

"I really like the photos you brought from Mom and Dad's."

She points to one of the two of us on the lake when we were little. "I think that was your first boat trip."

I smile at the memory. This house feels like the first solid thing I've ever built. "It's a great location too."

"And Carina?" she asks.

I'm tempted to share the truth, but I don't. "She's a good friend. Introduced me to people. Got me into yoga."

"I was telling you for years it would help your back," Brooklynn says.

"I know, I know."

Brooklynn will see right through both of us.

WE MAKE the trip to Paradise, sweating again before we even get to the beach, and Alex joins us for lunch. He and Spencer have been friends for a long time, but Spencer has never visited before. Bristol serves us with her usual local charm, telling us about the good places to go for water activities.

I see light in Brooklynn's eyes. She's never been to Florida and mostly knows only the Florida Man stereotypes. I see her wanting to experience more than strip malls and beaches. They'll be here for four days, plenty of time to make this trip memorable for her.

Once we're back in the air conditioning at my place after an afternoon hitting the tourist spots, she asks if we could check out one of the springs Bristol mentioned. "The one with the mermaid shows sounds like so much fun," she says. "But you have to work."

"Weeki Wachee," I say. "I got the charters covered."

"Yes, there! But I'd rather not kayak. Your accident freaked me out. I'd rather try paddleboarding. Do you think we could rent or take lessons?"

This is my opportunity and I know it. I've never been to

Weeki Wachee Springs. It's natural to invite someone to show us around. And even better if that person loves to paddleboard.

"Let me see if Carina wants to come. She'll know more than I do."

"You're sure she'll be able to?" Brooklynn asks.

"She'll probably love the chance to show off," I answer. I move away from the table and head for the door.

"Where are you going?"

"To ask her." I could call or text, but I need to see her. Need to hold her.

I walk around the fence and to the side door she leaves open for me. If she wasn't home or was busy, she would lock it.

I leave my shoes at the door and walk through her office, smiling at the smell of orange blossoms she probably doesn't even register anymore since it's everywhere she is. She's not there or her living room. I make my way up the stairs and see her bedroom door is cracked.

I push it open and she shrieks, jerking the covers over her bare chest. "Fuck, Orion. I thought you were an intruder."

"You left the door unlocked." I hear something vibrating. It's not her phone. "Really, Carina? It's been twelve hours." I'm impressed I can form words because my blood has rushed directly to my dick. I love the evidence she needs this as badly as I do.

"Longer than that, and that's rich when you're sporting wood." She gestures to my shorts.

"You really expect me to not get instantly hard knowing what you're doing under there?"

She shrugs.

"What were you thinking about?" I grab the back of my shirt and pull it off in one swift movement.

"Not you," she says with a smile.

She might not admit it, but I know I'm the only one for her. "Liar." I crawl toward her, pulling the blankets down so I can see her in her naked glory. She grips the wand vibrator. "Let me have it." She looks like she's about to fight me for it. But hands it over. "Is this the setting you like?"

"Yes."

I kneel between her legs. She's sitting against the headboard with her knees up. I place myself between them. She looks down at me. I came here for another reason, but seeing her wet and ready has pushed thoughts of anything else out of my mind.

I thrust two fingers inside her at the same time as I touch the vibrator to her clit. She comes instantly.

Holy fuck.

"That's not for you. I was close when you walked in," she pants.

"Sure, whatever you say." I sit up against the headboard next to her and pull my shorts off. "Come here," I order. I fist my cock. She turns to face me. "Nope, your back to me." I'm not done with her vibrator.

I hold on to her waist and ease her onto my length. Even the way her fingers wrap around my cock feel divine. Then she leans against me, and my arms are around her.

"You good?" I ask.

"Yes." She turns her head to kiss me and swivels her hips. If I'm not careful, I'll come too soon.

I grab the vibrator and adjust the setting down. With the slightest pressure, I rub it where we are joined.

"Fuck," she moans, leaning forward and bracing her hands on my legs.

"That's it. Use me, princess."

She looks back at me and I marvel at her. I can't believe this magnificent woman lets me this close to her. That she lets me do this to her. Fuck, I'm not even doing anything. I'm just holding on to her and her vibrator and letting her find what gets her off.

I thrust up to match her movements as her moans become louder. "Come on, Carina. Give me another one."

"The first one wasn't yours."

Sweat drips down her neck and I pull her back to me to lick it off. She tastes so fucking good. "My fingers. My orgasm."

"I can hop off you right now and finish myself," she says.

"Please don't."

She squeezes her inner muscles, and I might come right there, but I hold on.

"Come on, Orion. Beg for me. I bet you do it perfectly." The sly grin on her face tells me she knows exactly what she's doing.

I fucking love it.

And I don't hesitate. "Please, Carina. Come on my cock." I increase the setting on the vibrator and she pushes into it. "I need it." Need her.

"Oh god." It only takes a few more seconds and then she silently screams and pushes the vibrator away.

I come with her, holding her tight against me, loving how her skin feels against mine and the way we're both slick with sweat.

It's never been this good.

It'll never be this good with anyone else.

We lie there for a moment, then I reach over to turn off the vibrator. "That was..." I start.

"Yeah," she finishes. I kiss her neck. "You okay?" she asks, turning and brushing my hair away from my forehead.

"Yes. I missed you, that's all," I say.

"We spent last night together," she counters.

"I know." But it wasn't enough.

"Your sister..." she starts. She thinks that was stressing me.

"We're fine. She's always been unexpected and energetic. I'm happy she's here."

But I can't talk about my sister while I'm in Carina. I grip her hips and lift her off me. She makes a quick dash to the bathroom, and when she steps out we're both dressed again.

"You barely mentioned her. I didn't know if I overstepped," she says.

"No, you're fine. I came over to see if you'd come with us to Weeki Wachee tomorrow."

Her eyes light up. "Of course. Have you been?"

"No, not yet. Brooklynn and Spencer want to paddleboard. I thought we could rent and then you can give them some tips."

She shakes her head. "I own at least four boards. Two are inflatable. My board and your kayak can go on the roof. It'll be easy. No need to rent."

We spend a few minutes discussing logistics. Who's buying what for the cooler. What time we'll have to leave to attempt to beat the crowds.

If she's anxious about spending the day with my family, she doesn't show it. I hope at this point I know her well enough that I could tell.

twenty-nine

CARINA

WHEN I WAKE IN THE MORNING, I REACH FOR ORION. I SHOULD cut him loose now, before I start always reaching for him. He's there for me if I need him now. But that can change.

At least I have today with him. I'm not ready to let him go yet. It likely doesn't mean anything to him to have me around his family. He's not careful or guarded like I am. I shouldn't read into it.

I dress in a swimsuit, a pair of loose shorts, and a long-sleeved sun shirt. I take time to perfectly smooth my ponytail. It'll get messed up later, but I want to have put in the effort. I don't honor everything my parents taught me—my mother is horrified I leave the house in athletic wear instead of designer dresses. But she would be proud I take time with my hair, even if it's a ponytail. I packed my bag last night, so I only have to toss in my face sunscreen after I apply it. Orion is right about hats—I should research making them. He'll give me a hard time today, but I set a reminder on my phone to reapply sunscreen every two hours.

I text him to meet me at my garage so we can load the car. I back into the driveway and am in the process of lifting my hard-board to the roof rack when he appears with his kayak.

"Are you sure you don't want to take my SUV?"

"This is fine. The rack is designed for both. Plus, hybrid. Less gas than yours." He looks at me skeptically. We've fought about this before but I know what he's doing. He's feeling out my mood today. We work together to heave his craft on the roof and bicker the whole time. He thinks he knows the best way to secure them, but again, it's my car and my rack. I know what I'm doing.

"It sounds like you two need coffee." Brooklynn yawns. "Orion only has two travel mugs. Any chance you have more?"

"I do. Cabinet next to my fridge." I gesture for her to enter the house. "The cooler is ready too." Spencer follows her.

With his kayak secure, Orion turns to me. "Are we going to fight all day?"

I sigh. "I don't know." I'm not upset about the early morning or trying to make a good impression on his sister. I want to be closer to him than I'm letting myself, and I want him to hold me in his arms and kiss me.

And, frankly, I want to delay leaving twenty minutes so we can fuck. I've been imagining that future too much. One where things are easy. Where I open up to him and he stays to secure it all.

"We don't have to fight," he says.

We load the two inflatable boards into the trunk. We're doing a final check for towels and waters when Orion does something incredibly stupid.

"I'll take the keys." His hand is outstretched and open.

"What?"

Brooklynn and Spencer are about to get into the back seat, but they pause.

"I figure I'll drive since you never do."

I blinked a few times before responding. "First, it's my car. Why would you think I would let you drive it? Second, just because I don't drive much doesn't mean I can't. Third, you either sit your ass in the passenger seat or I leave without you."

He grins at me. "Sure thing."

He's fucking with me, but it's unexpected. He's never tried to take control. He doesn't have issues with women driving him around. It must be one last chance to remind me what we are to each other.

We hit the road. It's two hours to the park and involves driving through Tampa. But we watch the sunrise and have enough coffee that we don't truly complain.

Of course, Orion and I can't be in an enclosed space together without fighting. While discussing our favorite Disney movies, he counters all my opinions.

"No, *Peter Pan* is not a good movie," Orion argues.

"Didn't you dress up as Captain Hook several times?" Brooklynn asks.

"I knew it!" I exclaim. "You don't believe half the things you fight me on."

"Oh please. Because you really think my bushes are overgrown."

Brooklynn chokes back a laugh. I'm sure she thinks it's a euphemism. I shake my head.

"How long have you lived in Florida?" she asks.

"Um…technically since college. My family had the house since before I was born. We'd come here every summer and most family vacations."

"Aren't you worried about sea level rise? Hurricanes?" Spencer asks.

Orion gives me a look. I'm sure he had to answer these questions when he bought his house. He was probably told it was reckless and a bad investment because one storm could wipe out the whole beach. And it's not like homeowner's insurance is cheap.

"Of course. But that's why I do everything in my power to mitigate climate change. I built a whole company around it."

"You ever think you'll leave?" Brooklynn asks.

"Nope. The sea levels can rise. I'm going down with the island."

Brooklynn laughs. "You sound like Orion and the *Twisted Rigging*."

* * *

WHEN WE GET to the park, Orion and I take down our gear from the roof together. He doesn't complain and lets me tell him what to do.

"Is this like the boat thing?" I ask.

He shrugs. "I guess I'd rather you be relaxed on the water. Then you won't accidentally feed me to an alligator."

"This river doesn't have gators so it's not an option."

"Speaking of Gators." He pulls a hat out of his bag. "I bought this for you." He hands me a blue and white hat with a retro University of Florida logo.

"What's this?" I ask.

"You went there, right? And you liked it? If you can't endorse your university, then I don't know how to help you."

I should be annoyed. But I can't. He found a way for me to be protected from the sun and not go against my values and I love it.

"Thanks." I put the hat on. It's the perfect moment to kiss him but I keep my distance.

"No problem. I'll go pay the entrance fee," he says, squeezing my shoulder briefly.

We reapply sunscreen as I inflate the other boards. Quickly enough, we're at the water's edge. I give Brooklynn and Spencer instructions on how to navigate the paddleboards, and we're off.

thirty

ORION

I LOVE WATCHING CARINA TEACH. I'VE MADE HER WEEKLY CLASS A priority because I can't get enough of her. I love watching her do the thing she loves. I could get grumpy for an arbitrary reason, but I want to see her sharing her knowledge and her unconditional love of nature.

Of course we have a ton of fun. She's paddled here before and navigates us through the waters. She could go so much faster than the rest of us but pauses to point out wildlife. More than once, she's asked by someone passing if she's a tour guide.

She laughs, and I love everything about it.

I've fallen in love with her, and she doesn't even know. She won't admit we're more than fuck buddies and is still convinced I'll leave at any moment.

Soon, we'll have a conversation. I'll get through this trip with Brooklynn, and then I'll have Carina to myself again.

I pull up next to her. "You want to hand me your phone?"

She looks over at Brooklynn and Spencer who float a little behind us on the river. "You don't have to do this," she says.

"It's fine. This place is beautiful. You're dressed completely in your gear. Let me take a few pictures."

She thinks it over for a moment, then gets her phone from her dry bag and hands it to me with her hat and sunglasses. She paddles a short distance away so it's only her in the shot.

"You two do this a lot?" Brooklynn asks, pulling up alongside me.

"Paddle together? A few times," I say.

"No, the picture-taking thing," Brooklynn says.

Carina never asks me to, but I offer often. It's a chance to get her to show off. I'd capture every moment with her if I could. "A few times."

"He would make a very good Instagram boyfriend," Carina says.

She's said it before but this time it hurts. Because I want to be her Instagram boyfriend. I don't care how much time I spend taking pictures of her as long as I get to be with her.

"You can do a video," Carina says. "Then you don't have to get the exact moment. I'm going to do a headstand."

"Wait, what?" Spencer says, his eyes shooting between Carina and me.

Neither Carina nor I respond. It's better if he watches her.

I check the background, so she's centered. "Ready."

She places her forearms on her board, clasping her hands together, and braces her head between them. She slowly inverts, making it look easy when the board is moving and tilting ever so slightly in the river. She stays steady for several seconds and then falls out.

"You okay?" I ask. She's not in the water, but something might be wrong. I grip my paddle with my free hand, ready to be at her side in an instant.

"Yep," she calls back. "Can we go again?"

I give her a thumbs-up, and she repeats.

This time she doesn't fall, but instead inverts and moves her legs through several variations before landing softly on her feet.

Brooklynn cheers. "I can't believe you did that! That's amazing!"

Carina shrugs. "I've been practicing for years." It's the closest she'll come to self-praise.

We paddle back with enough time to catch the mermaid show in the underwater theater, and Brooklynn is absolutely amazed.

"I clearly missed my calling," she says. "I should have moved here and become a mermaid."

I look to Carina. There's one siren I'm completely mesmerized by.

The day passes slowly and lazily. We stop at the park's tiki restaurant for lunch. Carina is tired, and I'm sure that's why her chair rubs against mine.

"I should send pictures to Alex and Haley," Carina says, her mind always on work.

I was the one to suggest pictures earlier, but I wish I had her to myself. She shifts closer to me for a selfie, her head temporarily resting on my shoulder, and my breath stops.

In one second, everything in my life feels utterly perfect.

"You really putting that on the internet?" I ask. She's never posted a similar selfie in the time I've followed her Instagram.

"It's for me," she says, her head tilting as she considers the framing. I want to kiss her temple and ask her to send it to me but I see Brooklynn watching us.

We head to the swimming area, where I want to have Carina in my arms. I want to hold her as we float and find some spot to hide. She's all I can focus on.

Instead, we take advantage of the cool water to get a break from the heat. I'm amazed Carina is the first to suggest we go down the water slides.

Hours later, when we pack up the car, she hands me the keys.

"Really?" I ask.

She nods. "I might fall asleep."

"You sleeping okay?" I ask with a smirk.

"Yes. It's been a long day." Her lips press together as she suppresses a smile.

We stop for coffee on the drive back. I hate that my sister is here because I want to reach across the center console and take Carina's hand in mine.

Once we're back in Wendell Beach, I pull into Carina's driveway and help her unload the car. "You two go in," I call to Spencer and Brooklynn. "I'll put some burgers on the grill later so we can relax in the pool." They nod and go inside. "You want to join us?"

I want her to so much.

"I'll pass. I need to wind down on my own for a bit," she says.

I nod because I understand the feeling. But I'm also realizing that being with her is as restful as being alone.

"Have a good night," I respond. "I'll text you if we go to Paradise or something."

I take a leap and step in close to kiss her forehead. She doesn't object. She closes her eyes. It's affection for the sake of affection. It's not the deep kiss I want. With Carina, I'll take anything I can get.

"I'll see you soon," she says.

* * *

MUCH LATER THAT NIGHT, after dinner and beers, while Spencer watches college football, Brooklynn helps me with the dishes.

"I'm glad you're settling in so well," she says.

"I don't know why you were worried," I answer.

"Honestly, Orion, we thought you would set up the new business and move on."

I grind my teeth. "Is it so hard to believe I've changed?"

"When you told me you were doing this? Yes. But now I get it."

"Good."

"Will you come home for Thanksgiving, at least?"

I haven't been around for many holidays. I don't know why she suddenly cares now. "I'll see. I have a friend who's a chef, so Mom and Dad need to step up their food game."

"I'll tell them to practice." Brooklynn laughs. "And Carina?"

"What about her?"

"How long have you been seeing her?"

I put down the knife I'm drying. "A few weeks?" I'm not sure of the exact timeline at this point. If the first time on my boat counts as the starting point. She's been on my mind this entire time.

"Why didn't you tell me?"

She was watching all day. "It's not serious, and she wants to keep it a secret. She has a reputation to maintain."

"And you're, what, something dirty that needs to be hidden?"

"No, that's not it." I take a few breaths in. "You haven't been around Alex in a while. He and everyone else get in everyone's business. This is our chance to see if it's something before people start asking questions." That's what I tell myself. Until I can convince Carina this is more than a fling. It's something lasting.

"That's not what you said. You said she has a reputation to maintain. Look, I'm trying to take care of my little brother. And you deserve to be with someone who cares about you as much as you care about them. You clearly care for her."

"I do."

"And for what it's worth, I think she cares about you too. She wouldn't have let you drive her car if she didn't. That's why I don't like that it's a secret."

"I appreciate the concern. But we're fine. I'm fine with how things are with us," I repeat.

"Okay, if you say so."

Brooklynn lets it go. But I can't. So after the dishes are done and the football game is off and I'm alone in my room, I pull out my phone. My body aches. I'm not getting enough rest. I won't sleep now because I'll be replaying this conversation over in my head. I also won't sleep if I'm about to be rejected. But I hit send on the text anyway.

thirty-one

CARINA

Come over.

I FREEZE AT THE MESSAGE. I'M IN MY PAJAMAS AND WOULD BE IN bed, but I was making sure the doors were locked. This house has so many, I'm always certain I've forgotten one. I had left the side door unlocked. It's a habit at this point to expect his presence.

ME

Your sister?

ORION

She knows. She figured it out on her own. Come over.

I hesitate for a moment. I'm tired of waking up alone, but I don't know what he wants. After a long paddle like today, I'm exhausted.

ME

I'm not up for sex.

ORION

Come over. The front door code is 0815.

I don't even bristle at the order.

I grab a fresh toothbrush from a drawer and shove a pair of leggings and a sports bra in a bag. I leave out the front door and lock up behind me. His house is dark, so I enter quietly and walk up the stairs to his room. He's sitting in bed watching TV. I nervously place the bag by the door. He throws back the sheets for me to climb in with him. I do and he draws me close.

"We're really only sleeping?" I ask. His bedroom is done in slightly darker wood than mine but still keeps the same coastal decorative feel, especially with the gauzy curtains over the door to his balcony. He has white and light blue linens that are just as soft as mine and his walls are painted light gray. I almost never have time to appreciate how cozy the room is since we're usually in a rush to get naked.

"Yes." He kisses the top of my head. "Is that a problem?"

"No," I say. He spent all day with me. I don't understand why he wants more time with me, especially if we aren't having sex. But his body is the right kind of warm and he smells like paradise. "I have a six a.m. yoga class."

He turns off the TV. "We should sleep, then." He reaches for his bedside lamp and turns it off too.

I get comfortable underneath the blankets with his arm around me. He keeps his home a little cooler than mine, and even through his windows and the little extra distance, I can hear the waves crashing on the beach.

* * *

WHEN MY ALARM goes off in the morning, I'm in Orion's arms. I move out of them but he pulls me back to him.

"Stay," he whispers.

"I can't."

"Come over tonight?"

I roll to my back and look up at him. His eyes are soft in sleep, but that can't be desperation behind them as much as I want to believe it is.

I kiss him gently before I answer. "Of course."

I don't know what it means that he wants me around this much. But I'll take it. Because it's only a matter of time before he gets bored and moves on. Keeping him at arm's length isn't working. But I can enjoy the time I have with him.

I've fallen in love, and he doesn't even know.

ORION

SHORTLY AFTER BROOKLYNN AND SPENCER LEAVE, CARINA SHOWS up at my place. I wonder if she watches for me the way I watch for her. She has a determined look on her face that I hope will lead to sex.

"I need to see this suit you claim to have," she states.

Oh. That's significantly less fun.

"Sure. It's in the closet." I lead the way to my bedroom and into the closet where the suit hangs in a garment bag. She opens the zipper and traces the fabric with her hands.

It's amazing to watch her judge it. I'm not worried, but clothing is her thing and she's so incredibly sexy when she's doing what she's passionate about.

"It's nice. Can you try it on for me?"

"Why? Are you concerned?" She's stressed about something, and it's not the suit. But we're deep enough in that I can ask directly, and she'll tell me what she's thinking.

She looks at me and bites her lip, as if deciding how much to share. "We're less than a month out. Bachelor and bachelorette parties are next weekend. I had the final fitting for my dress this morning."

"Right." That is normal to me. But the worry on her face suggests there's something more. I take the suit out and head to the bedroom. I strip out of my clothes. The suit will need to be dry-cleaned since I'm a little bit sweaty.

Her gaze follows my skin. I'll let her stay focused on this for now, but when I'm done trying this on, I'm getting her naked with me.

Once I'm dressed, she steps in front of me, running her hands along the seams. "It's good. You look good," she says.

"Thanks." Her palm rests on my chest. I place one hand on it and the other around her waist.

"Why do you have this anyway?" she asks, letting me dance with her and not questioning it.

"Yacht clubs," I answer.

"You hang out at yacht clubs?"

"Not personally, but professionally. You know the value of networking."

"Yes," she says, a little breathless. I twirl her. "What are we doing?"

"Practicing for the wedding." Her body lands flush against mine.

"We can't dance like this at the wedding," she counters.

"Why not?"

"Because then everyone will know we're sleeping together."

"Is that so bad?" We've agreed to be exclusive. We've had the talk about our health and birth control. We might not talk about our feelings for each other, but we've been there for each other's low moments. I don't know what it will take for her to realize this is a relationship and not the fling she's making it out to be.

But she doesn't pull away and I'm thankful for that.

"When you leave…"

"I'm not leaving…"

"When you decide I'm not good enough…" she continues. I

growl and pull her closer. "Let's get through the bachelor and bachelorette parties and then we can discuss it."

I want to push her now. Her muscles tense under my hands. I won't get anywhere with her if the destination isn't somewhere she wants to go. So pushing her today is a mistake. She'll run. But I can't be at that wedding and pretend she doesn't matter to me.

"Are you excited for the bachelorette weekend?" I ask.

She hums, happy I've acquiesced for now. "It's been forever since we've gone to Miami. Are you excited about the bachelor trip?"

"I'm not actually going on the trip. I'm working it."

If it had been anyone else, I would have said no. But Beckett made me hosting the bachelor party a condition for the wedding invitation. And I want to go to the wedding to be there for Carina. Beckett's parents will pay for everything. Like with Carina and Alex, the Foleys can make or break people on this island. I agreed since it would only be four guys, and I trust Alex and Christian to not be complete fuckheads.

Christian is convinced he was only invited because he'd provide booze.

So I'm treating it as an audition. It's one step closer to convincing the Foleys to use Lost Craft Charters.

"Anything I should know about dealing with Hamilton?"

She tenses fully and pulls away. "Fuck, I forgot he's coming. You know I don't have any feelings for him."

"Considering how much you complain about him, I'd hope that's the case. Although I'm sure you complain about me."

"It's not the same."

"I'm not worried." I'm not. Not about him and her. But I will always be afraid she'll drift away from me.

"I feel like a failure every time I think about him," she confesses.

"What?" I hate that he continues to make her feel inadequate.

"I don't know. Like I should have tried harder with him. We were together for a few years. It should have gone somewhere."

I feel like I've been knocked on my ass. That wasn't where I thought she was taking this conversation. "If you don't have feelings for him now, then why would you want to have tried harder? He belittles your company every chance he gets. He doesn't respect what you've done or your values."

She rubs her forehead. "I don't know. I feel like it was a waste of a few years if it didn't work out. A mistake. I could have been using my time doing something else productive."

A full storm rages in my head. Is that what she thinks of us? That if this relationship doesn't end in marriage, it's a waste of time and a mistake? Is that why she doesn't want to tell anyone, because then it would be admitting failure? Is that what I'm fighting against?

Fuck this.

I grab her by the back of the head and pull her mouth to mine. "We're not a mistake."

"What?"

I don't respond. Instead, I pick her up and turn her to the bed. From there, it's a well-practiced race to get each other's clothes off.

"Your suit. We need to hang it up," she says, trying to sit up.

I pin her down. "It's getting cleaned anyway. Leave it."

I kiss my way down her body, feeling the vibrations in her chest as she hums her approval. She runs her hands through my hair. I'll never cut it. The longer it is, the more time I can keep her attached to me.

We're in my bed. I should be rough with her. She'll expect that, but I don't want to.

So I take her hands and pin them above her head. "I don't have a tie, so you'll have to exhibit some self-control. These stay here."

"No sailor's knots?"

"Not today." I nibble on her ear and she laughs.

I spread her legs and use one finger to find her already wet for me. I lower onto her and drown in the taste of her.

This is what I can do. I stay here and get her close to an orgasm over and over, until she's begging for it. And show her, even if it doesn't work out between us, that the time we spend together is worth it. She's not better served by researching fabric or practicing her handstand.

She's about to break, and the selfless thing would be to push her over the edge and have mercy on her. But I want to feel it when she does.

I thrust into her and it's enough for her waves to crash. I still and feel her shatter beneath me.

"You okay?" I ask when it's over. I'm dying to move, but I need to know she can take more. My forehead rests on hers.

"Yeah." Her breath is shallow.

"Good." I kiss her and roll my hips. Her arms reach around my back and her legs around my waist.

I can't let her go. I've known that from the first time. I've always worried she'll run, but I thought I had more time with her.

Today I start to wonder if the clock is already running down.

thirty-three

CARINA

Orion comes with a loud groan into my neck, right as my second orgasm hits me. I don't know how he always does it.

Something was different that time. He's thinking, and I'm not sure what about.

We're both exhausted and drift off to sleep. When we wake up a little bit later, he's watching me.

"Tell me how this whole thing started," he asks.

"How what started?"

"Why did you start your company? Your empire?"

"That's a different question." I kiss him and roll us so I straddle him. We could stay like this for hours and I wouldn't have to answer. We've always used sex as a distraction from our real problems. My only problem now is how much I want him.

But as much as I deny it, he knows me. Knows what I'm doing. "Carina, tell me."

"Or what?" I grind into his cock.

"No orgasm until I'm satisfied."

"You wouldn't."

He flips me onto my back and holds himself above me so we

aren't touching. "I promise pleasure until you pass out if you tell me."

"Isn't that what just happened?"

"Then you know I'm good for the threat."

"You're a manipulative bastard, you know that?" He lowers his body onto mine and I love the weight of him.

"You love it."

He's right. I do. I love him. I'm not sure when it happened, but it did.

"You can't hide from me, Carina."

"Fine." I push him off me so I can sit up and cover myself. "My parents are both successful people. My dad founded a million businesses and then sold them off once they were profitable. Now he mostly invests in startups as an angel investor, as you have figured out. My mother is a lawyer. Made partner young and was always chasing bigger and flashier clients."

"Okay, I get that. Both my parents work in real estate. I am familiar with the drive for more, more, more."

"Exactly. They were both always busy and—this sounds terrible so I'm saying it and I don't want you to react."

"Sure."

He'll react. I know it. "I don't think they cared about me. I know they love me. But I think they had a kid because it was expected, not out of any deep parental desire. I was in childcare a lot. When I aged out, it was after-school programs and sports. When we came to Wendell Beach, they thought the public beach lifeguards were as good a babysitter as any."

He takes my hand in his and squeezes before I continue.

"Even with the hands-off approach to parenting, they had one lesson for me: don't fail." It was drilled into me since I was small. Public failures were pointed at and ridiculed. I asked once if it was better to try. They told me that was done in private where no one could see.

Of course, this doesn't work for everything. I watched them

try for years to fix their marriage in private. It ultimately failed and both spent the next few years saving face in their social circles.

I was another asset to be divided up in the divorce.

"In college, I opted for business rather than law. My dad said he would give me startup funds as a graduation gift if I came up with a business plan. I spent four years brainstorming and researching, until I had a plan for sustainable activewear. It's a growing market and people will pay more if they think their clothing is doing moral good like taking water bottles out of the ocean. It felt fail-proof."

"So it's bullshit? You don't believe in your own mission statement?"

"No, I do. It's complicated. See, a successful activewear company is good. It empowers people to move their bodies and go on adventures and connect spiritually. But if we can do that *and* work against climate change? Even better. And with size inclusivity, I'm one step closer to a perfect company."

"And one step farther from failure. So your parents will finally pay attention to you."

I huff, feeling hurt. "Don't make fun of me. This is really hard to share."

His brown eyes fill with concern. "I know. I'm sorry. But you know this doesn't make sense. Your parents won't change their behavior."

I can't even remember the last conversation I had with my mom. She can't bill time for a phone call with me, so she sure as hell never calls. "But if I accept that, then I am accepting my relationship with my parents as is. It won't get any better."

He pulls me into his lap. "There is one person who thinks you're perfect as is." He trails kisses down my neck. "Who doesn't want you to change. Who would still kiss you if everything else in your life crumbled down."

"Then I would need you and your boat money."

He looks me in the eye and holds me steady. "If everything in your life fell apart, I would take you out on the *Twisted Rigging*. We wouldn't return until the only things you remember are me, my body, and the ocean."

I surge into him, capturing his lips. I need to consume him as much as he needs me. Our bodies are ready for each other. He's hard and I'm wet, and when we do this I can almost believe everything will be okay. That we'll make this last forever.

After, I rest my head against his chest. "How did you begin your empire? Or is it an armada once you have two fleets? Should I call you 'Commodore'?"

"It's not exciting."

"You knew the deal when you asked me."

"Yes, but I hoped to distract you with sex."

"That doesn't work with me. Single point of focus."

"I love being the object of your focus," he states.

I squirm. It's too good to hear. It's far too close to what I want. And he is the object of my focus far more than I could ever tell him.

I kiss him to distract from his statement and hopefully steer us back to safety. He leans away enough to look me in the eyes. I'm naked and wrapped around him with nothing between us.

"I always loved sailing. I got a job on a sailboat as soon as I could and trained for my captain's license. I took tours out into Boston Harbor. Saved enough to buy a second boat. Every winter, I traveled. The business grew. I hired more crew. I bought more boats. Some days were struggles, but overall, it wasn't."

"You poor, white man." Sarcasm fills my voice.

"I know." He shifts and pulls me against him. I'm pressed against his chest. His skin is warm against mine. "I have everything."

I want to believe that statement is about me, but I'm too afraid to let myself hope.

ORION

THE LOST CRAFT CHARTERS SHOP IS A TOTAL MONEY GRAB—WE stock the things guests forget, put our logo on it, and then overcharge. Plus, souvenirs and popular resort wear.

Our Nebula Athletics order came in. I'm pleased it's selling so well. It'll be another few weeks before we have our branded gear, but I like having a piece of Carina around me.

"Ohh. I love this brand," a woman from my last tour shrieks as she scours the rack with her friends.

I force myself to keep my smile internal as I review the sailing schedule. I'm so proud of Carina. If she'd let me, I'd spend all my time talking about how amazing my girlfriend's clothing is.

And she'd deny almost every word of my praise.

"Oh no," her friend bemoans. "They claim to use recycled stuff, but it's a lie. I watched a whole video on it this morning. I'm boycotting."

My ears start ringing, matched with a twisted feeling in my gut. Like the boat I'm on has suddenly been hit with fifteen-foot waves.

That can't be right. Carina wouldn't lie. Sustainability is

important to her. They must be wrong. There is some kind of mix-up. She'd be devastated if this was true.

"I'll be in my office," I tell Nathan, who's staffing the cash register, and head to the dock for some quiet. The *Twisted Rigging* is at the end, and I'm drawn to her. She's my safe space, and even if everything here in Wendell Beach fell apart, I will always have my boat.

I head out of the sun and into the galley and pull out my phone, searching social media.

It doesn't take me long.

Fuck.

Fuck.

Countless videos pop up showing how the current line is made from a different fabric. A TikTok materials expert demonstrates there's no way it's made from what the company claims it is.

I can't imagine she isn't aware, but I need to be sure.

We don't call each other often. It's always texting. But I need to hear her voice.

The phone rings, and when she answers, she sounds tired. "Hey."

"Hey, I'm sure you know—"

She doesn't let me finish. "Fuck, Orion. How do you know?"

"Some charter guests were looking at the display. A woman mentioned seeing a video."

She's crying. It's the worst fucking sound in the universe. Worse than the sound of wood cracking on a ship. Worse than the keel hitting ground. "I didn't know any of this. My supplier changed without telling me."

"I know, princess. You wouldn't do this on purpose. Are you at the office? Home?" I check my watch. "Do you want me to bring you dinner?" I need to be in the same space as she is.

She's stopped crying. "Dinner would be great. I'm at the office."

"I'll get you the chicken you like from Paradise," I offer. I don't know what she feels for me, but I can take care of her body. Usually it's sex, but today it can be food.

"I have to go. I have another call coming in." She hangs up before I can respond.

I grab the food from Paradise and head over to her office. It's busier than the last time I was here. Stacy and Jeannette talk to a young woman outside Carina's office.

"I brought Carina dinner." I hold up the bag. Paradise uses compostable takeout containers. I'm sure it was Carina's influence.

"Um…let me see if she's available," the woman I don't know says. All three women look confused. They probably aren't aware I'm her neighbor. I'm only the captain of the boat they took once, if they remember me at all.

Carina pops her head out of her office. "It's fine, Mackenzie. He can come back."

She's so fucking beautiful. I can't believe she's mine.

I close the door behind me and pull Carina into my arms. She must have gotten off a video call or done some filming because her makeup is perfect, and her eyes aren't puffy like after a cry.

"It'll be okay," I assure her.

She pulls away. "No, it won't. I don't know how I'll redeem the company after this. And it's not just the brand. It's me. My customers hate me."

I take her phone out of her hand and set it on her desk. "It's one day. You will fix the problem and you will regain their trust."

"How can you be so sure? You don't even know what the problem is."

"But I know you, Carina. You're a force of nature. You've never met a problem you couldn't solve."

"What if I can't fix this?"

"Then we take the *Twisted Rigging* out, and I make you forget everything terrible that's ever happened."

She smiles, however forced. She accepts the food container and sits down at her desk. "Did you get something for you?"

"No, I didn't want to distract you." I didn't know if she'd want me to stay.

"What if I want you to sit here while I eat?"

"Then I'll sit." I take the seat across from her as she opens up the box. "Do you want to talk about it?" As long as I've known her, she doesn't like to talk about her problems, at least not without serious coaxing. She'd prefer to hide behind arguments with me or by distracting everyone else by doing something so perfect that no one notices she did something wrong or that something is bothering her. That won't work with us anymore. We breached a new level in our relationship when my sister visited. She doesn't want to acknowledge it, but we are in a relationship. This is a partnership.

It's only a matter of time before I'll be able to get her to admit it.

It has to happen before the wedding. I was serious when I told her I can't be around her and the love on display and pretend I'm not sleeping with her.

I can barely pretend to her face that I'm not in love with her.

She sighs, which I think is a sign she wants to let something off her chest. "I drafted a statement. We didn't know. We trusted our supplier. We apologize our quality control didn't catch this. People will get full refunds. They don't even have to send the clothing back because that would be a waste of resources."

"How long before you can resupply?"

"I can't. Not in time to be meaningful." She shakes her head. "We slashed the prices on the website to liquidate it. It's not the whole line, regardless of what people say. Some people will buy because they are still good clothes. That, you know, polluted a river to get made."

I care about the river, I really do. But I care about Carina more. "Okay, it's not everything. What about future seasons?"

"It's isolated. Plenty of items weren't affected. But of course no one will believe us."

I won't manage her feelings. I know better. But I want to soothe her ache any way I can. She needs to talk this out. I can give her the space to do so.

"I lost the trust of my entire customer base." Carina looks like she's holding up now. Like she's accepted what has happened. But it's a lie.

It's not the money, although I'm sure she's concerned about her employees. It's the trust in the community she built. The community that shares the values they believe have been betrayed.

This could break her. I can't let that happen.

"Whatever you need, I'm here for you," I say. It's shallow and an echo of what I really want to say.

I love you. I'm not your partner in business, but I am your partner in life. I can take some of the burden for you.

But I don't think now is the time.

"I know, and I appreciate it," she replies, but it sounds hollow. Like she's responding to someone who means nothing to her.

She finishes her meal. I take my cue to leave. "Do you want to come over tonight?" We spend most nights together. It would be weird at this point for us to be separate.

It's getting habitual. It's getting comfortable.

My past relationships have been nonstop heat and adrenaline. Sure, some were longer lasting. But I've never felt the comfortable quiet I feel with her. The heat is better than I've ever had, but the space between is as important.

I need her to breathe. I need her around me. There is no getting out of this for me. This won't burn out. This won't ebb. This will never dissipate.

She squints her eyes. "Can we do my place? I'll probably log back in."

"Text me when you leave," I answer. It's not quite enough for me. I want a key to her place. I want to live in the same place as her.

I want her home to be my home.

But she'll never accept that. Not when she's convinced it could fail. She won't take another risk when she's had one fall apart.

I pause in the doorway, looking back at her as she turns her focus to her computer. "We could leave now. Head south on the *Rigging*."

She just shakes her head.

I smile at her, but I no longer have her attention so she doesn't notice.

thirty-five

CARINA

THIS DAY WOULD HAVE BEEN MISERABLE WITHOUT MY FATHER'S commentary. But that made me the most angry—that I couldn't even blame him. To him, my successes may not be my own, but my failures surely are.

For months he begged me to give up on the sustainability messaging and to pivot toward affordability. But that wasn't where my values lie. Sure, I want to be affordable. I participate in programs to keep girls in sports in low-income schools and do everything I can to help. I've done everything right and still got screwed over.

The buck stops with me. I take responsibility for what happened. I don't have a problem with that. But that doesn't mean I can't be angry about it.

I hate that my friends already know. Everyone has texted me. Telling me they believe in me and there is some rational reason other than my incompetence, negligence, or malfeasance.

I should feel grateful for their continued support. But I'm expecting it to fall apart soon.

And then there's Orion.

He showed up in exactly the way I needed him to. He brought

me food and didn't question anything. He trusted my explanation and didn't attempt to explain how I should have seen this in hindsight.

The rest of my friends feel the same way. They're asking what they can do and what I need. They are trying to help, but there is something about them knowing that gets under my skin.

I want this to happen in private. I want to suffer in quiet. But that's not an option.

This was supposed to be my legacy. I wanted to leave the world a better place than I found it. I meant everything I said to Orion about why I started Nebula Athletics.

Now it feels like everything is gone.

I endured a lecture from my father on my profits and everything we can do to recover from this. How I should pivot to a different clientele, one that isn't paying attention to the scandal and doesn't care.

That's not what I want to do.

Everyone keeps asking me what I want. I'm ashamed Orion's offer looks tempting—I want to rest in his arms and sail off into the sunset. We can get far enough away that we don't have cell service or internet and the world can forget about me. I'll come back rested and sated and everyone else will have moved on.

What I don't tell anyone is I'm terrified most of Orion.

I appreciate all he has done and know he cares about me. But there will come a time in the future when he gets tired of dealing with my drama and he'll leave. He'll sail away without me. I've always known this, but he's determined to convince me he'll always come home to Wendell Beach, even as he is constantly talking about some place he'd love to visit or a sailing destination he'd love to return to.

I used to think him coming home would be the worst outcome. That I'd be forced to see him live his life without me. But it would be much worse if he left and never returned. To think I drove him out of town.

I wouldn't blame him. I'd leave this mess too if I could.

He's waiting for me on my front step when I get home. It's late. The sun has long set. He looks exhausted.

He stands. I press myself into his chest to burrow in there. He places his arms on my waist and lets me be consumed by him.

Here, I feel calm. Here, I feel centered.

But I know the truth.

This is the eye of the storm. The worst is still to come.

ORION

I DIDN'T LIKE THE IDEA OF HAVING THE BACHELOR PARTY ON MY boat when it was proposed, but I thought I might grow into it. Maybe I'd get to know Beckett and wouldn't mind so much. It worked with Carina. Maybe I'd settle into the house and I wouldn't feel like the boat is the only place I call home. Having others on it wouldn't feel like such an invasion.

I still think he's a tool. But a tool Christian and Alex can keep in line, no matter how drunk he gets. The *Twisted Rigging* isn't just my space anymore. It's the space I share with Carina. I don't want her manipulative ex-boyfriend anywhere near it. But I don't have a choice since he's in the wedding party and was frat brothers with Beckett.

The women left earlier for Miami to go clubbing. I'm jealous of every man Carina dances with, even as I trust her completely. I wish she was in my bed at the end of each night. She's a part of every new memory I make, even when she's not around. I wish I knew it was the same for her. But more than my selfish needs, I hope she gets time away from her problems.

I'd tried to convince her to let me tag along and hide in her hotel room. She laughed and informed me girls' trips have strict rules and she would never break them. I didn't care about the disappointment I felt because she was laughing again.

We push off the dock right before noon. Beckett didn't want an early start, knowing the party would last late into the night. He has big plans for this sail, and then is heading to Wendell Beach Rum Works before hitting up as many bars on the island as he can before they close for the night.

To be honest, I'm surprised they didn't go to Tampa. It has more than enough strip clubs for them to get lost in. And selfishly, then they wouldn't be my problem. But his family is one of the largest employers on the island and a pillar of the economy, so he gets special treatment anywhere he goes. All he needs to do is flash his smile and tell everyone his name.

I should give Beckett more of a chance. I should give him the benefit of the doubt if for no other reason than Sienna loves him and Carina cares for her.

We make it to the gulf and I raise the sails. We're headed to an island south of us with calm water and beautiful beaches. I've taken plenty of tours there and everyone has fun. Christian opens a cooler and passes out premade cocktails while Alex is below deck getting food ready.

"Did Haley make the snacks?" Beckett asks.

"No, Alex got it catered," Christian says.

"Damn, I was really looking forward to her food." Hamilton downs his beverage quickly. He looks exactly the way I expected him to—his clothes look like they came from a website called NewEnglandYachtStyle.com. It's clear he thinks if he dresses the part, then the respect will immediately follow him. It's all slightly wrong for Florida. Carina loves this place so much. I can't see her ever happy with someone who tries so hard and gets it wrong.

I wish I could forget he was on this trip. Or that I don't know who he is to Carina. Every time she mentions him in relation to her business, I feel like he's giving her advice against what she genuinely believes in. And every time their relationship is mentioned, I wonder what she saw in him. But I know better than to state this to her.

"Why didn't you get Haley to make the food?" Beckett asks when Alex appears.

I swear both Christian and Alex look at me like I have an answer to this. Since it's my boat, it's my responsibility to deal with the dumb shit coming out of their mouths.

"She's busy with wedding planning and the bachelorette party," Alex answers with a tilt of his head, like he barely understood the question.

"I can't believe they're clubbing in Miami." Hamilton shakes his head. "You're not worried about Sienna?"

Beckett shrugs. "We're doing long-distance anyway right now."

"Carina is on the trip, right?" Hamilton asks. "When do they get back? She better not hook up with anyone."

I'm glad they aren't paying attention to me as I stand at the helm because they would have seen me roll my eyes. Hamilton has no right to ask anything of Carina. I should get annoyed with him thinking he does. But this man isn't worth being a thorn in my side.

"She is. Sunday night," Alex answers. Beckett hasn't been hands-on enough to know the details of their trip.

"Fuck, I'm leaving before then," Hamilton says.

"I'm pretty sure Carina can hook up with anyone she wants since y'all broke up," Alex says. "Years ago."

I focus on the sails and the direction of the wind, thankful Alex has my back, even if he doesn't realize it.

"We did. But I'm chartering a superyacht in February with a few friends. I'm inviting her along." He says it like she should be thankful he thought of her.

I face the bow and watch the angle of the sails and the way the waves dance on the water's surface, not just around the boat, but fifty yards ahead of us. I don't want to hear this guy talk about how he's planning to make a move on the woman I'm with. Or imagine how unpleasant he would be if he knew she wakes up in my arms every day. I'm not threatened by his invitation or any of the guys who might try to hook up with her in Miami. Only by the silence I'm forced to keep about our relationship.

"You really think she'll go with you?" Alex asks.

"It's a free trip for her on a superyacht. I won't tell her the sleeping arrangement until it's too late to back out."

"She'll go for it. If not for you, her dad will tell her it's in the best interest of the company," Beckett says.

"I know you're involved somehow with her business," Christian starts, "but she and I discuss business almost every day. I don't think that will work with her."

"Right, I forgot she's mentoring you and your little distillery."

Christian smiles. "You're enjoying my little distillery, so watch it."

Hamilton waves him off, but the flash of fear in his eyes tells me it's bravado. "If I don't get to talk to her soon, she's my date at the wedding. It's not like she can avoid me."

I grip the helm hard.

"I thought Orion was her date to the wedding," Alex says.

I can tell from the tone of his voice he would prefer me spending time with her. But I don't comment. None of this is fair. We're sitting around talking about Carina and she's not here to contribute.

"Who the fuck is Orion?" Hamilton says.

We were introduced by first names when he stepped aboard, but fuck him. "It's Captain Edwards when you're on my boat. And yes, I'm Carina's date to the wedding."

This isn't a regular charter where my goal is to be as polite and friendly as possible, but I still need to be on my best behavior. I can't have Beckett hate me if I want a good relationship with Coastline Beach House. And Carina wouldn't want me to get in a fight with her ex-boyfriend.

But I can adjust the sail and the helm. The *Twisted Rigging* picks up speed and tilts just enough to cause Hamilton and Beckett, the only two standing, to stumble into a bench and spill their drinks. "Hey! Watch the teak!" The railing is high enough that they weren't in danger of falling over or anything. I'm not that reckless.

"Sorry, man." Beckett grabs a towel and wipes up the mess. "You're not really her date. It was a numbers thing. You're her plus-one since she wasn't inviting anyone anyway. She'll be spending most of her time with the wedding party. Hamilton is her counterpart. Why would you want to spend the wedding with an ice queen like Carina? Sienna has a ton of hot cousins. And Haley is single again."

"I know how to get her warmed up." Hamilton tries to fist-bump Christian who keeps his hands to himself and glares back. "How do you even know her?" Hamilton drops his hand to his side while his eyes narrow to judge me.

"We're next-door neighbors." I have years of customer service experience. I can remain expressionless under his scrutiny. I know what I have with her. I'm not worried about him.

"Oh shit. I didn't think you'd be able to afford that place," he says.

I shrug. He doesn't need to know about the two thriving businesses I run. It's not worth my time to explain myself to him.

But of course, he can't stop running his mouth. Once he realizes I'm not responding, he continues. "I've been talking to her a lot with this whole fabric shit Nebula is dealing with. She'll take the trip to get away. She's so depressed about it. She'll take anything to cheer her up."

"Do you know what happened with that anyway?" Beckett asks. "She blew me off when I asked."

Hamilton lights up as if he's been waiting for the chance to explain this. "A supplier went behind her back. She should have listened to me in the first place. I told her trying to be 'green' would hurt her bottom line. It's a marketing strategy anyway. It doesn't make a difference. It's her fault, really."

My knuckles are completely white from gripping the helm. I wouldn't be surprised if I broke it. I've been the one taking care of Carina every night when she's terrified she won't make payroll. I've made sure she eats dinner when she's sick to her stomach over what people call her online. I've told her every day she is more than this. This won't define her. She's been so brave, taking full responsibility for something she had no control over. But she doesn't see it that way.

I need to talk to her. I need to see her face. Before the wedding I need everyone to know she is mine.

"Things will change when we get back together. She and I have so much history. We're inevitable," Hamilton states.

* * *

ONCE WE REACH THE ANCHORAGE, I head below deck. I need a minute away from these jackasses. I unlock the door to my cabin and shut it behind me.

I stare at the bed where Carina and I spend so much time. I'd cleaned up before today because it was what I could do to make it more sterile. But I don't want any of them in this sacred space.

There's a knock a minute later and Christian's voice comes through the door. "Hey man, you got a sec?"

I open the door. "Yeah, what's up?"

"You want a beer?"

"I can't drink and sail," I say.

He shrugs. "I figure we'll be here a minute. You could relax."

"I'll relax when this day is over."

Christian opens it instead. "They're off the boat. Alex is making sure they don't do anything stupid."

"Bets on how long that lasts?"

He laughs but doesn't comment further on the subject. "How long have you been with Carina?"

"I'm not," I lie.

"Right. I've done the whole secret thing in the past." He notices the look on my face. "Long time ago, way before Autumn. I know the glances and the excuses. You and Carina have something going on. You're not as subtle as you think."

I sigh and rest against the storage bench as he leans in the doorframe. I don't want to lie to him. But if he can see it, there's no point in denying it. I want to get this off my chest. I want to talk to someone about how amazing she is and how happy I am. He's married. I want his advice on how to convince her to tell people, and tell him how terrified I am she will dismiss us.

"She doesn't want anyone to know," I confess.

"That sucks," he says, taking a drink of his beer. "But I like the two of you together. She needs a little chaos in her life."

"She really does." Is that what I am to her? Chaos? Is that a good thing for her?

"You want to throw them off the boat?" he asks.

"It's so fucking tempting. But I'd be tempted if they were talking about any woman that way," I say. He wouldn't believe the amount of toxic shit I'm exposed to when I take out male-only groups.

"You never said how long," Christian says.

I should tell him the truth. It's been since the day I got here. That she's been under my skin since I first saw her. But it's her choice how this news comes out.

So, I lie, again. "A few weeks. It's nothing serious."

He nods. "I probably shouldn't do the 'if you hurt her' speech."

He's sincere. I appreciate that she has friends who care deeply about her. "We had this conversation once already, remember?"

"That was when I thought you were throwing rocks for the sake of rock throwing," he says.

"Like I said then, she can take care of herself. And I don't think I'll be the one doing the hurting in this relationship."

He looks at me for a moment. He's known her a lot longer than I have. I'm not worried he knows now. It's clear he has his own secrets. "I'm sure she'll come around. She won't be receptive to Hamilton making advances at the wedding. You two will figure it out." He claps me on the shoulder before leaving me in the cabin.

I wish I had his confidence this will work out.

thirty-seven

CARINA

I SNEAK AWAY TO THE BATHROOM AT DINNER. IT'S NOT THAT I'M not loving the time I'm spending with Haley and Sienna, but I swear I'm about to burst and tell them about Orion. But we have strict rules for girls' trips—dropping big news on someone else's day is a big no-no.

This is Sienna's trip. I can't make it about me. This is the last time the three of us will be together while we're not married. Our relationships will change, even if we want to deny Sienna getting married changes anything.

I'm fixing up my makeup when my phone vibrates on the counter. I really shouldn't answer it, but I do.

"Hey, babe," I say, the pet name I've never used surprising me. I miss him, so I go with it.

"Hey, I didn't think you would pick up." He sounds tired. It's past nine. The rest of the guys must be off the boat. Even if they didn't leave early in the morning, Orion likely was up at dawn for a morning paddle. It's been a long day for him.

"Then why did you call?" I ask.

He lets out a long breath. "I'd get your voicemail. I wanted to hear your voice."

246

I smile and bite my lip. I can't acknowledge that's what I want to hear. It's too close to feelings. "How was the trip?"

"Interesting. I learned you have a date to the wedding who's not me," he muses.

"I absolutely do not. Who?" But I know the answer before he responds.

"Hamilton thinks he's getting you to himself." There's no jealousy in his voice. Instead, it's nonchalant. Like he knows Hamilton is wasting his time.

Which he is. "Ugh, thanks for the heads-up."

"Of course. He also wants to take you out on a superyacht he's chartering. Thinks you won't be able to turn down an invitation like that."

I laugh. "Why would I need a superyacht when you have the *Twisted Rigging*?"

He chuckles. "Good girl."

I clench my thighs together. I cannot be horny during girls' night.

"Are you still on the boat?" I imagine him on the bed, reaching into his shorts.

"Yeah. I had to change the sheets this morning. It doesn't smell like you anymore."

"Shame. If only you had a key to my place and could sneak into my bed while I'm gone." I could give him the garage code. I have his door code. We'll be back late tomorrow. If he's in my bed waiting for me, I'd speed for once in my life.

I want this so bad.

"It is a shame. But I think before I accept a key we'd have to tell people we're together."

My heart stops. I don't want to have this conversation now. Not while I'm in a fancy bathroom and my friends are wondering where I am. I don't know how to respond to that statement. The only thing I know for sure is I love having him to myself. I love the way our relationship is now. It's safe and I can protect it and

I'm not worried about the fallout. Us failing was an abstract concept before, but now I'll be devastated even if no one knows. The shame will only be a part of it. After the public humiliation with my company, I can't have anything else go wrong where people can see it.

"Orion…" I start, but there's a knock on the door. "Shit. I have to go." I hang up before he can say anything more. Fuck, I should explain to him.

I open the door and ignore the glare of the woman waiting. I send a text in the hallway since there's no way I can at the dinner table.

ME

Sorry, I was hogging the bathroom.

ORION

It's fine.

ME

We'll talk when I get home?

ORION

Sure. Night.

Fuck, I'll have to smooth this over somehow.

When I get to the table, both Sienna and Haley give me dirty looks in the most loving way possible. Our food arrived, and they were waiting for me to start eating.

"What took you so long?" Sienna asks, her fork digging into her maple BBQ kebab.

"Sorry, I…um." I shouldn't lie. There's no point. "Orion called."

"Oh?" Haley's voice lifts into a question.

"Hey, no guy talk allowed," Sienna corrects. "Wait, why'd he call?"

"To check in. You want to hear how the guys' sailing day

went?" If I can get them talking about the sailing trip, then I can talk about Orion a little longer. I don't have to feel bad for thinking about him.

"Let me guess—Beckett and Hamilton got super drunk." Sienna knows her fiancé well.

"Basically," I confirm. Orion didn't mention it, but I know those two. "Also, Hamilton is looking to get back with me."

"That's nice of Orion to give you a heads-up," Haley comments.

"Yeah, he's a good friend." It's true. None of this is a lie.

"Did Orion mention anything else?" Sienna asks, with a certain tone suggesting she thinks I'm holding back.

"No," I lie. "Plus, it's girls' night. No boys allowed!"

"Fine," Sienna says. "Is he going with them to the distillery?"

"He sounded tired, so I doubt it. But if you want someone to track Beckett, I'm sure Christian will," I say.

"No, I trust him. It's just..." She lets out a heavy sigh. "I'm excited about the wedding. I'm ready to be married to him. But I'm sad my solo days are over."

Haley and I nod. "It's a change, and a big one. Of course your feelings are complicated," I affirm.

"I know. It sucks that my program is one more year. He'll be in Boston as much as he can. It feels like even though I'm taking this big step, I'm waiting for my life to begin. I want everything I love to be in one place. I don't even get that yet."

Haley places her hand on top of Sienna's. "Enjoy the moments while you have them."

* * *

ORION SITS on his deck when I get home. It's sunset on Sunday night and I'm completely exhausted. The wedding is in three weeks and we have so much to do. But we're almost there.

All I want to do is crawl into Orion's arms.

I drop my bags in the front hallway of my house and leave out the door, locking it behind me.

I don't say anything as I approach him. I just settle onto his lap and rest my head on his chest.

He plants a kiss on my forehead. "Good trip?"

"Yeah. I feel like shit though," I mumble.

"Carina Webb, are you hungover?"

"Not so loud." I bury myself deeper into his chest. His steadiness calms my roiling stomach.

His fingers stroke my arm. "I'd love to see you drunk."

"You've missed your chance. It happens rarely. Now that I remember it feels this terrible, it won't happen again for a while."

"I'd take care of you. Make sure you drink water, hold your hair while you're throwing up."

"Don't mention throwing up." I don't need reminders of my morning over the toilet before rallying for brunch. And then the drive home where every pothole felt like I was going to be sick again in the bright sunlight.

"Let's get up. I have ginger tea. It'll settle your stomach."

I take his hand and let him guide me. I wonder if this will be the time he brings up telling everyone that we're together. If he does, I won't be able to shut it down. I'm weak and I'll do almost anything for him right now.

My ability to pretend I'm not in love with him is fading fast.

* * *

ORION and I sit at a booth in the locals' section of Paradise. The bar is quiet ahead of tonight's Halloween party. Sienna arrives tomorrow for the wedding, and I've been getting as much done beforehand as possible. The last two weeks have been hectic. I've wanted to scream at Beckett so much. Every time I ask him for something, he's taking hours to respond. Or tells me his opinion doesn't matter when Sienna specifically said it did. I don't know how Haley has tolerated him for so long.

Orion has been incredibly patient through everything. He's made me dinner more nights than I should admit, considering he's working long hours on the boats. I asked him once if he was doing it so I don't jet off on a superyacht with my ex. He kissed me and told me he's not worried.

The fabric scandal died down, like Orion said it would. Sales have slowed, but not by as much as we feared. People moved on. My life may revolve around Nebula Athletics, but very few others feel the same way.

He doesn't mention telling anyone about us sleeping together. I think he understands where I'm coming from. But part of me believes he's biding his time. He looks at me with hunger and lust. I won't let myself hope for anything more. He's waiting to get through the wedding where he'll meet one of Sienna's hot cousins, or a rich friend of Beckett's. He'll be done with me. I'm a networking opportunity who gives him orgasms.

Now, we're waiting for Haley to meet me. We have a last-minute planning session. The only reason I'm with Orion is because he's meeting Alex. And since the two of them are running an errand together, it makes sense for us to wait with each other.

It has nothing to do with the fact we were having sex thirty minutes ago.

Across from me, Orion looks as tired as I feel. He doesn't hide from the world, while I've concealed the bags under my eyes, exfoliated my skin until it shines, and glossed my hair into oblivion.

I want to wrap my body around his and never let go.

"What?" he asks, taking a sip of his rum.

"Nothing," I say.

I wish I had taken more precautions against him. I've let him get too close. But a part of me knows I had no input in this—he came into my life and it wouldn't have mattered what I did. He's a force of nature. I have no protection against him.

But for a moment, I want to stay in this joy with him.

They enter the bar in a flash of light and panic. Orion and I don't have time to react. Haley and Alex's demeanors are enough to let us know something serious has happened.

Haley sits down next to me and takes a long swallow from my cocktail. Alex follows, stopping at the bar to grab four glasses and a bottle of Wendell Beach Rum—a bottle of the unaged one that usually only goes in cocktails. He cracks the seal and pours us each a drink. His hands shake but his years of bartending show and he doesn't spill a drop. He won't look any of us in the eye, but instead focuses on the table, the glasses, and the alcohol.

"What's—" I start.

Alex pushes a glass in front of me. "Nope, drink first."

I take a sip and it burns unpleasantly the whole way down. There's a reason this one usually isn't drunk straight. He and Haley down theirs in one. Orion gives me a look, but I'm as lost as he is.

Do you know anything? his eyes ask.

No, I answer without words or shaking my head.

Alex refills everyone's glasses, not caring that Orion and I have a full pour.

"We picked up the programs from the printer since someone insisted we use a union print shop instead of some online retailer," Alex says through gritted teeth.

"The source of our errand is not the issue, Alex," Haley interrupts.

I was the one who insisted on a union print shop.

"Anyway, we go to drop them at Alex's place," she continues, "and...ew. You have to say it."

Alex takes another drink from his glass. "Beckett and Kim were in my bed."

I'm glad I'm not taking a drink at the moment because I

would have spat my rum in Orion's face. Truth be told, I'd nearly forgotten about Kim. Alex hardly ever brings her around. I only remembered they were dating when I looked over the guest list.

This is the worst possible scenario for Sienna. She will be devastated. There are a million terrible ways to end a relationship, but cheating is the one Sienna would never be able to forgive.

"I didn't know you and Kim were living together." I'm reeling on the inside, but I have to stay collected on the outside. Everyone else is allowed to panic, but I can't.

Alex pours more rum. His hands are steady now. "We're not. But she has a key. She either doesn't care if I found out or was so sure I wouldn't."

"Fuck, man. I'm sorry," Orion says, taking a sip of his rum. He tries to catch my eye, but I can't tell what he's thinking.

"Does Sienna know?" I ask.

"I told Beckett he has one hour, or I'll call her." Haley looks sick at being the messenger.

"She'll be devastated," I say. Sienna was so ready to be married. But there is no possibility we wouldn't tell her. We won't keep this secret from her. None of us will protect Beckett.

"Any chance she won't call off the wedding?" Orion asks.

"No," Haley and I shout at the same time.

"Cheating's a hard limit for her. Her father had an affair. Beckett would've known," I finish. Affair is too simple a word for what he did. He had an entire second family that Sienna found out about in high school. I didn't meet her until after, but I remember the pain in her voice when she got drunk one night and told us what happened. I can't believe anyone who loves her could ever hurt her like that.

I thought Beckett loved Sienna. For all his flaws, I thought when the time came, he would put her first. Now he never will.

I look at Orion.

"Even if the wedding somehow does happen," Alex continues,

"I sure as hell won't be the best man." He's slowed his drinking at this point.

"Hamilton won't have an issue taking your place," I say.

Orion looks disgusted, like he doesn't want to imagine Hamilton as the best man. I don't blame him.

"Did he ever…?" Orion asks me. I know the question he's asking.

I shake my head. I don't think Hamilton cheated on me. But I have no way of knowing for sure. I don't feel anything at the thought he might have. He's so completely in my past.

I pull my phone out and notice several missed calls from Beckett and Hamilton. Both texted, asking me to call them back. Hamilton left me a voicemail begging me to help them make sure Sienna doesn't call off the wedding. I toss my phone on the table to show Orion the transcript of the message.

He scoffs. "Why would they think you would help? No cheating is the number one rule of relationships."

I shrug. "I don't know. Maybe they hope to appeal to my business sense. They've already spent so much money on the wedding."

"Beckett's parents paid for everything," Alex says. "And they're the example of happily married and faithful. They won't like this."

Bristol comes over and fills our glasses with water. We go silent. None of us make eye contact. The news will get around, but we're not ready to share before Sienna knows.

The front door opens and our heads swing toward it. I didn't realize I'm afraid Beckett will follow Alex and Haley here. It's the one place on the island they would seek sanctuary. We clearly share the thought. It's Christian who enters and we collectively breathe a sigh of relief.

But Beckett storms in after.

"Alex, we need to talk," he pleads.

"I don't have anything left to say to you," Alex says, his voice firm.

"It was a mistake." Beckett comes closer, his hair messed up and his collar askew.

"Doesn't change anything." Alex rises from the table.

Orion stands behind him, his fists clenched, ready for a physical confrontation. Christian forms a wall next to Orion and the two of them make eye contact and nod.

I tune out the voices. When did they become such good friends?

I want Orion all to myself.

It's good for him to have connections to other people. It will help when we fall apart. But I don't want to lose Christian as a friend.

"You're a fucking two-faced bastard and don't deserve Sienna," Alex says calmly.

Beckett takes a swing at Alex. He dodges. Christian grabs Beckett around the torso.

"You're still pissed I got to her first!" Beckett struggles, but Christian overpowers him.

"Fuck off, Beckett," Alex shouts.

Beckett knocks over a few chairs as Christian drags him out of the bar.

Haley's phone lights up with Sienna's name. She picks it up, and I move to follow her. But she waves me off before heading down the employees-only hallway.

"You okay?" I ask Christian when he returns.

"Yeah. He tried to elbow me in the ribs, but varsity wrestling prepared me for this moment," he says dryly. He pulls my chair out so I can sit and eyes the bottle on the table.

Bristol comes by, fussing over her brother. "What just happened?"

Alex is behind the bar, on the phone. Luckily, the chaos was contained in the locals' section so the rest of the restaurant didn't notice.

"I think we need food first," I say.

Bristol shakes her head but pulls out her notepad to take our orders. My stomach rolls from the alcohol and the indignity of it all.

It isn't long before Haley joins us, her eyes red from crying. We give her a minute and use the time to fill in Bristol and Christian.

"She's calling off the wedding. But she's still flying in tomorrow. Since she already has the time off scheduled." Her voice is raw. It's clear she's not done crying.

"Good," I offer. "Time off is important." Orion gives me a look because he knows how long it's been since I took a vacation purely for pleasure.

"She's furious. Beckett needs to join witness protection. He's not safe from her on the island," Haley says. "She wants us to help her call around and cancel everything."

I nod. "Of course."

We spend the rest of the meal making lists of the work we've done and now need to undo. This feels so public. We wonder if we should have seen the signs sooner. They've been together for years. I see Beckett on a weekly basis. Shouldn't I have known?

"We should do the sleepover you wanted," Haley says to me. "We'll invite Bristol and Autumn. Have a 'bash exes' night."

Christian gives us a look. "Autumn doesn't have any exes."

"Not even high school?" I ask. They started dating in college but there had to be someone else.

"Nothing serious."

"Whatever. She can still join us," Haley says.

"Yeah, of course." I open another list on my phone. "I'll make sure I have plenty of rosé for everyone."

"Don't worry, we'll have the parallel night at my place," Orion tells Christian and Alex. "My speakers are louder so we can overwhelm whatever noise they make."

It's a taunt. So, I know where I stand. It's with him.

"Barely," I say without looking up.

We walk home together on the beach. The back of my hand brushes his, but he doesn't reach to take it, just lets it rest against mine. We've never held hands in public and won't start now. But I love the touch of him. I love the calm when it's the two of us. When he's mine and I don't have to share him or us with the world.

I want to stay exactly like this. But I can't.

thirty-eight

ORION

WE GET TO CARINA'S HOUSE AND STAND FROZEN IN HER KITCHEN. That scene was such a disaster. We need a few moments to decompress before we can process it.

She looks at me, her expression carefully neutral. "Wine?"

"Sure," I say. I don't drink wine often, but I won't make her go out of her way now.

She pulls a bottle of white from the fridge and pours two glasses. I avoided drinking the rum Alex dispensed freely. I'm sober and in control, even as I feel the world spinning out around me.

"You okay?" I ask. She stares off into space. The window over the sink has a perfect beach view. The water is still. I won't catch a breeze tonight. There is no escape for me.

"Yeah, why?" she says.

I've gotten so used to reading her face, I'm concerned that now I can't. "You've known them a long time. You clearly thought Beckett was good enough for Sienna. It's a shock to me, and I just met them." I only met Sienna over the one weekend, but I like her. I don't want to see her hurt, especially when she means so much to Carina.

"Right, yeah." Carina shifts on her feet. "I mean, I always thought Beckett could try harder, but I thought he loved her."

"Apparently, love isn't enough," I say. It's not something I particularly believe in, but maybe it's what Carina needs to hear in the moment.

She looks at me like she doesn't understand what I'm saying, but she brushes it off. "At least she found out now and not after the wedding," she muses.

"Small silver lining," I agree.

"Anyway. Now that the wedding is off, we don't have to worry about telling anyone we're hooking up," she says. She turns back to the horizon.

"We'll have to tell them eventually." I'm tired of this game with her. I know how I feel about this relationship. And I have no problem letting everyone know. I got it when we were sneaking around, trying to figure out if there was something between us. Now we both know we have something special. Something to fight for.

It's more than hooking up. It's more than a fling.

"Why? It doesn't matter," she says to the window, her shoulder rising and falling in her denial.

It feels like a gut punch. "It matters to me. Do you want to keep this a secret forever?"

She finally turns to me. "Forever?"

I mean forever with her. "Maybe, yeah, Carina. I'm in this relationship. It's not a dirty secret or a fling. It's real. What am I to you?"

"You can't mean that." Her head tilts to the side in total disbelief. As if it clearly never occurred to her that she matters to me.

"Yes, I do."

"Oh come on, Orion. You're only with me because I'm here and you're there and you convinced me to sleep with you," she says.

My blood boils. She's being destructive, and I don't know how to stop it. She knows she's started this—I didn't convince her of anything; this has been on her terms. I would throw myself on fire for her. And I don't know how she doesn't see that. I haven't said more because I'm afraid of scaring her off, but I've been as clear as I can be with her.

"No, Carina. I'm sleeping with you because I want to be with you." I step toward her. The space of the kitchen feels much smaller than it is. I want to brace my hands on either side of her. Feel her heat rolling off her body. But I can't trap her in right now. She needs to choose this. To choose us.

"Fine, okay, you want to be with me. But it won't last. You'll change your mind."

"I won't."

"You always have before."

I take a few deep breaths. I won't get angry or yell because that won't help either of us. "I've changed. I feel differently about you than I have about anyone else. I'm not going to change my mind about us. We have something good here. Something beautiful. I won't let you destroy it because you're afraid."

"How the fuck am I supposed to know any of that? You've never said anything. And half of what you say to me is a lie anyway."

A chill runs through my entire body. She can make this argument if she really wants to. We've both been exaggerating annoyances and inventing grievances for months.

She could be doing that now. Maybe this is a game. Maybe she's pushing me to see how far I'll go. I search her face for some hint she's about to burst out laughing. *Gotcha, Orion! Let's go take a shower. I need to get Beckett's sleaze off me.* But she's still and serious, like she's never messed around in her entire life.

I know how this ends. I don't know how to make it stop.

I down my glass of wine before I speak again. "Carina, I should have told you how I feel about you before, but I was so scared you'd run if things got intense. If you knew how serious I am. You said you only do flings. I didn't know you wanted more. But I care about you. I want to be with you. For as long as I can. You know I'm telling the truth about this. This isn't a game to me, Carina."

She shakes her head. "You've been playing games with me from the start. From having a drink on your boat. To complaining about my hedges. To who can fucking orgasm first. This is a game to you, and sooner or later you'll get bored and sail away. I won't be left standing on a beach with nothing but wasted time."

Her face is set. She doesn't move away from me, even though I've stepped closer. She's holding her ground. Firm and planted. She doesn't fidget. She doesn't look away. She knows exactly what she's doing, and she won't back down.

"You were with me every step of the way. You were in on every game. You know when I'm telling the truth and when I'm lying for the sake of an argument. Don't do this, Carina." I repeat her name like I'm a hostage negotiator. "I've told you a million times I'm here to stay. Wendell Beach is my home. I'm not leaving at the end of winter or on a whim."

She told me I came into her life like a storm. That I'm the one who upended everything. I don't know how she doesn't realize she has always been in control. She is my home. And if I lose her, I'll be adrift.

"I'm not doing anything. I'm staying on this island. You're the one who's leaving." She moves, shifting away from me, like she's done with this conversation and she's ready to go about her day without me in it.

I want to reach for her and touch her. But I'm back to the beginning with her—I want her but I can't get near her.

"You are everything I want." I should tell her how I feel. Get it out there and then she won't doubt me. Won't doubt the connection we have. "I love you."

She looks at me. The full force of her gray eyes on me. Her

face is passive. This is the cold woman Beckett and Hamilton know. "Don't bait me, Orion. It won't work anymore."

I've never doubted my feelings for Carina. I've always known she was different from past relationships. But now I have irrefutable proof. The end has never hurt like this. I'm blown back and blown away and blown apart. There is no win for me in this argument. Not when her level of trust is so low. She feels something. I'm not wrong about that. But I was right to be afraid of being honest with her. "I don't know who's hurt you before, but you don't have to do this, Carina. You don't have to throw us away."

"There isn't anything to throw away. It's a fling. Never meant to last. No feelings involved."

"I just fucking—" No feelings involved, my ass. I'm cut loose from my tether, adrift to the winds and the tide. She's scared. Scared of everyone's reactions and that I'll hurt her. I've known that from the beginning. I've always known it would be worth it to jump with her. And we could get through this if she let her guard down a little bit more. She's so close but she's ebbing instead of surging forward. But I can't argue. I can't bait. I can't devil's advocate my way out of this. I can't make a wall move. "Fine. If that's what you really think is happening here, I'll leave. But don't expect me to come back to you. This is on you."

I want to kiss her one last time, because she'll never admit she's wrong. I want to prove to her this is real. That what we have is lasting.

But I don't get the chance, because she's looking at me like she doesn't care at all.

thirty-nine

CARINA

I THOUGHT MY WORLD WOULD END WITH THE FABRICS SCANDAL. But then I saw how it is possible for wounded things to carry on. Nebula Athletics has a future. There is so much more for me to do and grow with it.

Orion and I have no future. It was always going to end. I needed to do it on my terms.

I knew exactly what I was doing yesterday. I saw what happened with Sienna and Beckett. Time was also running out for Orion and me. So, I took the things most sacred to us and lit them on fire. There is no saving us.

I burned it down. The taunting that made me feel seen. The jokes that made me safe. The sex that was the best of my life.

It's gone.

He saw right through me even at my worst. But even he can't right this ship.

I believe he thinks he loves me, but I can't wait for him to figure out what that means to him. For him to realize we're the same as every other relationship he's had—that sometimes love isn't enough.

It's over, and I question if I did the right thing. I could have held on longer. Nothing could hurt worse than this. Holding on longer would have given me more time with him. I'd be left with the pain, but I could have had more joy.

At least now no one knows. And no one will. The next few days are about Sienna and her breakup.

What kind of friend would I be if I brought up my own?

* * *

I FEEL HOLLOW when I pick up Sienna from the airport in Sarasota. Haley and I didn't know what to expect—if she'd be sad or mad—but she hugs us both tight at baggage claim. I can't remember her ever hugging me before. At least not since college. Her long brown hair is disheveled and there are heavy bags under her eyes.

"That fucking bastard," she spits.

"I know," I say. "Fuck him."

On the car ride back, she lists the signs she should've seen and every excuse she believed. "I didn't think marriage would change him, you know? But I thought we were on the same page. And he fucking knows how much I hate my dad for what he did to my mom."

Haley and I agree and nod and add in "fuck him" when appropriate. We never thought there was anything ever fundamentally wrong with their relationship, but we did want more for her, someone who would give her the attention she deserves. But this isn't the time to tell her.

We spend the afternoon sorting through the vendors, canceling. We explain the situation, but most deposits are nonrefundable. I run errands, which is a mistake. I don't want time alone in the car. I play a podcast to distract me.

I was reeling yesterday. The chaos at Paradise had been my worst fears come to life. I replayed my parents' divorce in my head. The whispers I heard from my friends' parents when they thought I couldn't hear. Every time I doubt what I did, I remember why.

It was always better to fail in private than in public.

I don't hold any of this against Sienna. She's blameless in this. No one thinks it's her fault Beckett strayed. Orion isn't malicious the way we've learned Beckett is. But I would be held to a higher standard than Sienna. It would be my fault when he left.

I had to get out of the relationship before he left me. It was always ending, and I needed to do it on my terms. Before anyone found out about us. I thought I could save myself the public humiliation and the private pain.

But the private pain lingers.

No, it's better this way. His love will burn out and fade. I desperately wanted to backtrack when he said it. I wanted to throw caution to the wind and leap into his arms. But it was too late. Love has never been anything but temporary.

And I've fallen in love with him. I fight back tears every time I accidentally let the thought cross my mind. I will hold on to this forever.

I thought about saying it when we were at the table at Paradise yesterday, the two of us. It wasn't the post-sex haze. I reach for him every morning even when he's not there. I worry about him when he's out on the boat. I can't imagine a day without seeing him smile.

I have to tell myself this pain is temporary, even if I don't believe it yet.

I pick up Sienna's wedding dress on the mainland and explain the situation. They offer their condolences and provide a list of places to sell the dress. I think Sienna wants to throw red paint on it. But I'll make her wait before she pulls out the art supplies.

When I get home, I'm surprised to find Beckett's parents, Lisa and Mitchell, in my living room.

I step back to give them privacy, but Sienna stops me. "Wait, don't go. We're finishing up." All their eyes are red.

Lisa smiles at me. "It's so good to see you, Carina. Even under these circumstances." She pauses for a moment. "We were waiting for you to get back. I met your neighbor, Orion. We stopped at Paradise for lunch and Alex introduced us. He mentioned you made some branded shirts for him. We're interested in a similar arrangement. Something nice that says Coastline Beach House. People still ask about your classes. I can't believe I never thought of this before."

I smile, not wanting to cry at the mention of Orion and how he's helping me even after our breakup. "Of course. I'll send a proposal your way this week."

"Take your time," Mitchell says. "We want you to take care of Sienna first. We're not going anywhere."

Lisa gives me a conspiratorial look. "We promise you won't have to deal with our son."

Sienna sees them out. When she returns, she collapses on the couch. "They think he's is a disgrace to the world. They'll pay for everything nonrefundable," she explains.

"That certainly takes some stress off," I say, fixing the throw pillows. I can't imagine her grief. Not only losing the future she thought she had, but to find out it was a lie…

I don't blame her for being angry.

"They're also paying for the honeymoon and will transfer his ticket to someone else."

"Wait, really? That's incredibly generous."

"They made some suggestion that Beckett will be the one paying. Which I guess they can do since he works for them."

"Who are you taking?" I ask.

"You and Haley can flip a coin," she says.

I gape. It didn't occur to me she'd take me. Not that we're not best friends, but I don't deserve a free trip to the Maldives. Haley absolutely does. She helped Sienna pick the resort. She chattered on for days about how good the food is there, wanting Sienna to take pictures of everything and to steal recipes from the staff.

"Take Haley. She basically planned your wedding. She deserves it," I say. Orion will think I'm being a martyr about this, but this is fair to me.

"She did have to see Beckett's penis." She's thoughtful as she says it.

"See, something to bond over."

She's able to laugh and that assures me she will be okay.

* * *

THAT EVENING, Bristol arrives with Autumn. Haley spent the afternoon in the kitchen making our favorite breakup snacks. The rosé might have been opened early.

No rum or cocktails today.

I took the longest shower of my life, thinking I could get all my tears out of my system and they wouldn't plague me any longer.

It didn't work, but I smile as I play hostess.

"I feel a little weird intruding on this," Autumn says. "Since you're all single and I'm not."

"It's fine," Sienna says. "Christian is one in a million and we don't hold other men to his standard."

"Maybe we should." Bristol pours us each a large glass of wine. "What? I know my brother is a great husband."

We turn to Autumn. "He is. He is my best friend. I know he's more your friend than I am, and I'm not around you often. He and I have different lives. It's totally fine."

We feel tension in the room. Something is going on in her marriage that she doesn't want to talk about.

I can't help but wonder if, for a brief period of time, Orion was my best friend. The person I shared my secrets with and spent all my time with.

"Okay, I'm declaring girls' night rules," Sienna says. "No talking about men!"

"Men, or exes?" I ask. "Because you do have exes who are women."

"Men. The patriarchy is the problem, not the dating."

We blast Ashley Ferris and sing our hearts out to every one of her breakup songs.

"No one writes about love the ways she does," Autumn says, the superfan in the room.

I only hide in the bathroom once to get myself together. I want to explode and tell them everything about Orion. But I can't, even though every word, every chorus feels like a knife.

I bundle everything up and push it down.

forty

ORION

WHEN I OFFERED TO HOST A GUYS' NIGHT, I DIDN'T THINK I'D BE nursing my own heartache. I ordered pizza, since none of us felt like cooking. Alex is quiet about his feelings. I don't think he was serious about Kim. He only brought her around on a few occasions. Beckett is another question. There were days I wondered if they got along. But they had to—they'd been friends their entire lives.

Christian doesn't offer much, even when asked about the secrets to a happy marriage. He gives an answer I'm sure is rehearsed about friendship and trust and honesty.

"The thing about Beckett is…" Alex starts after a few drinks.

Christian, Alex, and I sit on my pool deck with the sun setting over the water behind us. If nothing else, at least I'll always drink well with these two. But the rum I should enjoy—and always have in the past—tastes wrong on my tongue.

They also don't question my piss-poor mood. We're not trying to make Alex feel better. We're letting him sit with whatever he needs to.

"We were only friends because our parents wanted it," he says. "There are two institutions on this island: Paradise and Coastline.

No offense to Wendell Beach Rum Works. It was expected our two families did everything together."

"Things are changing," Christian says. "The distillery is expanding. Carina is a force to be reckoned with. No one in town will respect Beckett after this. The resort will be fine, but he won't be the face of it."

I don't want to think about Carina. I've run through our conversation a thousand times in the last twenty-four hours. I don't know what I could have done differently. She had her eyes set on what she wanted and there was nothing I could do about it.

She didn't believe half of what she was saying. But I don't know how to convince her I know my mind enough to stay.

She didn't even react when I said I loved her. So I don't know how to fix this.

I did get to meet the Foleys out of this. They are the nicest people I've ever met—how they produced Beckett, I'll never know. They offered me an exclusive contract for the resort. We're creating a shuttle service. It's everything I've ever wanted.

"Does it always have to be Ashley fucking Ferris?" Christian groans as he slides down in his chair.

We can hear the music from next door. I don't know if she's baiting me. I wish she cared enough to bait me.

"She's a great singer and she's fucking hot. You don't like her because Autumn and Bristol are mad about the tickets," Alex says.

"Her music is fine. I just don't care about her love life. Every time I turn on the TV it's some new story. It's everywhere," Christian says with more emotion than I expect. He catches himself and adds calmly, "The ticket thing worked out."

"How?" Alex asks.

"I bought four tickets to her show in New York. I'm paying for Autumn and Bristol to take two friends for a weekend trip."

"But you're not going?" I clarify.

"No. The days don't work for me. I'm committed to a distilling conference with a friend."

I'm white-knuckling my way through the night. I hate the silence and I hate the secrets. I want to be able to express my frustration at the way she ended things. But instead, she's forcing me to keep quiet.

Carina gets a cathartic moment with her friends singing loudly and probably beautifully. I'm so fucking grateful she has that outlet, but she won't tell them she's hurting. Especially if she won't admit it to herself.

That's one thing we will share—the secret of our relationship. We'll both take it to our graves. But we don't have to.

I'd be more angry with her if I wasn't so sad for her.

I came to Wendell Beach wanting community and friendship and a place to call home. It was always a risk that hooking up with her would backfire and I would lose everything. But I didn't think it would be like this. That I would be here with the two friends I've made and still be cut off from them.

All because of her.

I should regret her. But I can't. Not yet anyway. Not when I'm still so full of love for her.

I send them home in a cab and collapse into a deck chair staring out at the restless water. The lights are out at her place, but I can still see the outline of her pool and feel all the edges she shared with me.

There isn't anything to throw away. It's a fling. Never meant to last. No feelings involved.

I can't go inside where my bed is empty and cold, and I would have never cared about that before. I should just walk to the marina and sit on the bow of the *Twisted Rigging*. The boat has never let me down before.

But that feels like running. I'm not running away from her or from this.

forty-one

CARINA

I CAN ALWAYS COUNT ON PARADISE TO BE A LITTLE EMPTY ON Sunday afternoons. I need to get out of my house because I want to stay in bed. But I will not let Orion take anything more from me. He doesn't get to change my life.

Sienna and Haley went to Sienna's mom's house. I bowed out, citing work. Which wasn't a lie. But I also didn't want to be around them.

I want to crumble.

I sit at the bar instead of a table. Bristol takes my usual order, and I hope she'll engage and distract me. She's about to make my cocktail when Alex walks behind the bar.

"Bristol, can you grab more limes for juicing?" he asks.

"Sure. You got Carina's order? Hemingway daiquiri." She walks away before he answers.

He takes one look at me and tilts his head. "You're the reason why Orion was a surly bastard last night."

My eye twitches. I didn't think he'd go around talking about us now. "If he was mad at me, he would speak up. He doesn't keep his thoughts to himself."

Alex grabs a cocktail shaker and mutters something. He's too fast and practiced for me to follow what liquids he's using. When he sets it in front of me, it's not the daiquiri I ordered. It's a dusty rose and has a lime wedge and a raspberry on the rim.

"What's this?" I ask.

"It's called My Pride. It's on the secret menu. It's time you swallow it."

"There's nothing between Orion and me," I grit out. I should have known Alex is like me. He doesn't give a lot away, but inside he's constantly churning.

"Normally, I would think Orion fucked up. But I know him and how he feels about you. He's never said anything. You tried to keep it under wraps, but that man would crawl over broken glass for you. He didn't fuck this up."

I want to deny it with my very soul. Orion doesn't get to force weakness out of me. But Alex is right. Orion didn't do anything wrong.

I take a sip of the drink and I know it's one of Orion's favorites. I've tasted it on his lips.

I won't let Alex force a confession out of me...but would it be so bad if he did? We've been friends for ages. I can admit to myself I'm miserable. Trying to fake it isn't helping anything. Why does it have to be so hard to admit it to a friend? Other people let things off their chest. I've been listening to Sienna cry for days, and she feels better for it. And for whatever manipulations and meddling Alex has done, he's never let me down.

Bristol appears again before I let everything out, and I plaster on a fake smile for her benefit. Alex walks away again, shaking his head at me.

* * *

I've been dreading this call. My father insists on check-ins every Tuesday to ensure damage control has been effective. I should appreciate knowing his criticism of me will be scheduled instead of spontaneous. But I feel raw. I'm not hiding anything the way I want to.

I checked the sign-up roster prior to attending class this morning. I don't want to be in the same room as Orion. I can lead myself through practice, but I want to turn my brain off and have someone else tell me what to do.

He wasn't there and I'm annoyed at myself for wishing he was. He said he wouldn't reach for me, but I'm so selfish I want him to.

I haven't seen him go out on the water. I thought he'd be out there every chance he got now that I'm not taking up time in his life. But my texts have been silent.

I was angry in class, and while I might have appeared calm on the surface, I was raging on the inside. I couldn't keep my mind centered. I pushed myself harder than I needed. If I'm not dating, then I need to focus my attention on my business and my yoga practice. I have goals—I should be pushing toward them with every second I have.

At the end of the practice, I should have been loose, but I held tension everywhere in my body. The instructor guided us to half-split pose, and offered up the modification that anyone who had a splits practice could move into that expression.

I've been able to do the splits for a long time. It's the way my body works with how my hips are formed and the way my tendons connect everything. My hips touch the ground and I lean forward over my front leg, searching for any type of sensation. I want my body to hurt so I can drown out the pain in my heart and in my head. I know better, but I move deeper than I should. The rules I give my students don't apply to me.

After class, I wince. I stretched too far and now I feel a dull ache at the top of my right hamstring.

I shower in one of the studio's changing rooms. Normally, I go home to refresh. But I'm avoiding my house. I knew this would happen with Orion. But I don't get credit for being right.

I'm in my office, finishing up my makeup, when I hear Mackenzie.

"Mr. Kane, so good to see you. I didn't know you were coming in today."

I freeze. There's no fucking way Hamilton is here.

"I'm in town for the wedding. I have a call scheduled with Carina. We might as well do it in person."

His voice and arrogance are unmistakable. And of course, he thinks the wedding is still happening.

"Oh, that's great..." Mackenzie starts as I step out of my office.

"Hamilton, come in," I say in my most pleasant voice. Orion would be so disappointed in me. At least I didn't call him Mr. Kane.

My ex smiles at me. We haven't been in the same room together in at least a year. Work communications were long ago relegated to video conferences and the phone. I understand he's an attractive man in his dark tailored suit and his perfectly styled hair. None of it matters to me.

It's so out of place in Florida.

"Carina, good to see you."

He steps into my office and I close the door behind him. I gesture for him to sit. My stomach clenches as I remember Orion sitting in the same chair after the fabrics news broke.

Orion brought me dinner. Hamilton could at least bring me coffee if he is angling for something with me. I have to assume that's part of the reason he's here in person.

He doesn't sit, but instead reaches for my waist.

I jerk away. "Don't touch me."

"I'm saying hello. No need to be jumpy."

"Do you touch your male CEOs like that?" I ask, sitting down in my chair.

He chuckles but sits across from me. "I haven't dated any of the other CEOs I work with. Don't pretend your relationship with the Webb Group is standard. You know you get special treatment."

I grind my teeth. I understand the implication—my business wouldn't get funded if my dad wasn't in charge. It's a pet project. A favor. "What are you doing in town anyway? The wedding is canceled."

"We'll see."

"I spent my entire Saturday canceling the vendors. The only way Sienna and Beckett get married is if they go to the courthouse. And I will absolutely stand up and object."

His eyes narrow on me. I dated this man for years. I know him inside and out. He has a terrible poker face.

"You wouldn't." He says it with absolute certainty. Like *he* knows *me* inside and out.

But he doesn't. It's only Orion who knows me.

Growing up, any time I shared my fears or worries with my parents, they brushed them off. I learned young that it was far easier to keep it bottled up. All those habits led me here. In this room with Hamilton. A man I could have easily married to please my father and because I thought he was good enough.

Things could be different. I could open up a little more. The ship has sailed with Orion, I can begin to accept that. But maybe I should have had Alex sit with me yesterday and let everything out. He's navigating his own heartache. Maybe we could have become better friends.

I'm not letting my dad, or my mom, or fucking Hamilton dictate my future any longer.

"Whatever. I only want to talk about business with you today. Let's get my dad on the line." I open the video conference app on my computer.

"Jeffrey won't make it today," Hamilton explains. "He's removing himself from your account. He wants me to take over. He thinks we're a better fit as partners moving forward."

My father had very little time for me growing up, so it's not a surprise to me that he's bored with the time he has for me now. I clench my teeth. My stomach queasiness turns to fire. I wish I was hurt. But I'm angry. I've used up all my hurt.

"Right." I pull up the latest numbers on my screen, turning the monitor so he can see. "We're doing fine. Customer surveys indicate they're satisfied with the handling of the scandal. Most will buy from us in the future. A few indicate they appreciate the additional steps we've taken to educate the public on how clothing manufacturing works."

"This looks good, but we need to revisit the change in marketing direction. We've discussed this on the phone. There are untapped avenues you can exploit."

"What makes you think I'm ever trying to exploit something?" I ask.

"Carina, you're being unnecessarily hostile today."

"Oh fuck you, Hamilton." I don't think I've ever sworn in front of him. He wanted a pretty princess who designed her cute little yoga clothes and never made a fuss. I'm not that, and I won't pretend anymore. "You don't understand what I'm trying to do with Nebula Athletics. You never have. I don't want you on my account if you are ignoring my vision."

He sucks in a deep breath. "Jeffrey won't like this."

"Then he can take it up with me." I don't think my dad will cut my funding. But even if he does, we've been profitable for years. I don't need him the way I used to. I can make it work. I won't compromise on my values anymore. I won't bend myself backward to get him to notice me. I stand. "Any additional discussion can be completed over email."

"Carina, come on," he protests.

"That's your argument?" I step around the desk to open the door, but Hamilton grabs my elbow. "Don't touch me!" I can't stand him on my skin.

I spent years with him, thinking I would end up marrying him because I wouldn't find anyone better, or because I had already given him so much of my time and I didn't want to start over. But I'm done. I miss Orion, but even if I made a mistake, it's not worth it to go back to this man who doesn't see me.

Hamilton puts his hands up in defense, like I'm the one who's done something inappropriate. "We can reschedule when you've calmed down. I'm here all week. You don't have much planned, aside from anything with the wedding."

I shake my head. I'm done engaging with him. I'll accept the consequences, but I'm not letting him—or my father—make decisions for me or my business anymore.

ORION

I SEE HER WALKING HOME FROM THE GROCERY STORE ON Wednesday. Her groceries are in the same oversized tote on one shoulder. It's hot as hell out even though it's November. Her usual perky ponytail is drooping and her skin is covered in a sheen of sweat.

I roll down my passenger-side window. "Carina, let me give you a ride."

"No!" She doesn't even look at me.

"Seriously, we're going to the same place. It's not a waste of gas."

"That's a slippery slope," she says in a mocking tone.

That's when I notice it. Her limp. She's favoring her right leg and it's not the bag. The grimace I thought was annoyance at me is really pain. "Why are you limping?"

"I'm not limping."

She's definitely limping. "No strings attached. Let me drive you home."

She doesn't answer. She keeps walking.

"Fucking hell." I drive the remaining two blocks and park in my garage. I wait in front of hers.

No matter which door she goes through, she has to climb stairs. I don't want her to lift her groceries and hurt herself any more than she has. I'm right here. I can help her.

She greets me with a glare.

"Give me the bag," I say.

She doesn't fight me when I reach for the strap. "What are you doing?" she asks.

"What does it look like? I'm helping my hurt neighbor with her groceries. Isn't that a normal thing for friends to do?" I'll prove to her we can be friends, even if the breakup didn't need to happen in the first place. She might have always thought I would leave if things ended, but I'm not going anywhere.

I shouldn't wish to convince her I'm staying. I don't know if she'll ever accept it.

"I don't need your fucking help."

Once in the kitchen, I set the bag on her counter and lean against the sink. Here, I'm out of her way but I can watch her move. "What happened to your leg?" I ask.

"None of your business." She methodically unpacks her food. It's obvious every step is painful.

"Maybe not, but you took care of me when I was hurt. Do you really think I'd be able to see you in pain and ignore it?"

She braces her hands on the counter. "It's a high hamstring strain. It's a common yoga injury."

"Okay, should you see a doctor? I can drive you."

"No, I just need to rest it," she says.

"Then why did you walk to the grocery store?" She has a perfectly functioning hybrid. She doesn't need to be this stubborn.

"I didn't ask for your opinion, Orion." Her voice changes. It's perfectly pleasant. As if my presence means nothing to her and whatever we had before meant nothing.

I should let it go, walk away now and preserve whatever friendship or neighborliness I can. But I don't. Because she hurt me. She refuses to see what's directly in front of her, and I'm done giving her the benefit of the doubt. She's afraid. I need her brave.

I need closure.

"No, you're right. You never did ask for my opinion. But I've always given it. So, listen to me now." She may take emotion out of her voice, but I let her hear my anger and my pain. "I'm sorry I ever made you feel like you weren't enough reason for me to stay. I'm sorry I've been downplaying my feelings for weeks. I thought you knew. Or knew enough. I'm staying anyway, but I would stay for you alone."

"I didn't ask for any of this, Orion," she says. "You can't blame me for your feelings because I didn't start this. You're the one who blew into my life like a hurricane. I didn't ask you to move next door. Or to kiss me on your boat. You were always there. And I didn't choose any of this. I was fine before you. I'll be fine after you."

I lean back again, the wall catching me so I don't fall. I'm not sure she believes the last thing. "You were with me every step of the way," I say.

"Maybe, in the moments. I never had the chance to stop and think about what I wanted. We agreed to a fling. That's all I wanted. It's fine. You don't have to worry about me," she says.

She kissed me first, but I let her know I was open to it and she walked through the door. I've always been afraid I was convenient for her, that any obstacle would have prevented us from hooking up. If I lived a few streets over, or heaven forbid, the mainland, we would have never connected the same way, even if we had the same friend group and I was around the same amount. But I'm done playing games and not saying everything I feel to make her comfortable. She can either handle the full force of my emotions or she can't. She can hide from her friends, but she's never been able to hide from me and I won't let her start now.

I set my anger and my pain at what she's saying aside, because she's so woefully transparent. She wants this. But she's so scared to take what she wants for herself. She's afraid she'll lose it. Lose me. She's pushing me away instead, and she will take me down with her. "Choose me now. You're hiding behind your rules and your fear, rather than admitting your feelings. You could have everything you've wanted if you pick me now."

She growls. I swear she fucking growls. "It's not that simple."

"Yes, it is. Be in a relationship with me. Without boundaries and without reservations."

"You can't possibly want me back." Her voice is disbelieving.

"I love you, Carina. We can work this out, but you have to give me something."

"I have nothing left to give you." Her voice is barely a whisper. "There's no point in trying for more."

"Right. You've already given everything away. Well, I tried. I gave you a chance. Twice now. At least I'll always be able to say that." I've fought more for her than I have for anyone else. Every moment of it was worth it.

But I won't sail where I'll run aground. There is no passage forward for me here.

She stares at me blankly, clearly done with me in her house. I walk out, wondering if this is the last time I will be inside these walls. I thought I understood her. But if she won't even look at herself, then I don't know what I can expect from her.

* * *

In the end, the wedding would have been ruined anyway.

It wasn't anything they could've prevented, but the reality of living in Florida and it being fall—Tropical Storm Thea formed in the gulf in the days leading up to the weekend, and I did everything I could to prepare.

I have my checklist. I know what needs to be done.

I knew this was a risk when I moved here. It was one reason why people told me it was a bad investment to buy a house on the beach. But I deluded myself into thinking I had more time before it would impact me. I thought I'd appreciate the beach more and the way the waves collapsed on the sand. I thought I'd be able to memorize every dune between my house and Paradise.

I thought I'd be able to keep Carina.

I field phone calls from my family asking if I'm going to evacuate. We don't have orders to, and I decide to stay. Carina's voice echoes in my head.

I'm going down with the island.

She doesn't mean that. She'd be the first person to heed an evacuation order. She wouldn't risk having to be rescued and taking resources away from people who truly needed them or putting the lives of first responders in jeopardy.

I take care of the boats in the marina, securing them as much as possible. There is a chance I could lose them. But that's what insurance is for, I remind myself. I run my hand over the helm of the *Twisted Rigging*. I always thought I'd be devastated if I lost this boat. This once was my home, an external manifestation of my soul.

But nothing currently compares to the anguish in my soul at losing Carina.

When I pull into my driveway, I see Christian putting up shutters with her, and I'm so thankful she has help. They also placed sandbags in front of all her doors. She'll be safe, but I want to ride out the storm with her.

Christian waves at me, and then with a nod from Carina he hops the fence into my yard.

"You got everything you need?" he asks.

"I think so. Boats are secure. I have water, batteries, nonperishable food."

He looks back at Carina moving her patio furniture to the garage. I cringe thinking about her leg. Has she rested enough?

"You're more than welcome to stay with Autumn and me. We have a guest room."

He knows the answer I'm going to give. But he had to ask.

I stay where she stays.

"I'll be fine," I say. "The storm surge shouldn't be bad."

He nods. I've obsessively checked the weather and radar for years. The most important part of sailing is knowing the wind. But for the last couple of days, we all have obsessively checked the models and the predictions. I can talk spaghetti models and if we should be paying more attention to the Euro track all day.

"If you change your mind, let me know." He claps me on the back and then heads back to Carina's place.

I go inside, to the house I thought I'd give up everything for. I thought this place would force me to put down roots and invest in the community around me.

I could lose it all. Not in this storm, but there will always be another one. Carina has always been right.

I don't care about the house or my business or my boats. It means nothing if I don't have her.

My phone vibrates on the table with a text.

ALEX BARNES

Hurricane party at Paradise! 5pm!

At least some people aren't concerned.

I look at the gulf where the waves roll fiercer than I've seen before.

A lone figure stands on the beach, with her blond hair whipping in the wind.

forty-three

CARINA

I'VE ALWAYS LOVED THE WATER DURING STORMS. I'VE BEEN through enough to know which ones to be concerned about.

This one won't be a big deal. Not for us, at least.

I've done my storm prep. My house is secure. Sienna left for her mom's place in Sarasota, and Haley is with her parents on the mainland. Both offered for me to join them, but I couldn't.

I've been surrounded by people for days. I need some time in my own head.

I reached for Orion so often since I saw him last. I pretended he meant nothing to me. But he saw right through it. I have no one to blame but me.

I can do most of the preparation by myself. I have a hurricane kit. I can do this. But I can't reach all the shutters on my own. I wanted to call him. He would have helped. It's the neighborly thing to do.

I thought I understood what it meant to be alone. After Hamilton left, I didn't have this aching sense of loss. My life continued the same way as it had before. But with Orion, everything has changed. This life I thought was fulfilling is empty. This time in my own head is teaching me one thing: I want Orion here with me.

But I don't have any rights to him anymore. He needs to take care of the boats and his house, and I don't even know if he's staying through the storm. A lot of people leave. It's less stressful that way. To not deal with the wind and the rain and the constant fear that something will go terribly wrong before it gets better.

So this is the worst I will feel. But I will never have it as good again as I did with Orion. It's not that no one else could make me happy, it's that no one else will ever push me and cherish me the way Orion did.

I fucked up. Worse than I ever have before.

I called Christian for help with the shutters. He's always willing to assist and he's the type of new Floridian who has his ducks in a row long before a storm comes. And Autumn can handle the grocery stores for anything else they need.

I can live on my own, but I don't want to. I want Orion in my life. Not as my neighbor, but as my partner. I'll get through this storm and then I'll go to him and beg if I need to. I'll admit I'm scared, that he scares me more than anything. I built these walls with the assumption they would protect me. I wanted to preserve my image at all costs. Now all I have is a friend who helps me with my shutters and my sandbags but doesn't ask how I'm feeling. I shouldn't have pushed Orion away in the first place. I should have admitted from the beginning that he could be everything to me.

No one besides Alex has said anything to me to indicate they have noticed a change in my relationship with Orion. But when we saw Orion in his backyard, Christian looked at me sympathetically before crossing to him. Does he know more than he's letting on?

I stand on the beach as the waves crash over my feet. The air is sticky warm and electric in the coming storm. It's not raining yet, just wind and waves and this body of water that I love so much, that has the power to destroy everything that matters to me.

"Carina!" Orion's voice barely carries over the violent waves. "What are you doing?"

I could fight him on this. He'll tell me I'm not safe. That I'm taking too big of a risk. I do take risks. Risks I completely calculate and have determined that the odds of success are great enough that it doesn't feel like chance anymore.

Standing in one spot shouldn't feel dangerous.

"I'm fine, Orion," I yell back.

He comes up next to me and braces himself against the wind, his hair blown about. Mine must look just as messy.

"This isn't safe." He stands close to me so we can hear each other.

"I've done safe," I say. "Look where it's gotten me."

He takes a deep breath like he's steeling for an endless conversation about my feelings and my needs, and we won't touch his feelings and his needs.

I've been so selfish.

"I didn't think you'd stay," I shout. He told me he never had before. Why would he sail through a storm if he could avoid it? I didn't see our relationship as any different.

"We're not under evacuation orders. I want to be here. Make sure everything is okay."

"No, I meant with me. I thought you'd leave, and I'd be left here, and everyone would tell me I was an idiot for falling in love with the sailor who was always leaving."

His eyebrows scrunch together and his arms cross over his chest. He'll probably tell me I didn't listen to him and then make sure I'm safe in the storm, because that's what neighbors do.

"How many times did I tell you this is my home now? I'm staying here. And even if that wasn't my plan at the beginning, how could I leave you, Carina?"

We stare at the waves together. He has been with me for every storm I've faced since he came into my life. Even the ones he created.

"You could lose the house," I say.

"Not this storm," he replies. He's not wrong. The latest forecast has it weakening and heading north.

"The next one, then."

"Maybe. Doesn't matter though."

"Why?" I'm finally ready to hear what he's saying.

He sighs. "Fuck it. Carina, you are my home. You are my anchor. I don't care about anything else if I don't have you. You were right. This whole thing was a mistake because I hate living so close to you and not being able to have you. I'm spiteful enough that I'll stay. Because I always intended to stay and you're the one who didn't want me to."

"What do you want me to say to that?"

"Nothing, Carina. I'm done asking you for anything." He turns and walks in the direction of our houses.

"Wait!"

He turns back, but any hope he once had is gone. He's truly given up on us.

Maybe I can fix this. My whole body shakes. "I was wrong."

He doesn't move. "About what?"

"I was scared. I was spiraling. I didn't know how to make it stop. Every other relationship I've seen has fallen apart. I picked a fight because I was so scared we would break and I wouldn't recover. I'm not recovering from losing you. I won't ever. I didn't mean it when I said there wasn't anything to throw away. We have something here. I know that. I've always known that."

He approaches me. "We don't have to end, Carina."

In my desire to keep my perfect facade up, I showed far more of my fears than I thought possible. "You'll take me back? I said some horrible things to you. I twisted everything. I wouldn't blame you for wanting me to crawl on broken glass just to prove that I would. I'd give up my home. My company. Anything."

He looks at me for a long moment. Rain starts to fall, and it might have been safe a minute ago but conditions are rapidly deteriorating.

He sees that as well, because he wastes no time stepping close and wrapping his arms around me, pressing his lips against mine. He tastes like home. How could I have ever thought to give this up?

"I don't need you to give anything up. I need you to commit. To promise that *you* won't leave. A guarantee that we're partners."

I nod. "Yes. I'm committed. I love you."

He silences me with a kiss, but I know those aren't the last of his terms.

"I know all of you." He takes my hair and makes a ponytail with his hands at the nape of my neck. He's holding me together like he always does. "I know all your flaws. Each one of them is perfect to me."

I've done nothing to deserve this man. But I'll take everything that he gives me.

"I know. That terrified me. But I don't want to be anymore," I say, shaking and trying my hardest to control my tears. But I fail at that.

He holds me tight. "I've got you. I promise."

"What happens when you want to sail off to Key West?"

He laughs. "You'll come with me. I love you. We can figure everything else out. But I promise you, if I leave Wendell Beach, I'm taking you with me."

"I love you too." He smiles, and I hate every second I let pass without telling him the truth of how I feel. Every second I let myself hide from this.

"I promise you'll always know what I'm thinking," he says. "I will still argue with you for the sake of arguing with you. But you'll always know."

"I'm sorry I said I didn't trust you. I do. I know you. I know what we are." I need this man. He won't leave me. He won't change his mind.

"We should get out of the storm," he says. The rain plasters our hair to our faces.

I nod, letting him grab my hand and pull me toward the street and our houses. When he bypasses mine, I stop. "Why yours?"

"I know what my liquor cache looks like. I don't know yours." He pauses. "And I have a feeling this will be the only storm we hunker down in my place."

"Why is that?"

"Mine is ready to market as a rental. You've said it a million times. Yours needs work."

"Did you just invite yourself to move in with me?"

"I told you I'm in. I'm not saying I'm moving *now*. I know how much that house means to you. You don't have to give it up for me."

My heart swells. I should have always known that I could count on him to be exactly what I need, even when I don't know it myself.

With that, we head into his house and straight into the shower.

 forty-four

ORION

We meet at Paradise that night for the hurricane party. Sienna also claims it's her dodged bullet party. She and Haley both came back once the worst passed. I told Carina it's not a hurricane but a tropical storm, just to see how she'd react. I endured a long but naked lecture on colloquialisms, dark humor, and the importance of community in the face of danger.

I've never been happier.

Carina and I spent the day in bed. I didn't realize it would be different, being able to press into her and tell her I love her. But it is, and it's amazing. I'm adjusting to the knowledge that I get to do this for the rest of my life. Then she rolls her hips and asks me what else I have for her.

Everything. Absolutely everything I have is for her.

I was prepared to make cocktails for her throughout the day. I paid enough attention to her drink orders at Paradise to know what she likes. Mysteriously, the ingredients are always in my fridge. She refused, claiming it was too much effort and she only wanted to drink the rum that brought us together. I didn't mind licking my favorite rum off her nipples and hearing her giggle.

Also, hearing her giggle for the first time.

I have everything I've ever wanted—Carina in my arms, wild and free.

She was more than a little tipsy when we walked along the roads to get here, rather than the beach. The rain had stopped but the wind blew fiercely. Carina laughed the whole way. Giggling over the way my hair wouldn't stay out of my face, and how she'd teach me to braid it if I let it grow a little longer.

We immediately join Christian and Autumn who stand a few feet apart from each other. I don't understand them. I've been forced to keep my distance from Carina in public and hated every second of it. *How can you be in the same space as your wife and not want to maul her?*

Even now, Carina is leaning on me like she needs me to stand. But that might be the rum.

"Finally," Christian says under his breath.

Carina pulls away. "Excuse me?"

"Oh, um. He knew," I admit.

"What?" both Autumn and Carina exclaim.

"You two aren't as sneaky as you think you are," he says.

"Why didn't you tell me?" Autumn asks with mock hurt in her voice.

Christian shrugs. "It wasn't my secret."

My arm wraps around Carina's waist, holding her close to me. She reaches up to whisper loudly into my ear. "Come on, let's get you something to eat." At least she has the sense to know what we need.

She leads me by the hand to the bar. Alex and Bristol are busy, simultaneously making drinks and taking orders. The place is as crowded as I've ever seen it and the atmosphere is festive. I laugh when I see the special cocktail of the night, Foley's Folly. I'm not sure I want to know what Alex put in it.

I find Sienna across the room. She looks happy as she talks animatedly with Haley. Then she glances up and her eyes go wide. She and Haley make a beeline for us.

Carina shocks both of them by giving them hugs.

"I knew it," Sienna shouts over the noise. "Why didn't you tell us?"

"It's against the friend code to bring up good news when a friend is going through a bad time." Carina sips her water.

Sienna laughs, deep and full-throated. "Fine. If that's how you want to play it." She turns to Haley. "Called it."

"I didn't argue with you!" Haley turns back to Carina. "How long?"

Carina and I look at each other. She shrugs. "There's no sense in denying it now."

I take the full green light and kiss her temple. "Since the day of the charter."

"No you didn't!" Haley says, her eyes full of giggles.

"I didn't know you had it in you! I need to know everything," Sienna exclaims.

"Later." Carina's hand drifts to the waistband of my shorts.

Sienna is pulled away, and Haley gives Carina a sign saying she's watching us but goes to talk with Christian and Autumn.

Carina turns to me with fear in her eyes. "What if I fuck up again?"

"We'll work through it," I assure her.

"What if I want kids and you don't?" She shakes her head like this will break us. Like I forgot something fundamental about her and I'll come to my senses and call off this whole relationship.

"I want kids. Do you want kids?" I admit.

"Maybe. Yes."

"Great. That's dealt with." Her arms wrap around my waist and mine are around her shoulders. She is absolutely everything to me. My home. My anchor. My whole life.

Now everyone will know.

Epilogue

CARINA

SIX MONTHS LATER

WE HIKE up the trail in our swimsuits and water shoes. No cameras in our hands and no phones. No one around to capture the moment. When we get to the top, I take a deep breath. Not from the physical exertion, but from the beauty of it all.

Orion and I stand on top of a twenty-foot cliff overlooking the Atlantic Ocean. The water is turquoise and sapphire blue. With barely any wind, no waves crash below, just gently lap at the rocks.

With the lack of wind, we got to this spot using the motor on the *Twisted Rigging* instead of sails, but we've done plenty of sailing in the weeks since we left Wendell Beach for the Bahamas. I'm starting to think I'm pretty good at it. I can't believe how much sailing Orion has done on his own. At night when we're anchored he holds me close and whispers how happy he is I'm here.

"You sailed across the ocean with friends before," I remind him.

"Yes, but there was significantly less cuddling."

We're away from home for over a month. It was my idea, surprisingly. He made arguments about how he needed to be around for high season. But spring break had passed, and he could step away like he had before. The boat has satellite internet, so I can work remotely when I need to.

The last few months with my dad have turned out better than I thought it would. I was assigned another project manager, who seems to think that as long as nothing goes wrong, then he doesn't need to be involved.

I wish I could say I made attempts to repair my relationship with my parents. But I haven't. If they haven't noticed something is wrong, then it's not on me to fix everything. I don't always have to be the responsible one.

Plus, Orion's sister Brooklynn and his parents have more than welcomed me into the family.

I step to the edge. "This is a terrible idea." I'm not exactly afraid of heights, but there is something about leaving the safety of the ground to free-fall.

Orion laughs and pulls me close to him. "You'll be fine. Remember what we talked about. Jump out and breathe out. Keep your mouth closed. You'll stay upright and the water is deep enough that you won't hit bottom. It's safe."

He's right. We've been practicing for this. It was my idea too. I started with the bow of the boat, and we've been working up to this. I rest my head on his shoulder and trace the outline of the tattoo on his left pec.

Six weeks ago, he came home with a bandage over it. I peppered him with questions for hours until it was time to take it off. He leaned against the counter in our bathroom, the windows open to the gulf breeze, while I revealed that he had orange blossoms inked around the anchor. I'd looked at him, confused—what did it mean, Florida? That he liked my yard with its trees?

"It's you, Carina."

My eyes had welled up with tears, but neither of us moved to brush them away. Instead, I lifted up on my toes to kiss him. We've talked about marriage and kids and everything, but neither one of us is in a hurry. This is forever. We're fine not putting additional external pressure on our relationship.

And I really don't want to plan a wedding.

On the cliff, his thumb rubs on my rib cage, right below my bikini top. It's where a week later, I came home with the Orion constellation, permanent on my skin.

He's mine. Forever.

"Come on, princess. You can do this. Think how much you want to prove your bikini will stay in place," he taunts.

It's not real. He's putting up a fight. I've always known the difference.

"Oh please, you want it to come off," I respond.

"Of course I do. I always want that. But I can get it off myself. You don't have to jump," he assures me. "It's a beautiful view. We can hike back down and call it a day."

"No, I want to." I pull away and step to the edge. I need to do this now and not wait any longer.

He grabs my hand and looks at me. "On the count of three. One."

"Two," I continue.

"Three."

We jump.

I let go of his hand as we fall—the momentary weightlessness taking over everything.

I hit the water faster than I expect, suddenly disoriented. I find the light and kick toward the surface. Once my head is above water, I look around for Orion. He surfaces a second later, a few feet away. When he sees me, he swims for me, pulling me against him so my legs wrap around his waist.

"You good?" He brushes my hair out of my face, his eyes searching mine for any sign I'm not okay.

My heart races, from the adrenaline of the jump and from him so near to me. I'll never get used to it. I don't want to. I want to always appreciate him in my life. I almost threw everything away for my fears. I won't do that ever again.

"I'm good. I can float on my own." I won't fight him on this, other than this performative protest. He needs to hold me so he knows he didn't push me too hard.

"You're amazing." The awe in his voice is obvious. This shouldn't be a big moment for us—it's just another day of sand and salt water. But it's us and our love and we'll never let it go.

"I love you." I kiss him.

"I love you too. Boat?" It's not a question of safety. It's how fast can we be naked with each other? How fast can we be wild, vulnerable, and free?

"Boat," I agree. I disentangle from him, and we swim for where the *Twisted Rigging* is anchored.

It's not his home anymore, but one of ours. The place where we first came together and one of the places where we will always return. He reaches her before I do, and waits for me to haul myself up before getting out of the water himself. He heads for the cabin knowing I'll follow him anywhere.

I take a moment to run my hand over the helm. Orion has given me so much since we've been together. Never once has he disappointed me.

I follow him below, past the pictures of him sailing in Greece and my yoga retreat in Thailand, to our cabin. Knowing the next memory we make will be my favorite.

Until the next one.

carina's pride

3/4 oz simple syrup
1 oz lime juice
3/4 oz raspberry liquor
2 oz rum of your choice
Raspberry
Lime wedge

Add first four ingredients to a cocktail shaker. Add ice. Shake for about twenty seconds. Strain into a cocktail glass. Garnish with the raspberry and lime wedge. Toast to not letting fear get in the way of your happiness.

Note: Orion drinks Diplomático Reserva Exclusiva, but play around with different rums to find your favorite.

acknowledgments

The funny thing about writing a second book is that I thought I knew what I was doing, but I really didn't. The most extraordinary thing is how many more people I have to thank for this book because I have met and been supported by so many incredible people in the last year since my first book came out.

The Spellbound Writers Group for getting me out of my house once a month and being almost like therapy and for all the incredible writers I've met through this group. Especially the ones who let me dm them random questions and took the time to answer me. Spellbound Bookstore for stocking my book and giving me the opportunity to do signings and meet so many incredible readers. Dani and Sarai, you both have made me feel like I can do this when I wasn't always sure.

Sarah, Bess and the rest of the Pubbers from Wednesday Write Ins. #TeamTea.

The Procrastination of Romantics and within them, the Contemporary Cuties. Thank you for holding my hand and telling me I'm pretty when I was convinced I didn't know how sentences work. For workshopping the first chapter and the breakup scene and being as excited for Carina and Orion as I am. Also, for putting up with my particular brand of chaos this year and becoming some of my closest friends. I should also thank Sarah MacLean for teaching a class on conflict last year since that's how I met you all.

Captain DJ at USail of Central Florida. All sailing errors are my own.

My Vinyasa Practice for the 200 hour yoga teacher training I took for research. It also deepened my practice and helped me to become more authentically me. All yoga errors are my own.

The team over at Qamber Designs for bring Carina and Orion to life. And for being incredibly patient with me as we designed this cover while I was in the middle of buying a house and moving.

My beta readers, Hayley Fleming, Hillary Noelle, Andie James, and Ly. Nicole McCurdy for giving great notes and for being such a champion of this book. Julia Ganis for helping me level everything up. Laura Helseth for taking my unhinged texts when I'm upset about grammar.

Kaely, Jessika, Sam, and Cody for helping me come up names of places that sound particularly Florida. Kaely was also the first person to take me to Florida back in 2015.

My parents and sisters for being more supportive of my writing career than I could ever imagine.

My in-laws for renting a house on the beach for a week in 2021. That house became Orion's house. That beach became Wendell Beach.

My therapist, Samantha, for that look you gave me when I said there wasn't much of me in Staged. Wait until you read this one!

And, finally, my very sexy accountant, Wesley. Thank you for asking "who hurt you" every time you walked into a room and found me crying. Writing a book is hard so it was usually that. But sometimes it was Taylor Swift. Thank you for holding me and telling me that I could do it. I promise I won't try to write off alcohol on our taxes next year.

Standalone
Staged: A Cupid/Psyche Fake Dating Novella
Alma Blake and Will Caron

Wendell Beach Series:
Rum Sips and Salty Lips
Carina Webb and Orion Edwards
Coming Soon: Wendell Beach Book Two

about the author

Rebecca V. Archer writes contemporary romance about characters who are afraid of their own emotions. She lives in Florida with her soulmate, drinks copious amounts of tea, and is always looking for a new cocktail or food recipe to try.

Check out her website for updates.

www.rebeccavarcher.com

You can also subscribe her to newsletter for bonus content, writing updates, and sneak peeks either at

https://rebeccavarcher.com/newsletter

Or by scanning the QR code

instagram.com/rebeccavarcher

threads.net/@rebeccavarcher

facebook.com/rebeccavarcher

tiktok.com/@rebeccavarcher

amazon.com/author/rebeccavarcher

9 798988 524731